Down and Out is a heartfe
dilapidated America we live
where the dream remains alive. How Briseño manages to
leave us feeling hopeful is nothing short of a miracle.

—Colin Winnette,
author of *Haints Stay* and *The Job of the Wasp*

Down and Out's momentum churns on such a cruel
premise for a reality television show—about poverty and
suffering deliberately exploited for mass entertainment—
that we know it could and must be true. As a new economy
violently supplants the old, a parade of hardworking people
is caught between twisting gears and unspooling
film. *Down and Out* delivers these quiet episodes of small-
town desires, failures, and dreams, which we are lucky to
witness as one season of this world fades into the next.

—Dolan Morgan,
author of *Insignificana*

In *Down and Out,* J. Andrew Briseño sees something like
hope where others would merely gawp. This book is sad
and funny and an outrage and the good kind of weird and
at the end of it all just really really human, with images of
small factory-town life that sit somewhere between the
bible and a Springsteen song getting all defrauded and
wrong through a reality TV lens that refuses to look away
or stop meddling in what might be good if it could just be
let alone. Deep down, it's a book about what it is to be
moral, how we're always losing it, how we sometimes get
it back that way. I need J. Andrew Briseño. We all do.

—Zach VandeZande,
author of *Apathy & Paying Rent*

DOWN

AND

O
U
T

a novel

by J. Andrew Briseño

For Travis, who was better than all of us

Pilot

It started with the city, which was really barely a town, a halfway stop between Fort Smith and nowhere. It started with the factory in the town, Doyles' Gear, stamping out cogs and sprockets and knowing the difference. It started with the people inside the factory, all two hundred employees, the fireflushed dozen in the furnace, the stampers, the toolers, the die casters, the foremen, the secretary/accountant/sales representative, the manager. It started with the assembly line, humming at a steady third-of-a-mile-an-hour as the gears we made were polished and packaged and set to ship. It started when all of that came to a stop.

We did not choose this place. None of us. Paris, Arkansas, is a thing you're born into, handed down generation to generation, like colorblindness.

From on top of Petit Jean Mountain, not fifteen miles outside of town, there is a break in the trees that frames all of Paris. If you climb out onto the rocks like everybody does, you can see in the distant west the shape of the abbey bell tower, the tallest thing in the county, and east of that the first and second ridges that arced around us, cut us off from the rest of the river valley and the land south. You can see Route 22, and the factory just outside of downtown, and the football stadium, and if you look real close the high school. You can see downtown dignified in its old age, and both stoplights and the traffic that sometimes builds up because folks prefer to be polite and wave their neighbors through. If you know where you're looking, like all of us did, you can see Old Military Road, and Meinrad Ave.,

Church St. and Watkins St. and on those just about every house in town. There's not a child older than five that can't point to his own house, his own place in this world. From that distance it seems to make sense.

And then, like it snuck up on you, you see the river, our river, the hesitant Arkansas, saddled across the land like a forgotten strand of twine. It seems too lazy of a river to have carved out the valley, but like all great rivers it moves only when you're not looking at it, or when it swallows you. You could ride a boat clean from Fort Smith to Little Rock, but since the freeway had gone in—six miles past the river, just out of sight—you wouldn't hardly see a boat on the river.

But you would see our bridge. Our grandfathers built it with relief money from the Depression, poured the concrete, welded the girders. It straddled the river at a point inconvenient to both nature and man, and its construction had been in its time the state's crown jewel of technological achievement. It took four hundred men six years to cross the river. Back then, the state was two lobes joined only notionally. Crossing meant Fort Smith, or Little Rock—an honest case of you couldn't get there from here. Individuals separated by as little as five miles might as well have been in other countries. No county in Arkansas is on both sides of the river. We were told then that the new bridge would bring new business, new families, new growth. It had brought Doyles' Gear.

Traffic to Paris was rare, but what there was of it came across the bridge. And if you happened to be looking from that bridge on just the right day, early in summer when the dust and the fresh sunshine add a sheen that makes damn near everything cheerful, you would have seen a rush of

Down and Out

identical white-panel vans. There must have been eighty of them, which means that those who saw claimed there were two, three hundred, sometimes more. None of the vans had windows. All of them were headed one place. The place where most of us already were.

Doyles' Gear was a one-and-three-quarters-story metal building with a metal roof, stretching a quarter mile down the side of the highway. The building is unassuming, made of the corrugated tan-painted sheet metal that means a brand-new garage, a temporary classroom, or good hard work. If you drove by, you would not know that inside slats of SAE 1144 induction heat-treated, billet steel were melted, forged, and formed into gears that spun damn near forever, the guts of half the motors on earth. There was a time that every man in America owned at least a dozen Doyles' Gears without ever knowing. We were a small but moving part of forty-eight NASCAR cup champions, six Tours de France, and the landing gear for every single space shuttle.

Driving by, what you would have known was what the factory meant to the town. From the highway, it was the only building that looked like it had a fresh coat of paint. It had a parking lot bigger than the Walmart, and should you be around long after dark, you'd see that lot full and light slipping out of the windows, some of us at work even then. Doyles' Gear had donated the trash cans in our park, the scoreboards at the baseball diamond and the football stadium. The name was on billboards and company vehicles, and pretty well everybody's navy blue button ups.

It wasn't just familiar, it was natural and presumed, a strand of barb wire long since surrounded and consumed by a tree, the two made one, that single strand of wire you found standing after violent storms tore down the fence and scattered the posts and every other remnant of life as it was all down the valley.

Everyone knew what Doyles' meant to Paris. Nobody knew what Paris would mean without Doyles'. But like you were guessing already, we are all about to find out.

At 6:15 that morning those of us on first shift left our homes, got into our trucks, and drove to work. We were there by 6:30 or so, plenty of time to stretch, get a second cup of coffee, nod pleasantly, inquire as to the health of one another's parents and children, the latest news with the State College's football, basketball, baseball, track team, who had seen whom doing what. We didn't remember what we talked about. None of it foreshadowed anything.

At ten till, the third shift rolled off the floor on ragged wheels, tired yet energized by the sight of the sun streaming through the breakroom windows. We said our hellos to them as we passed to clock in and take their places. We rolled our necks on our shoulders, and waited for the signal that the shift had started, the siren that meant the conveyor belt would soon shudder to life.

Lyle Younse was the man who sounded that siren. He was our foreman, which meant he did every job and not just one. He was a tall man, what we would call skinny because he wasn't fat but lean and drawn taut from all of his sixteen years at the factory. Lyle was the youngest foreman the factory had ever had, but none of the older employees minded much, because he worked harder than they could and was always respectful. Truth be told, Lyle thought his job was easy. No one was late without an acceptable excuse, no one ever minded more than was reasonable when they were asked to learn a brand-new job after twenty years of doing things in just such a way. When management came up with new products we would sell, new methods of manufacturing that were designed to save us time or energy or some other important thing that can be measured but not weighed, Lyle would spend as long as it took to understand it and then tell it back to us, make us see the wisdom in it. When someone was sick, which was uncommon, or too injured to do their job, which was fairly regular, Lyle stepped into their place in the human machine and did their job and his, and if anything we were just a little quicker then.

Even at thirty-three, gray had flecked its way through Lyle's short hair, particularly at the temples. He had steady brown eyes and a smile you saw on the regular. We had known he was good looking since Lyle was a baby, but it never seemed to occur to him, which of course made him that much more desirable. Like all of us, he had married young and for love.

Lyle was good at his job precisely because he didn't put much thought into it. Like any good athlete, which he'd been back some years ago at Paris High, he had learned to forget the target, just swing. Lyle did everything that was asked of him and more because he never asked himself if he could, always kept his thoughts on what he was doing now and ought to do next. Reflection was one of the few tasks that his job did not require.

Another thing Lyle would never have thought of: that day was the first time since he had walked into the factory the week after high school graduation that Lyle ever looked back to wonder if he'd done something wrong. It was the first day that something happened that he had not in some small way planned for.

Briseño

Two hours into the day, forty minutes short of the coffee break, someone other than Lyle hit the siren that told us the line was stopping, that work everywhere was stopping—a siren that meant in this context only a horrible injury or a malfunction severe enough to threaten the day's hours and thus our paychecks. All of us silently said a prayer in case the former, did a quick calculation as to what we might have to deal without if the latter, looked to Lyle to show us what was happening. But Lyle was confused, a sensation he found both new and displeasing, and went to find instantly who or what had changed things, to start the immediate and necessary process of returning things to the way they ought to be. He walked to the control station from the forge room and found his boss, Martin Gossett, standing at the siren, next to him a man in a silk shirt, which meant that Lyle had never seen him before.

Martin Gossett wasn't going bald, his hair was just thinning. He wasn't getting fat, just getting thirty-five. Truth be told he was still good looking in that father-of-two kind of a way, and he looked for all the world like a state senator in the making. He looked like an asshole from fifty feet off and your best friend from five. He could smile at you and make you believe that he believed in you, which is powerful enough to be dangerous. He was blond headed just so everyone would know he came from money, and despite marrying the first Mexican that the city of Paris had gotten to know well, both of his daughters had hair the color of a square bale.

His official title was Operations Manager, which meant that, according to him and everybody who could hear him, he managed to keep things operating. We didn't know then how true or false that was, only that Martin was polite,

8

decent, and hadn't fired anybody since Jamie Mallett's mama. We didn't look up to him, but we were glad it was him that we weren't looking up to. He was only a year or two older than Lyle and younger than damn near half of us. But we listened to him because he was from here, and that meant something, even if his daddy didn't work here with our daddies. We listened to him because he tried his best never to lie to us, and never to treat us like we were too damn stupid to know what was going on.

Today we listened because Martin was the one who came forward and hollered at us to gather around, all of us. We looked to Lyle, and when he nodded we did as we were told. It was seventy-five of us on the first shift. But when we turned around, there were the seventy-five on the second and the fifty that kept the plant running over night, the maintenance men, the three truck drivers, the secretary/accountant. The inside of Doyles' Gear was fifteen thousand feet square, enough room to park any two airplanes, but it felt crowded.

"Folks," began Martin, and he looked down at his hands, already displeased with the way he sounded. "Folks," he started again, "I don't have great news. You probably might have guessed it, but things haven't been doing well around here for some time. I have been doing my damnedest," he turned to the man in the silk shirt, asked if he could say that, got permission, went on, "my absolute damnedest to keep this place on its feet, trying to bring in new revenue, new ideas. And I want you to know that whatever I asked and however I asked it, all y'all were always there for me. Always there for Doyles' Gear. So thank you." Looking back he wished he'd paused here—give some space to add sincerity to those words. But no space was given. "I won't pretend there's an easy way to say this," Martin said. "The factory is shutting down."

Martin stopped then. We were silent. Looking forward. When he'd said there was bad news, we didn't figure anything else. We had guessed it already. We said nothing, and that dismayed Martin, made him look down at the floor, look up at what we didn't know, and then add, "Right now." That seemed to produce the required effect, as all of us started to murmur and wonder, to look at those near us and ask without saying more than a whisper if any of this could be real. The words severance and notice floated out above us. And it was then that the first cameramen peeking out from the platforms above us, started pacing through entrances and exits like cats on the hunt. Surrounded us. Focused on us. But we didn't notice because Martin was back to mumbling at us.

"Listen, I know that all of this is a surprise. And that none of it's good. I want you to know that we, all of us, have done the best we could." It sounded like he was telling himself. "We did everything, everything. And if there was any way to keep this factory running, any way at all, I would have found it. I would have. You have to believe me. You have to." He paused here to gauge our belief. He was far from bolstered, and at this he nodded. It was going exactly the way he had imagined it.

"There's not a lot more to say. Doyles' Gear closes today. Clean out your personal belongings. Pick up your last check in the business office. I know..." he started and trailed off. "I know." He started and trailed off. "God bless."

He started to walk away, and we started to descend into whatever you call it when your job of ten, twenty, thirty years is suddenly as absent as a missing limb. But then

Down and Out

Martin remembered one last thing, and turned back toward us all. "Oh," he said. "And this man'd like to say something to you too."

The man in the silk shirt walked to the front, shook Martin's hand even though it wasn't really being offered, and waved. He had a microphone—we couldn't figure why as plainly he'd just seen Martin talk to us—but he talked into it just the same. He smiled and looked us over and nodded. This is what he'd been looking for. He was pleased with that which he had found. And he leaned into the microphone and said, "Ladies and gentlemen, I have the greatest news ever."

He looked like one of those people who run on a treadmill for a living. His tan was too even, his stance more level than it had a right to be. He said, "First let me tell you that I'm sorry about your jobs. I know how long many of you have worked here. You don't know it, but we've had our eye on Paris for a while now. And I know that a change like this is never easy to take."

This apology was the first time we'd actually thought about it. It's funny how you don't know things have happened until someone is telling you they're sorry for it. We looked around at the folks with whom we now had nothing in common. We were on a wave-when-you-pass-each-other basis with pretty well everyone in the room. We were keeping it together for each other, and trying only to whisper to those nearest us about what we would do now. Only a few had started tearing up. Jamie Mallett, who worked the forge like his Daddy, or used to, had his lips curled back.

The man went on, "But like every struggle, this is also an opportunity." Most of us could think of a struggle or three that lacked this upside, but we listened rather than saying so out loud. "My name is Miles Francis, and I am the Executive Producer of a brand-new television show, and I would like you to turn to the right and left and introduce yourselves to our shows newest stars: You!"

He said the last word through a smile so white it looked blue. We looked at each other. At Jason and Tammy Johnson, who had found each other in the crowd and were holding hands, whispering back and forth as their eyes wandered the room, pointing at the cameramen. At Lyle, already the cell phone in his hand to call Cathy back at home. At Martin standing sheepishly next to the man, wishing he could do anything useful.

"America loves the story of obstacles overcome. They want to see you rise above this day, and we want to show it to them. Make no mistake, the road in front of you will not be easy. You will suffer, and I know I don't have to tell that to you. But we can share that suffering, let the whole country see it as what it is—the story of us all. The story of the American Dream, live from the trenches, realer than anything out there. We have an opportunity here to show America to itself—and all that starts with you.

"We will show America your lives, we will open the door and let them see and share in your struggle. When you look for new jobs, America will look for new jobs. When you are hungry, the nation will hunger with you. We have the chance to break new ground in reality television, and that all starts with you people."

By now most of us had seen the cameras on us. Men stood up and drew in their guts, women wished they'd known, that they could have dressed for it. A few of us waved. Jimmy Starling leaned into Steve Womack and said,

Down and Out

"You're going to be a TV star, son." Steve said nothing back. He was too scared to think.

"Now I know this is a lot to take in, so I won't keep you very much longer," said Francis, and suddenly we knew his name because we knew why it was important to remember it. "Now of course, participation in the show is voluntary. If you'd prefer to not be on the program, if you're a private person, we certainly understand. We ask that you sign a waiver for today's filming, and we'll not bother you again. For those who do want to participate, I want you to know that you will be compensated for your time on the show. Everyone who signs up today receives five thousand dollars right now." He stopped there and waited, and we realized we were supposed to clap and so we did.

"In addition, you'll be paid for any footage of you we use in the program. For every show you're in after this one, we'll give you another ten thousand dollars, which means that if you're in every episode this season, you can make $135,000 in the next eight months or so." He paused again, and again it took us a second to figure out and to start to cheer. But this time it wasn't that we didn't understand why he'd stopped, but because we were all of us caught in thinking. That was more money than Lyle made in a year by three, and he got a dollar seventy-five more an hour than pretty much everybody. Even Mr. Gossett was staggered, in spite of himself, knowing more than the rest of us. Still we cheered once we'd gotten our head around the idea, cheered loudly for this miracle that stood in front of us.

"Each of you who chooses to participate will go home with a film crew today. We should have almost enough, though a few of you might need to wait so that we can film every homecoming. We appreciate your patience in advance. But before I let you go, I want to tell you the secret to being a great reality TV star: Don't be a TV star. We're here because we want to see you, the real you. It might feel strange to be personal in front of a camera, to share that much of yourself. But that's what makes the drama happen. That's exactly what we need. And that's what will lead to you being featured in more episodes. Just relax, try to forget that the cameras are there at all."

That led us to counting, and we saw the scope of what was being done here. There were some three hundred people in teams of four surrounding us in a tight ring. They'd been creeping in while Francis had talked, and were now in full ambush position.

"Okay, so that's it for now. As you wait, please refrain from using any cellular device or contacting your family. Anyone who does will be disqualified from participation." He said that last part like it was an afterthought, not a large issue, and so we took it as such. Or tried to.

We stood in line. It was just after 9:45 in the morning when production had stopped for the last time. The last of us didn't get home until after dark. But they went as fast as they could, and after all when you get five thousand dollars for waiting in line, you'll find your patience expanding as necessary.

When our names were called, after we'd signed the form nine different ways and had what they called a head shot taken, and had been filmed saying what our names were and what we had until recently done at the factory, we drove home with a cameraman in our passenger seat. We were all asked the same questions. What did working at the factory mean to you? What will you do now? Do you have anything to fall back on? None of us had good answers.

The pilot of *Down 'N' Out* set the tone for much of what was to come. Gritty shots of the factory with half the color faded out. Our parking lot, the rusty sign that announced where Old Military Road met the highway. Our factory, bustling that last morning. They had been there without us knowing. Had shots of the packing line slowing to a stop as the siren sounded. They had footage of us gathering together, and of Martin telling us how sorry he was. Throughout, we were cut in introducing ourselves. My name is Lyle Younse, and I was the foreman for Doyles' Gear. My name is Whitney Tevebaugh, I drove a forklift. I'm Tammy Johnson and this is my husband Jason. I worked the packing line, manned the forge, operated the gear stamper. All of it in the past tense, just like we'd been told, none of us allowed to look right into the camera.

America watched us drive home, the lucky ones of us who had thought up something worth listening to—Jason and Tammy running through their savings accounts, trying to figure out how long they could keep the lights on with what they had, Tammy sobbing quietly and convincingly; Lyle saying that his job was all he'd known, that he'd been working at the factory since three days after he graduated from high school, that he didn't know if he could find more work here, didn't know if he could make himself leave.

They showed all of us opening our own front doors, those of us who had family looking at the people we shared our lives with, staring and really seeing them for the first time maybe ever. They showed all of us looking down, all of us mumbling. The factory closed. We were out of a job.

Briseño

We were unsure of what would happen now, what would become of us. But we would figure it out, somehow. We would. We knew.

Season 1, Episode 2:
Shining City at the Bottom of a Hill

At first, in spite of everything, it was exciting. White vans dotted the streets like magnolia trees. In addition to the plant's employees, other businesses and townspeople were put under contract, which meant almost everyone in town was on the show. For the first time it seemed like it wasn't just a bunch of individuals, but an *us*, a whole town of *us*. And at first *we* were doing not so badly at all.

As soon as the news hit, the town took off like kudzu— there were long lines for perms and dye jobs at the beauty parlor, for tune-ups and oil changes at Crash's Muffler Shop, and even the IGA, long suffocating under the low prices of the Walmart, found a boom in business. It seemed like everyone in town just couldn't wait to spend up the last of their old money looking good for their new jobs. And of course there were those out-of-town folks who wanted to see the cameras and the crews that operated them and perhaps to even catch a glimpse of themselves someday on television—all of which led the *Paris Express* to dub the city the "Hollywood of the River Valley."

We liked that, being a place that people wanted to visit. We liked having that reason to check our appearance when we passed the mirror in the hall, the one next to the family pictures that we were proud to say we had recently found the time to dust. Being on television was like getting all our New Year's resolutions to come true at once. We'd been finding lots of time for lots of things. Jason Johnson had bought his three boys a swing set and jungle gym requiring more than some assembly for Christmas back three years ago, which had since taken up permanent residence in the rafters of his garage, still shackled in the plastic packing straps.

Now, with his camera crew nodding along, Jason cleared a square of earth next to the old clothesline post in his backyard. It took less than three hours for the All-in-One Fun Station to go from notional concept to reality, complete with Junior and Ricky hanging off the monkey bars while their little brother, Dale, begged for a turn. Jason could see himself, or at least he thought he could, from a few yards away, his crew now ahead of him, now at the side so as to capture his profile in the arc of his swinging hammer. He liked to think about this being on television. Possibly when televised this would become a montage, or something with music behind it, which got him wondering about what the theme song for the show might be. Country probably or maybe old rock 'n' roll, some Lynyrd Skynyrd knockoff. If it were up to him he might want something with a touch more personality to it, gospel probably. Like Elvis. Jason thought these things and watched himself smiling as he pieced the swing set together.

Seeing him over the fence, Jason's neighbor Jamie Mallett struck up a conversation, and ended up coming over with his own hammer to help hang the giraffe-shaped crossbeam. When they finished they both stood back and nodded slightly at each other and at the swings and slides. Jamie said, "You know, I think there might be enough shingles left over in my garage for a new roof on that shed."

That was how the wandering work crews got started. Fences were mended, lawns mowed. As more of us saw the work, more of us joined or started going around on our own doing about the same thing. We patched concrete and cleared drains. We cleared ditches of trash, nailed down loose boards, and covered everything in a fresh coat of the cheap white paint someone had found in an outbuilding.

It took not long at all for the city to sparkle. Where things could be accomplished with hard work, water, borrowed shovels and lended ladders, they were. Within three weeks of that first swing set, the town looked like a commercial for itself and since it was so clean, so near to perfect, we took care to keep it that way, everyone doing the little things. We grew proud of our town, the way the pansies in the window boxes caught the dusk light, the weedless cracks in our driveways.

Thus it surprised us when we saw the opening credits of the show and what we learned were called establishing shots. So long after it all seemed over, we came to see a different city than our own. Some of the shots were taken before the cleanup got there, with the grass still in clumps and screen doors mildly askew, clapping in the wind. Some were even older, from before we thought the filming had begun. They'd been watching us for longer than we knew. Other shots like the one of the house leaning casually to the left, or the trailer with all the dogs—no one could place them, and we were forced to conclude that they weren't here at all—someplace altogether different. We talked about it amongst ourselves and someone even called the production company to ask about it, but the person who answered the phone didn't seem to understand our concern. We were *overreacting*, she said, no one had stolen our city. It was just storytelling—the magic of television, and perhaps it would be best if we didn't watch the show so closely, if at all. We hung up, dissatisfied yet partially unsure why we called in the first place.

All the same, it was unsettling. Seeing what was on the screen, knowing better, didn't make the effects of the dissolves and the hard cuts any less effective. We felt as though what had happened had happened elsewhere, to other people just like us, and that made it all the worse, watching not-us making all of our mistakes, each somehow more wrong because of that dirty city they'd found for all of that to happen in. Worse, we knew that even without our vanity, these familiar strangers would still become us. Like it or not we knew what was coming and we cringed.

But all that came after.

From the very beginning, we were surprised by how much they had to say to us. They sent each of us home with a binder full of rules and regulations. There was a page to cover everything we were supposed to do, and we signed something that said we'd read and understood it in full before they would give it to us. They made us read this page before we could leave the first day:

Telling Your Loved Ones the News

Down 'N' Out is a television show and you are one of its stars. Though you were unaware, we've been examining yours and other facilities for some time now. We've come to know you, and feel that your story is unique yet universal. We have chosen you, and we have done so for who you are.

So please, try not to withhold that great personality that we have come to love so much. Many people instinctively put on a false front when they're first filmed, worried about how they'll look later. Remember, it's you we love, so please try not to act like somebody else.

That means also—don't hold back! Remember that human drama is what makes television great. Crying in front of the camera or having a fight with your significant other might not seem like they speak positively of you but it's just this sort of reality that we think will make *Down 'N' Out* a hit for seasons to come.

For this reason, it's important not to let your family know that you will be compensated for your appearance on the show until after we've filmed their initial reactions to the news that the factory is closing. Though it might be hard to keep this from them when telling them might help to calm them down, you have to stay strong. We want our presence to have as little as an effect as possible, so the advantages of being on the program should remain hidden. We promise to finish in as few takes as possible. Remember, making the show great is great for all of us! **

For most of us, our husbands and wives were near us when the show started. Most factory families lived on two incomes, and thus most of us were lucky in that we only had to break the news to our children, many of whom were too young to fully understand what it meant. Still, four dozen wives and husbands had to hear it that way, that the factory had closed and that they had precisely one more paycheck coming and very little prospect for other work, and had to be filmed hearing it that way. Only then could they hear why none of that was exactly the case.

These shots were of great use to the production team. Having so many of them meant that they could speak to the size of the town, and by that they meant the scope of the show. Dozens of them were burnt up in the opening episode, but there were still plenty leftover. Enough, in fact, that each of the first four episodes of the season started the same way. A knock on the door. Whatever each of us said to our loved ones when we said it, and then the inevitable doubt and confusion.

The second episode began with Lyle, whom the producers had spotted early as having great potential. They liked his clean-cut good looks, and the way he looked hopeful when he was frowning, which was most of the time, and how his dark curly hair, which would have hung in ringlets if he'd let it grow that long, would have crowned him like the thorns of Jesus.

They filmed him walking out the door to his truck and they filmed him driving away. They sat in the cab with him. They listened to him explain that he was the foreman of the factory. He was in charge of how things had run there. The day-to-day of it. He was good at this job. Good at anticipating what might happen, of seeing threats before they became as much. They filmed the road in front of him, two lanes wide, lit only by his headlights, dotted with mailboxes and blister-packed by pine forest. They filmed him saying he wasn't so sure about what now.

His house, a post-manufactured home. It was a double-wide trailer that had been modified and added to in the ten years he had lived there. There was the porch in back, the windowboxes and the shutters, and right where the door had once been, a gigantic picture window, and in it Lyle's wife, Cathy, watching the white van follow her husband home.

When the crews saw her in their viewfinder, framed in plate glass and muslin curtains, soft colored hair spilling over her shoulders, the small mouth and the eyes that got larger and maybe more blue when she was worried, they knew they had their star. It helped that she was beautiful, that her husband was as well. It helped more that, according to the data sheet Lyle had filled out, they were both just past thirty and had no children. But what it really was, what really led the showrunner to radio to the producers to pick up their live feed and confirm what they suspected, was the way that she looked at them, shed a single strangely visible tear, and nodded. She packed her whole emotional response into that one moment without ever being coached into it.

Lyle opened the door the way he always did. It was never locked, but he took his keys out of his pocket anyways, pulled the knob right before left. He saw her and his face lit like a match in the dark and he said, "Thank you."

She walked up and held him as always and said, "I love you too," the two of them long ago agreeing that love and gratitude were awful close. She kissed him hard, just the way she kissed him every day he came home from work, and you can tell because this kiss has a piece of all those others.

He tells her, tells her just the way they wanted him to, with all the bad parts first and foremost. She doesn't need to nod. Others of us in town reported later that when they heard the news their wives and husbands became intractable, took to swearing and screaming, unsure of what to do with this awful thing. Cathy waited. She could feel the steadiness in his eyes and turned it right back to him. She knew there was more to the story than the tragedy. She beamed her strength into him and waited for him to stop crying and to finish the story. She looked as though she'd known the whole time.

She hadn't known. She hadn't any idea. But when she saw tragedy writ large across his face, she knew she had a job and she made to do it right away. And they showed three full minutes of her and Lyle holding each other and whispering in each other's ears that things would work out. They would find a way. The news of the factory, the job, it was almost expected. It was one of the many contingencies that she had foreseen, if not planned for. She held him until they both grew still, certain that the two of them were strong enough for this.

Then they turned the cameras off and explained about the show. And as soon as this second explanation came, even with its promise of money, with absolute proof of a sort that the faith she had just now relied upon was well founded, it emptied her out. She couldn't think why exactly, but something in her screamed to flinch, and at each added explanation she fell deeper into worry until she realized the sobs she heard were hers now and that they'd started filming again so as not to waste such valuable footage.

In post-production they edited this scene so that the calm reactions came only after the tears and worry. It made for a well-rounded scene. The husband comes home, the wife suspects the worst. The husband reveals the problem they will have to deal with, the wife becomes distraught and breaks down. Together they comfort each other and convince themselves that there is yet reason for hope. The truth of it, so far as there's any of that going around, was the opposite. She suspected something she could plan for, and almost got it. She provided stability and comfort to him, convinced him that his job was less than essential. Her worry only came about as a response to something else she didn't yet understand. What ought to be remembered is that the tears were the end of it all and not the beginning.

When they'd filmed for about an hour, and were absolutely certain the Younses weren't going to start fighting until at least tomorrow morning, the camera crew thanked them for their time and let themselves out. Cathy and Lyle sat next to each other on the couch just out of touch. Neither moved for some time until Cathy was overcome with curiosity and opened the large binder that the crew had left on the coffee table on their way out the door.

Section II: Life as a Television Star

As we begin this journey together, remember that change—and lots of it—is only natural. Keep in mind that change is good; change is, in fact, one of the things we are here to capture. But while certain changes are important—even vital—others can be harmful to our shared goals. If, for instance, a family of Down 'N' Outers left town and moved far away to stay with well-off relatives, this might not be a positive change. Not only does this prevent that family from interacting with the larger *Down 'N' Out* community (for more on interacting with other cast please see CHAPTER 4) they also in a sense cheat. While the rest of us are here in Paris getting by how we can, this one family sits around in a house they haven't paid for, eating someone else's food. This is unfair to the rest of us, and more importantly it doesn't make for great television.

For these reasons, and to help you, we created a list of good and bad changes. Here are some Dos and Don'ts for the next six months:

Do:
- Make your own food
- " " " clothes
- " " " household goods
- " " " games and toys
- Tighten the old belt
- Hold a bake sale
- Hold a yard sale
- Hold a craft sale
- Get rid of unnecessary possessions
- Ride a bike instead of driving
- Reuse, recycle, repurpose
- Sacrifice to make ends meet

Don't:
- Move away from the target area
- Rely on savings
- Seek aid from charitable organizations
- Accept book deals, interviews requests, or promotional agreements
- Wear clothes with copyrighted logos of any kind
- Take a job
- Accept monetary or material aid from friends, families, or other persons discussed
- Discuss this document or the contract it contains on camera or at all with nonparticipants

To help residents follow these guidelines, each family's camera crew will also act as a reality checkpoint, offering guidance and suggestions on how best to participate. To best do this job, crews may ask for copies of bank records, financial holdings, address books, email contacts, phone records, etc. Noncompliance may lead to contract cancellation.

That very next day, while Lyle was outside looking for something to do and the cameras followed him around, Cathy Leann Younse prayed, which was not something she was used to doing. She and Lyle attended service semi-regularly at the Catholic church downtown near the old optical shop. But what she really cared for was the music; God the Almighty maker of heaven and whatever else wasn't something she gave much thought to. But this was different and new to her and so she knelt down in the front room in front of the couch and said out loud, "Dear God, this is Cathy. I don't know whether or not to give my money to the TV show. They made it seem like it was nothing out of the ordinary, a special account. But I just don't know."

She'd been up most of the night reading the handbook. While most of it seemed vaguely ominous, one thing in particular stuck on her mind. According to the book, she was required to hand over any saved sums of cash greater than five hundred dollars for holding. It was necessary to do so to keep the audience from asking questions. Some families being able to stay afloat longer than others would be confusing to viewers at home. And so all savings usage was limited. Any balance over five hundred dollars would be held in a special account, they said. She would get the money back in six months or less. But there were yards of tiny print at the back of the handbook, something she'd been raised to be wary of. She worried that if she went down to the office and handed them her money, she would never see it again. What did these folks from the coast care about her and her money? How easy would it be for them to misplace a few measly thousand dollars, call it an oversight? It is no little thing to trust a stranger, and it bothered her deeply to see all of her neighbors so willingly participating in this little adventure.

But more than that it was where the money had come from and what it was for. It was true that Lyle made what amounted to good money in Paris. It was why they owned this home outright and how they'd managed to add the porch and the picture window and the shutters. But even still, no one here had extra money, least of all her. Saving as much as she had had meant sacrifice, plain and dirty. She'd been cutting her own hair for four years, something the ladies at the beauty salon took as a personal insult, and which led to her being mildly estranged from the few girlfriends she'd retained since high school. She'd been washing the dishes by hand because the soap to run the dishwasher cost a little bit more, been sewing together everything that came apart until some of her underwear and a great deal of Lyle's socks were more darning than darned.

She had been living without for longer than she could think to count by now, the results of which were in a manila envelope taped to the wall behind the box that held her wedding dress at the very back of her closet. Forty-six hundred dollars. The words had a magic to them, the sum potential energy of all that wishing. Or at least they had, until last night. Now she wanted to dig the money out just to make sure it was there. But of course she couldn't, largely because Lyle didn't know about the money at all.

It broke her heart not to tell him about it, the first and

only secret she had kept from him in the twelve years they'd been married. But it had started a great deal smaller than it was now, as a simple gesture, a putting back of a tiny amount of extra money she had. She told herself it might be for a trip or a special present or just so that he couldn't see how much his Christmas presents cost when they balanced the checkbook together. She didn't let herself even think about what the money was really for, felt like saying it would mean someone could take it away from her. And that was it, of course, she couldn't think about it, and so she certainly couldn't have told him about it. Not that he would have been surprised.

Not that any of us were. If you asked us about Lyle and Cathy Younse, and the camera folks asked all of us, we would tell you first and foremost that they were good people and good neighbors, that he was a fine foreman and that she was a sweet woman who volunteered to decorate for the Christmas party every year. We would probably mention that they lived on Old Military, that they were both born and raised here, children raised on factory salaries themselves. And before long, if you kept asking for more, and probably if you didn't, we would mention that they had no children.

We didn't talk about it, not that often. Of course sometimes when we'd see her bringing an extra-large casserole over after a funeral, or the Christmas wreath of pine boughs she'd found the time to make, we'd let it slip. We didn't mean it cross, just as a simple statement of fact— it must be nice. Sure would be easy that way, wouldn't it? We never said the other part, never accused her of being less of anything, and really it was a kind of jealousy more than anything.

But Cathy didn't hear the jealousy. She only heard the whispers, and the every-so-often hinting questions from someone who felt her age gave her the right to ask such things forthrightly. No, they didn't have any children, but they would love to. She resented very much having to confirm that yes, they were trying, wanted to rise up against the gross invasion of privacy such a question represented. But she didn't, because she knew that she couldn't. She knew that our quiet, well-meaning whispers would turn only too quick to something else, had seen so firsthand.

She wanted more than anything to scream the truth at them—that she and Lyle had been trying to make a baby since even before they were married. They had names picked out a decade back. But no children had come. Not so much as a whiff of one. Her period came regular as the mail every month. Lyle was compassionate and honest about it, wondered openly if it wasn't probably his fault and not hers. She watched his nostrils contract as he fought to ignore emotions when he told her how sorry he was, that if their insurance covered such things or if there was a way, any way at all, that they could afford it, that he would be the first to volunteer for medical examination at the nearest fertility clinic down in Little Rock.

She watched him say this to her once or twice a year, a sort of unscheduled ritual between the two of them. He apologized to her and then she apologized to him and then he cried for the both of them and then one of them said something about a miracle. Then one day she was driving back from some far-away errand and saw a sign in front of the Baptist church in Camden that said, "Miracles don't happen. They are worked." That was the day she took

Down and Out

twenty dollars from the grocery budget and put it in a hiding spot. She didn't even know exactly what the money would go to—doctors' visits, adoption fees? But she couldn't stand to have a problem and not at least try to solve it, figuring the first step was always to pick your foot up and move it away from where it'd been.

And that was how there was $4600 hidden behind her wedding dress. And that was why now she was praying to Jesus while Lyle was outside. And it was why, without really even deciding to, because some things happen to you, even things that will always be your fault, they still happen to you, she wrote o in the box on the form that said "cash on hand," and it was why she looked worried and like she was acting when Lyle came back in and asked her if something was wrong.

Season 1, Episode 3: The Greatest Daddy in Logan County

Martin Gossett's father, Albert Gossett, was our optometrist—the one in the shop downtown. Back then, Doyles' would halve the cost of custom-fit safety glasses, which meant everyone had a pair, which meant that the Gossetts were one of the wealthier families in town. Two thirds of Martin's graduating class at Paris High school—twenty-four of thirty-five—filled out applications at the factory the week after commencement; Martin had applied to colleges all over the country. He had cars, clothes, anything we could think to want. But most found it hard to begrudge Martin his privilege; he had too level a head, kept too quiet, was too honest and too helpful and too busy smiling at everyone. We all agreed that the credit was due to Dr. Albert.

"This town has been good to me and mine, damn good," we'd heard the Doc say—at Lion's Club Meetings and church fundraisers, and to his son when he thought no one was listening. "It's been damn good, and you never get finished paying debts like that. Never."

Martin walked around like he had that tattooed on his eyeballs. When we hung around him, we got to feeling like it was us that had it easy, that we were glad that we were riding shotgun in the new Mustang and not driving it. When he did go off to college, Martin went to Joplin, the tiny liberal arts school on the other side of the mountains. He left that August, and we assumed we would all but never see him again, and for a while we were right.

Martin didn't come back for summer breaks, or for more than a few days at Christmas, or at all on most Easters. When he was home, he didn't see anybody, didn't run into folks at the gas station and the Walmart. He even quit coming to church, which when we looked back on it should have been the first sign. If you happened to catch him someplace, get to talking to him, it was always the same Martin, too kind to accuse of anything, but he had a nervous look about him, like you'd caught him in a lie just by waving at him.

The talk was that after he graduated from the university, we'd see even less of Martin, that he'd pull away and soon enough it would be his parents who would be the ones traveling on holidays, flying off to who knows where to see grandkids we'd only know from wallet snapshots. And really, we didn't hate him for it, not that much. It was what we'd all have done.

But instead, Martin came home, and he brought a woman with him that he swore was his wife.

They'd met, he would tell us, one day after class, when Martin had followed a pair of hips out of his comparative literature class and found they were the property of a girl with hazel eyes and golden-brown curls, a wide pretty mouth. Her name was Marla, and she was where he'd been when he wasn't at home.

Of course we'd known that Martin couldn't help but marry well—better, probably, than the town could offer. But when we pictured the future Mrs. Gossett, we hadn't seen that winking smile, the tattoo peeking out from the left sleeves of her blouses. For starters she was both from the city and from Texas—Fort Worth, she said—and it showed in her bare shoulders and her vocabulary. We were proud of the way we stopped it there, left it at a regional issue. But once, back when Mrs. Mallett was still driving, she'd run into Marla at the market and remarked in her absolute most politest voice that we hadn't seen her at church yet. Marla gave too big of a smile and said offhandedly, "I gave up the church a long time ago"—right there in the Save-A-Lot. The owners of the Double Deuce reported that she had once visited their establishment—by herself—and tried to order a whiskey at four o'clock in the afternoon. Joanna down at the courthouse reported in a hushed whisper that, according to their mortgage papers, Marla hadn't even taken his name, was still, in the eyes of the law, Marla Esperanza Sanchez.

We had to admit that the two of them, Martin and Marla, were certainly fond of each other. They spent every moment they could find together, always sat on the same side of a booth at the Grapevine. If you ever saw one of them meet the other, you saw their eye teeth, that big awkward unfakeable smile. Some swore they'd seen them kissing while stopped at the red light. And certainly, she was beautiful, certainly gifted and intelligent. She volunteered at the animal shelter and brought unpronounceable but delicious dishes to all the company potlucks.

We all had to admit, she made Martin happy.

So when they threw a second reception here in town, we all danced at what we called their wedding, all told Martin what a catch she was. We all made room for them the best we could. Surprising us all, Martin took the business degree he and his father had compromised on and got on in the office at Doyles', and before long he was the

Down and Out

Operations Manager in name, and the only one who mattered in practice. The Doyleses themselves were still in charge of the company. But Martin pulled the strings, Martin made the reports, Martin told people when they were fired and when they had to work overtime. We all called him Boss and nodded at him when we saw him on the floor of the factory, measuring our efficiency, giving a tour to investors or school children.

Marla opened an art studio in the old strip mall next to the Supertire, and a few of us sent our daughters to her for lessons, even though at first she didn't think that's what an art studio was for. We invited them to our barbecues, and when we passed each other going opposite directions down Route 22, we waved.

But there were always whispers, like there had to be. Probably a lot of things were said but most of all we told each other one thing, whispered it after we'd left their dinner parties, after we saw their car in our rearviews. *It can't last*, we all said, and even when we didn't say it, our smiles did, or the way we took her credit card when we changed her oil, the way we signed checks for the lessons we had to teach her to teach our children. *How could it?* we thought, and without even knowing we were doing it we started thinking about Marla as Martin's first wife.

To Martin, this meant damn near nothing. He'd known before the first time he'd touched Marla that it would never be easy. He knew above all where he was from and that this meant a thing. Yes, the two of them could have moved elsewhere, but he knew what Paris meant to him, just like he knew as soon as he saw her that he would love her every day of the rest of his life. He knew that these two things contradicted each other, and he knew that he could live with it. When he was smiling so politely, bowing his head his whole life and forcing us to like him even though probably we shouldn't have, Martin got to know this town better than most, like only those on the edge can know something, from the inside and the out. And because he knew, he could live with it.

For Marla it wasn't as easy. Her love was as strong as his, maybe stronger, but she was also from Southside Fort Worth, which was far enough away that it might have been the other Paris for all it meant to us. When she walked the aisles of the Save-A-Lot, picking over the dusty onions and turning peaches, you could see her in an intimate urban grocery buying all the produce she asked for that we'd never heard of, shopping in a place we'd only recognize from a movie. She brought the city with her, its light and its vibrancy, but keeping that light seemed to grow wrinkles on the skin beneath her eyes.

That must be it, we said. Of course we didn't think of it as a race thing, we repeated. We treated her just the same as everybody else who was from out of town, every city person, every Texan.

Marla never told us, of course, what it was like not to be from Paris, probably because we never asked. When she and Martin were newlyweds, we saw her on the phone constantly, staying in touch with friends from college and what she kept calling "the real world." Over the years, with the kids and the studio, we noticed that she was on the phone a good deal less. Whether she still kept up with her other friends we couldn't say. She didn't seem like she was lacking human contact, and she certainly had a loving family. We assumed that this was enough, that even if she wasn't from here, she was happy. Who wouldn't be happy married to the best man in Paris?

She found a way to make Paris work, and it was in this that she belonged the most. He got every promotion there was to have out of the Doyleses. Children came, first Layne and then Stacey, both beautiful in the same way as their mother. They still didn't come to church, but Marla learned to say that they were just too busy, and most of us learned not to resent her too much for it. We didn't try to turn her out, even if we thought about it. Almost certainly she couldn't have known how we all thought about her. We called them neighbors, and we saw Martin as a part of the work that we did, and Marla in turn as a part of Martin. All of us settled in together, and we thanked Martin, and through him Marla, for running his side of the factory the same way that we ran ours.

And no one ever even tried to deny that we did a hard day's work, nor did anyone ever claim that the gears that we made were of any but the highest quality. Martin told us as much every year at the Fourth of July picnic, at the Christmas party. He led us to feel pride in the things that we did, told us that there was an us, that we had earned the right to think and talk this way. He told us, and we often repeated, that at one point, Doyles' Gears were found in almost every American car, seventy-five percent of tractors, most bulldozers, a fair number of diesel trains, and in every single oil derrick the whole world over.

What Martin didn't tell us was that what cost a dollar from our plant cost fifty cents from China, shipping somehow included. Of course those gears were less precise, broke sooner and with far graver results than did ours. But for the automakers and the tractor companies and even, over time, the oil derrick welders, obsolescence became a feature rather than a failure. Why pay more when all it meant was that one particular part could outlast the whole rest of the shoddy machine built around it? By the end it was a single bicycle company and a handful of custom engine builders who still wanted the unmatched quality that Doyles' had come to represent.

Martin never told us that every single day the furnace burned seven thousand dollars' worth of coal, that to blow it out and relight it cost twice that. No one knew that because of this we kept stamping gears well beyond what the order sheets required, kept stamping until warehousing what we made and couldn't sell became its own financial burden. Only Martin and the secretary/accountant knew for certain that the factory had long since become unviable.

Martin did everything in his power to keep the factory alive. He pitched his product to every mechanical manufacturer that would listen and several who wouldn't, spent countless hours and thousands of dollars he knew we didn't have researching ways to modernize and retool the factory, to find a thing that it could make that people needed.

Some of us even thought it strange when we saw in the pilot just what all he'd done to keep the factory working. His name wasn't on the door, and his Daddy hadn't even worked at the factory like so many of ours had. But Martin drove past the old square on his way home, past the old Gossett Optical shop. Martin's parents, who had passed on just after meeting their second granddaughter, had sold the shop to a junior partner when Martin came home. Since then the partner had moved the practice out to Clarksville where there was more work. But even now, if he looked just right, Martin could see his own name written into the

Down and Out

bricks, a cleaner part of a rusty stain.

As a child, Martin had only rarely been punished, and even then his father never hit him. When it was necessary to make a point, as Albert would have said it, Martin went with his father to the office early on a Saturday. His father opened the door, handed him a square of soft felt, and went to the back room. Martin would slide out the wide heavy drawers, open each Naugahyde case, and polish every individual lens. Some of the frames were thin spindles of golden wire like librarians wore, others wide tortoiseshell plastics that were seen in their way as stylish. But almost every case had a pair of wide black safety glasses, almost every receipt was stamped "Bill to: Doyles' Gear." Martin's father never checked his work, just like he never lectured him afterwards, or said a word to him until after the job was finished. Martin often wondered, well into adulthood, if he had learned the right lessons.

He thought on it frequently as he mulled what else might be done to keep Doyles' Gear alive. But long before he let himself admit it he knew that no lack of sleep or extra effort would do the trick, that there was no answer to find. The factory would close. He made plans, canceled the coal orders, ran numbers on severance checks. He was thinking of when to tell us and what, when he got an odd phone call.

The very first camera crew took an after-hours tour of the factory in February, drove through and around town all night and into the following morning. They weren't in a white van then, but a rental car with darkly tinted windows. They filmed through the back glass, taking in almost every street in town. Martin, able salesman that he was, tried to steer them towards the finer points of town, why he felt that his factory and its employees were uniquely able to provide this product and service. But the two men in the front seat had a conversation Martin could only barely follow, snapping back and forth about pass-through saturation, location monetization, coverage ratios, wireless radii, and so on until Martin didn't know if they were even sharing information or just passing the time in a language of their own creation. They dropped Martin off at the factory ten minutes till nine, said, "We'll be in touch," as they drove away.

Two days later a purchase order came into Martin's office for a hundred thousand dollars' worth of gears from a company that he'd never heard of. The purchase order did not specify the size, or even the number of gears that were required, only a factory in India to ship them to and a date of expected final delivery—six months. A week after the purchase order, Martin got a contract that asked him to agree have to his life videotaped as part of a potential reality series relating to Doyles' Gear, along with a short note: "It will take time for production to begin. Keep things silent until then."

News of the strange purchase order spread instantly through the factory and then the town, and probably we should have been more suspicious. But like most folks who have been sworn to secrecy, the accountants had let slip that how bad things had gotten, how close it might truly be, and the news had spread through town like a toxic cloud. This new purchase order blew it away, turned it back into the rumor it was. We forgot, if we'd ever known, that it was Martin who had filled in the details regarding what sort of gears we'd be stamping, and set instead to what we then did best.

That night before the last day of the factory, the first

official camera crew went home with Martin. It was a Monday, which meant vegetarian, and Marla had settled on a Mediterranean theme, prepared a spread of hummus, couscous, baba ghanouj, and dark rich olives. She had bought all of this in Little Rock, a two-hour drive down the interstate, a trip she made twice a month to buy organic produce and Portuguese white wine and conditioner that worked.

Because he had been told to, Martin had not informed his wife that he would be bringing strangers with video cameras to dinner, just like he hadn't told her yet that the factory was closing in the morning, that the town and everything in it was different now whether they knew it yet or not. The producers had explained that this was vitally important, the surprise factor, they called it, and had insisted no matter how Martin argued. It was the first time he'd ever kept anything more serious than a Christmas present from Marla.

She saw them pull up through the front window, saw the four men in matching green polo shirts pile out of the white van and start taking establishing shots. Her reaction was allergic, the sight of the boom mic liked to make her throat close up. Then Martin rung his own doorbell and waited for her to answer. When she did, she found her husband standing there, his mouth a small crooked line, his outline black against the floodlights. "Honey, I have some bad news," she heard him say. Then the camera crew led itself inside, took aim on the inside of the door, and told Martin to back up and do it again. She tried to ask what bad news, but by then there were five production assistants and a boom operator resetting her foyer, and she wasn't even sure who exactly she was asking, though certainly no one answered.

When the crew was settled enough to create a sense of seamless continuity, Martin and she were seated on the couch, and then, when that didn't have the right light, at the dinner table, and she finally heard about the factory. It hit her like hailstones in May, glancing off more easily than you'd think, the damage less than you'd figured, it being only the roof, just the dog that's bleeding. Still it was hard to look away.

She says, "It's gone?"

Martin talks into his drink, "I tried so hard."

She starts crying, and the camera spreads over the dinner table, the food untouched like a moonscape, oil pooling in the center of most of everything. She gets up slowly from the table, walks even more slowly to the door.

"Wait," says Martin, as her fingers twist the silver knob. "Don't go. Not like this. I love you."

She turns around, looks at him.

The camera looks at him.

The door closes.

That's what it looked like on the show. And really, if the truth is told, the editors did good work. There were so many more pauses and coughs, so much fat to trim. What was left behind was a cleaner thing. Something that made sense to us. The truth of the matter came through. The camera captured the look of bewildered shock and pain in that first moment of opening the door to a television crew, even if it left out Marla saying, "What the fuck is all this?" after the crew piled in without explanation and really, what's lost in that?

Who had need of watching Marla pour herself a juice

glass of brown liquor and drain it undramatically before she asked him, "It's gone?"

What would it add if you heard him yell back, "I told you that, didn't I? Do you like hearing me say it? Is that it?"

She said, "I do want to hear it, just once, without the self-pity and the martyr face, one goddamn time." She gestured to the camera, was told not to. "What, is that some kind of an imposition?"

He stood up hard enough to knock his chair over, but he didn't pick it up. He walked to the bar, poured his own glass of liquor, took to drinking it like it was work. He didn't pull his eyes away, and he said into his drink, "I tried so hard."

Marla's face broke like dry earth in a rainstorm, and she went to him, stumbling over the chair into his arms. "Baby, I love you," she told him, "like it hurts. So much."

They held each other for long enough that the cameraman lost interest, drifted the shot around the room to where Layne and Stacey sat coloring. From his arms she said, "But you know that this is over now."

He grabbed her arms and found her eyes, and she nodded long enough to make his face crumple before she said, "The factory."

He didn't understand.

"The town, all of it. It's over now."

He pulled away. "Not yet. Almost, but not yet."

She walked back to the liquor cabinet, but he stopped her, sat her down, took her glass, filled it only a third of the way full. She took the drink from him, stared him right in the eye, and drank it down. "The fire goes out tomorrow. No more gears."

He shook his head, "There's more work to do yet."

"This," said Marla, gesturing wildly with her drink in the general direction of camera two, being told not to, "is not work."

He makes to explain, but she holds the glass up, cuing silence.

"I followed you to here. To the rusty buckle of the fucking Bible Belt, to Paris fucking Arkansas. And I did it"— she dropped her glass—"I did it for you. But I won't follow you to basic cable." Her empty hand kept the shape of the glass on the ground. She gestured to the camera again, was told not to. "I think I've been watched enough around here as it is. I put in my time. When are you going to follow me?"

Martin hung his head. "It's just not that simple."

Marla went back to him, and held him again, again for longer than the camera had use for. "That's just it," she said. "It is that simple. We leave, and it's gone. You tried, you did your part, and now we go."

"I'm under contract," said Martin, and he was reminded not to mention his contract. "If I leave they can call off the whole thing."

"Didn't you say they had sixty camera crews watching the whole factory?" The production assistant told her not to mention the cameras and she showed the camera her middle finger. She was told not to do that, that they couldn't use footage like that. Marla showed the other camera her other middle finger, so that her arms were spread wide, one in each direction. "Do you really think they would quit, now? Would they give up? Doyles' needed you, maybe, but this will be well enough on its own. You know it."

Martin walked over and picked her glass up off the ground, polished it against his shirt, set it down neatly on the bar. "You don't get it, Marla. I can't take that chance.

Down and Out

What if I leave and they cancel everybody's contract, what if they use it as some sort of an excuse not to pay them? What would they do? We might could move along, but they don't have savings accounts because I didn't pay them enough to save. They gave that factory their whole lives for nine thirty-five an hour, and were lining their kids up to do the same, and I didn't even have to say thank you. I won't take any chances."

"Mr. Savior." She swung her chair to the left. "Mr. Hero." She swung it back to the right, and the camera got a good view of the flush on her face. "Logan County's own personal Jesus Christ." She started to cry, and the camera focused in on her, watched every tear pool at the corner of her eye. After a silent minute the camera spread over the dinner table, the food untouched like a moonscape, oil pooling in the center of most of everything.

Martin went to hold her again, but she pushed him away. "You don't get it," he said.

"What? What don't I get?"

"Commitment, human fucking decency, what this place really means."

Her face darkened, the corners of her mouth pulled up in a snarl. She started out crying, and in a moment she was furious, at Martin and at the town and at the cameras, and then something melted across her face and what's left behind was a sense of unsettling resolve and a crooked mascara trail.

"This town is the only thing you'll ever understand," she said, and then stopped and composed herself, willed straightness to her limbs.

She got up slowly from the table, walked even more slowly to the door.

He jumped up and followed her, the camera shook as it hustled to get them back in focus. "Where the hell do you think you're going?" he said.

"I didn't sign anything. I'm not going to be a clown, it won't happen. If you won't come with me, if you want to doubt my goddamn commitment, then you can deal without me."

"Wait," said Martin, as her fingers twisted the sliver knob. "Don't go. Not like this. I love you."

"How else is it going to be?" she said. "Tell me, if I stay and wait this shitstorm out, and let everyone I know see me, what then? Would you go then? Or would you find something else that needs you, some other way to hang on? Go ahead, tell me, Martin, tell me there's an end to this." She stood with her hands on her hips. Then, when she saw that he really couldn't answer, she walked back to him, kissed him once, hard, then turned back around.

She opened the door, turned around, and looked at him.

The camera looked at him.

The door closed.

The Gossetts always kept to themselves, so it took a while for us to hear either version of the story. It came, the way it always does, but when it did, our version ended up more like the one on television, so none of us were really surprised when this became the climax of our pilot, weren't surprised when we won a prime slot in the weeknight lineup. A mother, leaving her children, and on some level we knew it. Hadn't we been telling this story for years? And if we hadn't been the neighbor to Marla we should have, wasn't it because we had been right about her and Martin this whole time?

Down and Out

But we were surprised that the rest of the story never made the show. When Marla showed up the next day with a used pickup truck, loaded up her belongings, and headed off back to Texas or wherever, and when she and Martin fought in the yard until the sheriff came—we felt for sure this would make the show, but it never came up. A month or so later, when Martin got the divorce papers, he walked downtown and drank the better part of the storeroom at the Double Deuce, and again this was, for whatever reason, not a part of the storyline. Even the parade of semi-eligible women that kept finding their way over, just to see how the girls were doing, all were left out like so many blinks and farts.

Yet Martin was still in almost every episode. Part of it was the girls. They had their mother's darker skin tone, but hair too light a shade to last, and were always willing to giggle on command or hold a fish by the tail and pretend it smelled bad. But most of Martin's screen time came from his willingness to be involved in the show. Martin was always willing to volunteer to try and cook something using only cornstarch and a can of cream of mushroom, and then eat whatever it was that he had left in the pan with a smile and a few saltines. Of course, we all did as we were asked, but Martin had a knack for doing it in just the right way. They asked us all to ride bikes around during week eight and to say that it was for saving gas, but Martin left Marla's ten-speed in the garage and instead put the training wheels back on Stacey's drop-bar cruiser before pedaling the six miles to town. A clip of this was released as a teaser on YouTube and garnered thirty million views before the show debuted. Some wondered why Martin tried so hard, guessed privately that his contract must include some clause we didn't know about, but we were told not to discuss our contracts. But it seemed like every time that Marla called to talk to the girls, the family was busy living in front of the cameras. Still, it was not lost on us that the one who needed the money the least would, per the contracts we signed, get paid the most.

Anyhow, when the camera crew asked him to look into the camera and say, "I met a man who was willing to trade my television for a mule," he turned into the camera and said it, and without further prompting and only a few audible sighs, he went to his front room and unscrewed the television from the wall.

Folks from far enough away assume that everyone in the South or from a town of less than three thousand souls is at least a part-time farmer. The truth is that an optometrist's son from around here knows about as much about animal husbandry as an optometrist's son from just about anywhere. But even Martin knew well enough to be wary of mules, that they were mean enough to have a word, ornery, seemingly reserved just for them.

Martin pulled up to a shed in a cloud of red dust. To get there he'd taken Old Military down past Jamie Jack Landing to a part of the county he hadn't seen since he was in high school, cruising the dirt roads connecting corn fields to cotton patches, drinking tall beers from sweating cans. He honked his horn, and an old man came shuffling out of doors, already giggling.

It seemed pretty clear to Martin that his fifty-two-inch plasma was worth two of any animal on the property, and every business sense he had screamed out when the man led over a scarcely animated carcass with more ears than teeth. The animal and its owner shared the same dusty gray color, and both seem crooked like trees that had stood in the same wind too long. When he saw Martin balk, the man giggled again and said, "Don't forget, mister, that includes that trailer yonder," spitting in the direction of the trailer, just as the production crew had asked him to.

For his part, the man was more amused by this than anything, had been amused since that morning when the sissy had knocked on his trailer and proposed that if he would agree to part with the sorry animal visible from the road and also take up chewing tobacco for the afternoon, he could net a new TV and a thousand dollars besides.

Oh, thanks, thought Martin, looking at the rusted horse cart sitting unevenly leaned against a pile of used straw. He looked out of the corner of his eye at the camera crew like they'd taught him to. He wanted to take his television home, to screw it back to the wall, or at least to demand something else in barter. But then he considered in what certain ways the camera crew was likely to let him sweeten the bargain, and so instead he sighed heavily, shook it off, smiled at the camera, and said, "I guess we got a deal."

When he got home, the crew suggested that the animal would be much more comfortable if he let it out of the cart. It took him twenty minutes to unlatch the door. While he worked, the mule eyed him with practiced disinterest, and when the door finally sprung open, the mule stood with the same look on his face. Martin has presumed that the animal would take full advantage of his newfound freedom, but the animal seemed content to stand in the shade of the trailer and watch Martin for as long as he could.

The old man had included what looked to be a full assortment of harnesses and reins, but the ball of leather straps seemed, at the moment, more trouble that it was worth. Martin tied a rope around the mule's neck, and pulled for all he was worth. The mule stood chewing its tooth like it was muttering prayers to itself and flicking flies with its tail.

Try talking to it, the crew suggested.

Martin gulped, and his thoughts ran to polishing row after row of black safety frames, and said, "Woo Mule sooie! Come here, boy," though it occurred to him and embarrassed him that he hadn't sexed the mule before purchase. "Come on out, Mule," he said, pulling harder on the rope, clicking his tongue like he'd seen in a movie, and when clicking didn't work, whistling. The mule stood entirely unaffected other than tilting its head to one side as to regard Martin more clearly.

Martin fetched a sharp stick, walked to the back, and tried to poke the animal through the air vent, but he couldn't quite reach. He was preparing to fist fight the mule, if only for a sense of catharsis, when he heard his daughters giggling from the front porch. The mule rushed past him, knocking him into the mud and running right to the girls' outstretched arms.

"What's the horsey's name?" asked Layne.

"It's a mule, sweetheart. It doesn't have a name."

The animal rubbed its long muzzle against Stacy's blond head. "Let's name him Horsey," she said, and giggled in a way that reminded Martin of the man who was no doubt watching his television this very moment.

Within five minutes both girls were riding without reins or saddle. Horsey cantered around the yard at an agreeable pace, bobbing his head and making slow loops around the production van.

On the forth lap around, Stacey cried out, "This is the

best present ever. And you're the best Daddy in the whole world," and then, because they thought it might have been cute, they had her say "the best Daddy in Arkansas" and a few others, a new exclamation every time the mule made a lap, until it was too dark to film outside.

They had no fence, so that night Martin tied the mule to the porch, half hoping the thing would break loose and wander off before anyone knew whose problem it was. He went back in, then came out again with a juice glass full of brown liquor and sat drinking in the company of the mule, trying not to think about Marla. Instead, he wondered what, exactly, a mule was good for, not just for him, but for the show. He knew well enough that letting the girls ride it around could only be a start to something. The size of the animal alone filled him with an unfamiliar kind of dread.

Horsey seemed to sway with the wind like the trees did, seemed unfairly comfortable in his loose and shedding hide. Martin found himself looking into the mule's eyes, surprised and disoriented by the depth of their sorrow. He looked much longer than he meant to, and when Horsey finally broke the stare to chew at the crabgrass near his feet, Martin felt as though the mule had somehow gotten a point across, whatever it might be, and they both stood there drinking up the darkness.

Season 1, Episode 4:
Everything Will Be All Right

Jamie Mallett was the sort of man who took pride in how few questions he asked. Good news or bad, it was coming either way. He had worked for the last thirteen years in the forge, where we turned raw metal into usable lumps. Six men per shift tended to and worked in the furnace, rotating in and out in half-hour shifts, it being illegal to work any longer than that. His job was to use a pair of three-foot tongs to reach into the fire and turn loose the unformed lumps, and to retrieve the tray he'd dropped them onto once the metal had melted into the mold provided. The furnace was made of concrete, walls four and a half feet thick. To reach inside was to bend from the waist and to lean towards four thousand degrees Fahrenheit. That kind of heat travels like electricity through everything it touches. It can lick through the creases of the thickest leather gloves and aprons, and settle permanently into the folds along the back of your neck.

It was a heat that molded the men who served it to its needs. They learned to shave close because the heat can melt your whiskers to your face if you're not careful about how you take your gear off. Their faces took on a flush that never went away, a tan deeper than a tan that in Jamie's case gave life to his cheeks and made his green eyes stand out like Christmas ornaments. Jamie's hair was coarse and black where it hadn't gone to silver early. We didn't know if we could blame the heat for the look across his face, the way he seemed to demand and be granted more space than most men. We wondered this because we knew the heat lingered long after you'd swear it must have slipped away. The tongs Jamie had been using were still hot enough to sear flesh twenty minutes after he'd been let go from the one job he'd ever had.

It was a job that Jamie had inherited, passed down to him from his father, Jim Mallett, who had been the first forge master the factory had ever had and who held the job for some forty-three years. Half of us were second- and some third-generation employees, but Jamie was the only one to work literally in the shoes his father wore.

It had begun, as really most things did around here, in high school. Jamie was a little taller then, walked with a looseness in his step. Things had gone well for him. For starters, he wanted for nothing. This was not only because his parents were the first two-income family in the history of Doyles' Gear, but also because his father was renowned for his willingness and ability to pick up extra shifts. It was largely agreed that if they had let him, Jim Mallett wouldn't ever have stopped working.

Jamie had carried that looseness with him to high school, where he'd been an average athlete with great effort and an average student with none at all, lettered in baseball and football, been elected the prom king, and been given a half scholarship to the local university.

He arrived on campus that August and was for the first time assaulted by the huge variety the world could offer. He hardly knew what it was that he was supposed to do with himself. Jamie discovered that he enjoyed his classes much more than he would have thought, that they caused him to consider entirely new things. He sat stupefied by the simple beauty of the things he learned about the movement of the soil and the basics of chemistry.

He could feel his life begin to accelerate and to widen. The surge of potential that seemed to flow through every day was easier to scoop up than a bad bunt. If he'd stopped and thought about it, which was still not a trait he'd acquired, he would have said he was exhilarated and barely able to stand thinking about what might could come next.

Then what came next came. He was down at the field house lifting weights with the baseball team and trying to explain to one of the catchers what tectonic plates were about, when his roommate ran in out of breath with his hands on his knees and said between gasps that Jamie had to call home right away.

And before Jamie knew it he was wearing his father's second-nicest suit, staring down at his father wearing the other one. Heart attack, they said. Died right there at the forge. Worked all the way to the end, the most honest and decent of men. God could rest easy now, as Jim Mallett would be around to take care of any overtime. We were so sorry for his loss. Jamie barely heard or saw any of it.

Instead a single memory kept playing through his head. It was the last time a bad storm had blown through town, when Jamie was thirteen maybe. Straightline winds had torn down the valley at eighty miles an hour, along with howling rain and hail the size of golf balls. These were things that happened here, perhaps not often, but often enough that Jim Mallett had dug out a storm shelter in the yard on his day off, lined the sides with concrete, fashioned a door from sheet iron and six-by-twos. It was scarcely large enough for him, his wife, their son, but it felt plenty large that night to Jamie. He had watched his father dig the hole, brought him water, and plugged in the radio so he could have something to listen to, had asked and had learned why it was necessary to build such a heavy door, had brought the hose to mix the concrete, done other small accessory work. Young Jamie looked around in the dark, not seeing much, but feeling safe and secure and proud of his part in creating such a feeling. He smiled through the darkness and whispered, "Golly, we're lucky we have this."

Out of the darkness and yet closer than he would have imagined came his father's voice. "Goddamnit it, son, you've brought it on us now."

It was probably an hour later, but it felt like right then that Jamie and maybe everybody else for a mile around heard a thundering crack that rose above the howl of the wind.

It was a pine tree, and not a small one. The wind had liberated several of them and shot-put them into or through whatever happened to be nearby. When they climbed out of the shelter, the house seemed fine from the back, was fine from the back, and Jamie was foolish enough to think that his father might have been wrong. But when they opened the door they found roots and trunk where the living room ought to have been. It had smashed out every window on that side of the house, and caved in that half of the roof line. Mrs. Mallett had a collection of Precious Moments figurines that had since been rendered into a pile of shards and remnants with parts of faces and limbs and the heads of animals sometimes still whole. The living room furniture was all relatively intact given the water damage, just shoved well out of the way into the kitchen and the hall and the wall that used to separate the two, like the tree had politely cleared a space to lie down before it fell through the roof and then the floor.

Mrs. Mallett couldn't bring herself to talk, just worked her jaw in a little circle and looked from pile to pile. Young Jamie saw everything and then saw the road through the hole the tree made, and people slowing down to look at what all the storm had done, looking at where the Mallett's living room ought to have been, looking right in at Jamie. That's when he started to cry, not even making much noise.

Up till then, Jim Mallett hadn't done or said a thing. Since he'd shut the boy up he hadn't even breathed through his mouth, let alone spoke. He had followed the boy and his wife into the house, almost certain of what they'd find there. But when he saw tears running down his son's face, he lost his temper and hauled off and slapped him backhanded.

Jamie was shocked silent even though he wanted to cry even more now, but he was afraid to. He looked at his father, unsure exactly what it was he was allowed to do.

Jim Mallett looked down at his son, and maybe he saw the fear in his eyes and took pity, or maybe he just said what was on his mind, or maybe he was just talking to himself, or maybe, and this is what Jamie wanted to think now, he was explaining a few things. He said, "Everything will be all right. Because all right's how we'll call what it'll be."

Jamie didn't know what he meant then, and he didn't know at the funeral, but he found out shortly after. It started when the factory foreman at the time, a quiet man named Mr. Bates, came up to Jamie when they were standing around eating after and said that while normally they'd promote from within, that it had been agreed that Jamie could take on his father's job and start as soon as he had things settled. Bates didn't ask him if he wanted the job or even imply that there was a question. He addressed

Down and Out

Jamie as he would any other employee.

At first Jamie felt almost offended, angry enough to fight the man and the presumption at the goddamn nerve and not an hour after they'd laid his father to rest. But he tucked that away as well and said nothing and nodded and shook the man's hand and wondered if he did actually have a say in the matter.

It turned out that he didn't. His mother made it clear that his father's income was the half of his tuition not covered by the scholarship, along with the pocket money and the clothes and the everything. She could keep the roof over her head, she was fairly certain, especially with the insurance policy, but he was on his own. He was just nineteen and thought for the first time in quite some time that he was lucky, in that he had an opportunity.

He reported for his first shift at 7:00, bright and early the Monday after they'd buried his father. He'd spent an hour filling out paperwork, an hour getting his job explained to him, and had started doing the work his father had done his entire adult life at just before nine in the morning. By ten he was ready to run. He asked for a bathroom break, and was granted one after being told his father had never once made such a request. Once away, he threw off the protective clothing he'd found in his locker, the leather and the nomex and the thick-soled steel-toe boots. No one had told him that he would be throwing himself into a fire hotter than anything that seemed like it had a right to be. No one told him about the way the heat pried its way right into you, shot through, left a hole that kept your guts feelings cooked even still, the air coming out of Jamie's lungs so much hotter than the air coming in. His only thoughts were to find coolness, to find the tallest cliff over the deepest spring-fed pool and to dive, dive deep until the water was cold enough to soak the heat away, and be damned if he never came up for air. He was already leaving the break room with its bare tan walls and scuffed tables and multitude of microwaves, already out of the door, on his way to he barely knew where. But every step grew heavy, and then he wasn't moving at all, just standing and thinking about what he was really doing. He could go, right out the door and past them all, let them say what they would, could find that cliff and could jump into that pool. But there would always be a tomorrow, and there would always be a need to keep going. He knew right then that there was only one real way he could go, that being back to the furnace, and it was then that he met his father man-to-man.

Jamie had thought his father enjoyed his work in some way or another, that he must've as often as he spent at it. But two hours in his apron and Jamie knew for certain that couldn't have been the case. Breathing in the fire, sweat leaking out the eyelets in his work boots, hissing when it hit the floor—it was a thing that couldn't be loved or enjoyed, that could yield no satisfaction beyond its end. Jim Mallett must have felt the same urge to run, the same deep animal requirement to move away and fast, must have felt it every moment of every day, and yet he held that ground, and came back for extra as often as they would have him. Jamie couldn't fathom the depth of will such a thing would take, and he was certain he could never be the man his father was. It was the first time Jamie knew all the way through that he would die.

It took not five minutes from start to finish for Jamie to realize all that, and that left plenty of time for him to summon enough fortitude to go back to his father's job. Knowing what he knew didn't help him stomach it, made it not one degree cooler. But it gave him a thing to think about as he worked, and he did so and tried hard to keep his chin level. In only a short period of time, men who had known his father well began to nod their silent approval— all of us pleased at the way he'd managed to fill Jim's welding gloves so admirably.

Jamie said little from then on, took on a scowl that never seemed to lift. But he was polite enough, and a hard worker, and so we nodded at him when we drove by all the same. He kept largely to himself, but went hunting and fishing with Lyle Younse on weekends. He was not often seen in church or the bar, but was welcome enough in both places.

When the factory died and the show began, Jamie volunteered to be the last one driven home. He sat in the break room patiently, asked no questions and answered shortly when ones were asked. When the camera was finally mounted in the front seat of his truck, the production assistant crammed into the jump seat behind Jamie, and the camera started rolling, the assistant asked him the first question on his list: What do you think you'll do now?

Jamie found himself quoting his father, and in so doing gave the show its first great soundbite. "Things will be all right because all right's what we'll call how it'll be" became not only part of the opening montage and the first bump, but a sort of recurring theme. They would play the clip over the end of anything we tried and failed at. They would show it as Jamie's truck faded into the background as an ending to episodes four, nine, and thirteen. He only said it the one time, but like several things it tended to take on more meaning that he might have intended.

Season 1, Episode 5: The Date

Cheryl Mathews had quit smoking three years before the show, and when it started she saw this as the greatest of blessings. She managed to quit by using a combination of nicotine patches and a book that promised to induce self-hypnosis. While she didn't feel hypnotized, she found the book useful in that it told you what to do when you had a given problem. When you wanted a cigarette, you were to picture setting $100,000 on fire, the idea being that if you stayed tobacco-free you would save that much in your lifetime.

Since then she had pictured setting that pile of money on fire more times than anyone would bother to count. It had gotten to the point where she fantasized about setting the money on fire and what that would be like more often than she thought about cigarettes. She had the details all worked out, how she would pile the money into a neat triangle like she'd learned in Girl Scouts, set fires at three corners, and wait. Sometimes in this dream she would roast a marshmallow, other times put the fire out with the nicest wine she could get her hands on. She liked that every day she was not fulfilling this fantasy, that she could choose through lighting a single cigarette to burn away more money than she could even think about, and she liked even more that every day she didn't make that choice. It seemed a fair trade-off for not getting to smoke.

Since she had given up the cigarettes, though, she had taken up the lottery. She bought one ticket every day, a single draw at the big interstate prize. She stopped every day on her way home from work at the gear factory, bought the ticket, and put it in her purse. When she got home, she would put the ticket into the big ashtray that she hadn't had use for since she quit. Once the ticket was in the ashtray, she left it there, never checking to see if she was a winner. She reasoned that if she had won the jackpot somebody would tell her about it, and that any other minor prizes, three dollars here or there, weren't really worth her trouble. She liked not checking for the same reason she liked not setting a hundred thousand dollars on fire, and with no cigarettes to buy she could damn sure afford it. It seemed again a fair trade-off. When the factory stopped, the stack of lottery tickets was two inches thick, required a paperweight to keep from toppling over.

Then of course the show started and Cheryl signed up because right then it seemed like the thing to do. You weren't supposed to stay unemployed and so she took the new job just like everybody. What set Cheryl apart from most was that when they asked her who would be waiting at home for her to tell the news to, she said nobody. Not that she was the only one without a family, but she was among the youngest and the only female. In a town like Paris, the general theory was that a single woman, especially a pretty one with a good paycheck, must be in need of a husband.

And of course, that was just where the show started in. When they followed her home and confirmed that she was being honest, that there was no sign of a boyfriend at all, they immediately embarked on a task that at some point all of us had engaged in—trying to get Cheryl set up.

That was the way we talked about it—set up, fixed with. Cheryl both could and couldn't understand why nobody believed she had little need of a man. On the one hand, she thought it was ludicrous the way we nudged her and suggested, brought up every eligible cousin and distant relation and friend of a friend of an acquaintance. It was almost funny if it weren't so sad, the way everybody genuinely didn't seem to understand that she might enjoy being single. On the other hand, she also had grown up around here.

So she often found herself giving in to please people. For even in a town where everyone was already settled, there was always someone we could think of who could help Cheryl. We of course knew what Cheryl was all about, even if she wouldn't admit it. She talked all that independence and her own space business, and, sure, that must have its advantages. But really we knew, all of us, the whole town, that it hadn't anything to do with that, and everything to do with senior prom 1997.

Like so many other things around here, explaining Cheryl meant returning to high school. Some might call that absurd or sad, but the first thing to remember is that it was normal. More than that, it was inevitable. No one but Marla had moved *to* Paris in some time; our growth was all internal and that meant that you graduated from high school with the same people you went to kindergarten with, and that for most of us you still worked with those people at the factory. And high school, however long ago it was, was the time when you started being you for better or worse. It was in high school that Martin Gossett had run for and been elected class president, when Lyle Younse and Jason Johnson had been co-captains of the football team, which was always more important.

And it was in high school that Cheryl Mathews had been the second-prettiest cheerleader, right behind Tammy

Starling. Since Tammy was dating Jason, and Lyle was dating Cathy Wells—a non-cheerleader who was still popular in the quiet way—it meant that Cheryl was supposed to date the captain of either the basketball team or the baseball team, and both of those were Jamie Mallett.

Through stammering and note passing, Jamie had managed to ask Cheryl out sometime halfway through his junior year and dated her almost until graduation. They shared popularity, beauty, and a certain kind of awkward bluntness. And it was this third thing that made us sure they were made for each other. Both had a way of saying just what they were thinking when they probably ought not have.

We assumed they were going to marry, and you cannot blame us. Two in five marriages in Paris stem from relationships at least as old as high school. Rodney and Cindy Allen had been dating since the seventh grade. Lyle and Cathy, Jason and Tammy, two dozen other couples from the factory, all of them met that far back, have been making their way in pairs for all that time, and who doesn't love hearing about a couple's fiftieth wedding anniversary? When these relationships work, they add a sweetness to life that can't be had other ways.

But of course sometimes they don't work and sometimes that's because of Jamie. We all knew the whole story. It was the night of senior prom, always a special time in Paris. Every year, the young ladies of the city drive with their mothers to the dress shop in Clarksville, where they choose the second or third most expensive piece of clothing they'll ever own. Being as there is only the one dress shop, these young ladies choose from one of the three available patterns and four available colors, but none of that seems to bother them.

As the prettiest girl in the class, Tammy Starling was the heavy favorite for prom queen. But even back then, Cheryl was asking questions, one of which was, "Why not me?" She and Tammy had been friends since the first grade and she would never wish any bad thing on someone she'd known so long. In all that time, it was agreed upon that Tammy was the prettier of the two. It had been repeated so often and in so many subtle ways that most of us took it as true without thinking about it. But Cheryl couldn't see any reason why she *couldn't* be prom queen, and that was enough reason to hope. Besides, it was common practice to vote in a couple so as to not cause painful strife, and while Tammy was every bit a prom queen, Jason Johnson looked less the part of a king. Certainly less the part than young Jamie Mallett.

Jamie was still far from hard on the eyes—with strong features and fierce blue eyes—but back then in high school he was a tiny piece of perfection. Years of the sports that valued speed over strength had left him agile and lean and toned. His hair was still jet black then, thick enough to shine in the sun, and if someone ever looked like a prom king it was him. He was Cheryl's ace in the hole.

Until, of course, as the story goes, Jamie broke her heart that very night. As we tell it, he came over to her place and explained in a callous manner that since he had recently learned that he was going to the University that he had no use for a local girl, and so he might as well cut it off then. He left her there on her own doorstep, still wearing the corsage he'd just pinned to her, and they hardly ever spoke again.

Cheryl never bothered to contradict this version of the

story. Never mentioned how it really went, and of course neither did Jamie.

The truth, if you believe in that kind of a thing, was a bit more muddy and uncertain. Yes, Jamie came over to her place and pinned the corsage on her and then left alone and went to the dance without her, that much happened. But the spaces in between can tell a lot of stories.

When Jamie arrived at her home, he did just what was asked of him, waited with her father, nodded at his threats, pinned the corsage, and let her mother take a picture. Then they walked outside and were halfway to his car when he started to cry.

She asked him what was wrong, and he said between the tears that he loved her. That he didn't care who knew it, but that he did, and that from that point on he would love her for the rest of his life. And that was when she panicked. That was when she ran back inside, shouting, "I just can't" over her shoulder. And after then, when she wouldn't come out no matter what anyone said, Jamie went to the prom alone, and told a lie.

For Jamie's part, he hadn't understood most of what was going on. The tears that had come had surprised him more than everything. He couldn't believe he felt the things he heard himself saying he felt, couldn't believe it was all happening just like that.

For Cheryl's part, it was a great deal more simple. Jamie had told her he would love her forever, and she knew what that meant. She knew that it meant a wedding that next spring and a child the winter following and then that child growing up and either pinning a corsage or having a corsage pinned and it was more than she could think about, and so she ran back inside.

Down and Out

Jamie had gone on to the dance because he didn't know what else to do. That he left a few months later to go to the University was the last sealing detail. The two separate incidents were married, one explaining the other, and so it was and had been for some fifteen years.

Thus the town assumed that Jamie and Cheryl were our one unsettled romance, the two people in our town that were meant in some way to be together and yet weren't. And clearly the show thought the same.

It was not a week in to filming before they suggested to Jamie that he ought to call Cheryl and ask her out. Yes, they had heard from all of us about their past, but probably they would have made the same suggestions anyways. They were after all the only two single people their age in the whole town. They were both pretty and uninvolved, and that alone might have made it a forgone conclusion.

Jamie was more than willing, we assumed, not bothering to ask him. For if there is little space for the feelings of women who don't care for romance, there is none at all for men who don't care for company one way or the other. Still he said yes when the show asked him, if only because it got him out of his house, and away from his ailing mother. The truth of it was that Jamie might well have still been in love with Cheryl if he'd ever gotten the chance to be. But that was far as he ever let it go when his thoughts shifted that direction.

Cheryl was less easy to convince. The show tried all their normal tactics, which is to say implying, suggesting, and then asking outright. But no matter how many times they tried, or how many times Jamie called and asked her, she wanted nothing to do with it, and it had to do with all those lottery tickets.

Briseño

They were her first thought when she heard Martin say the factory was closing, not as a source of hope but as a source of regret. She immediately wished that she'd saved that money, or weirdly that she'd even spent it on cigarettes—anything that she would have taken advantage of. But of course at the same time it was obvious to her that she may already be a winner.

And so as soon as she got home she looked right at the camera and explained. She told all about quitting and hypnotizing herself and that degree of control and how she liked, maybe needed, the freedom required not to care about those lottery tickets, to just let them sit there. She said that now that she was unemployed, probably the first thing she ought to do was to look through and see if maybe she had money she didn't know about.

In her mind she could already see the episode, her standing in front of the lotto machine in the IGA, showing barcode after barcode to the electric eye, getting told time and time again that, sorry, she was not a winner. She saw it as a symbol of how the first thing to go is the comfort, the sense of being in charge that came with it. Instead they asked again if she was single.

And so when Jamie called, she was less than agreeable, and told him to go right to hell, though it wasn't him she was swearing at. She thought insistence would change Jamie's and thus the show's mind. It only worked halfway.

Jamie heard her curse him the first time and nodded. He hadn't asked for further explanation that first night and he didn't see how he could ask now. She had chosen otherwise, and he wanted to, needed to respect that. He could never understand the idea that women saying no meant any other thing than no, and from that very first refusal, he had been trying with limited success to move on.

But the show had other ideas, and so they turned to an unlikely go-between, Tammy Johnson née Starling. Tammy and Cheryl had been close in high school, remained close after. Cheryl was the maid of honor at Tammy's wedding, and since they both worked at the same place it was easy to stay in touch through all the years. Yes, it was true that life had dealt them different hands, as they termed it when talking, had given Tammy a husband, Jason, and three young boys, Junior, Ricky, and Dale, and had given Cheryl a tiny house near the river that she had paid off in full by the time she was twenty-nine, making her one of only a handful of people with no mortgage or rent to speak of. But it was also true that they had shared more years together than they spent apart.

It didn't hurt any that Tammy Johnson was awful happy to find herself helpful. Part of this, of course, was her natural post in life. She had from birth been trained to be thankful for advantages she had that others lacked, and to be helpful where she could. She was the daughter of a prom queen and was told from an early age that she was expected to follow suit. That meant a lifetime of campaigning. Though no elections had been held in quite some time, she was still on that trail, still asking everyone to think the highest of her. That was a part of it.

Another part was Jason Johnson. Co-captain of the football team along with Lyle and thus likewise raised to expect greatness of himself. We always imagined that it bit at Jason that Lyle was the foreman and he was just another man on the line. When the show came along, we thought we could see Jason trying to step back up into co-captaincy.

In any case, it happened like this. Tammy went to see Cheryl and talked to her about going out with Jamie while Jason walked next door to Jamie Mallett's and asked him to call Cheryl. Of course, Jamie had already called Cheryl a handful of times by then, but Jason thought it best to make sure, and strangely when we finally saw the show on television, it was this last attempt they showed, Jason trying to whisper things into Jamie's ear, Jamie pushing him away confused.

Tammy and Cheryl hugged at the door and ended up sitting down on her couch and talking about how things were going now that the factory was gone. Cheryl was then still finding benefits of her unemployment to focus on. Two years earlier she'd gotten a set of exotic teas as a gift at the company Christmas party. Since then she hadn't bothered, but now that the factory was gone and she had hours stretching in front of her, it seemed just the right thing to do, and so she had poured both her and Tammy a cup of Earl Green Tea—half Earl Grey, half green tea, she supposed—and was trying to figure out whether she liked it or not.

Meanwhile, Tammy was explaining how it was in everyone's best interest, but most of all Cheryl's, that she go out on a double date with Jamie and Jason and her. "That way if Jamie starts acting stuck up or funny, then I'll be there to help you, Sugar," explained Tammy. "And besides, you two always did make a smart couple."

Cheryl sighed deep into her tea mug. She thought again about telling Tammy how things had really gone that night, that Jamie wasn't the one who had acted stuck up. Instead she just thought about the tea. This was her second cup of this particular variety. The first time she had almost poured it out. In fact, she'd picked this variety hoping it might keep things shorter between her and Tammy, as since high school it had always seemed that shorter worked best. But the tea was growing on her. And she was plenty smart enough to see what was coming. She had a knack for that, and it was why she among all of her classmates had gotten hired as office secretary/accountant. Surely, she reasoned, she would keep getting bothered about it until she gave in. Surely there would be no other way around it.

And so rather than fight it, Cheryl smiled and said, "Well, why not? What could it hurt?"

When they finally showed the date on television, they built it up maybe even more than we had in town. They showed half a dozen of us answering in a complete statement that we could certainly think of one couple that we wished would get back together. Cutting back and forth between various contributors, they strung together the story of senior prom and of the love lost between Jamie and Cheryl. There were some of us who tried to blame Jamie for the breakup, and others who tried to blame Cheryl, but all that was left on the cutting floor. They found a picture of the two of them in the yearbook, blew it up, and showed everyone. Then they showed the bar.

The four of them met at the only place in town to meet, a skinny little bar we all knew as the Double Deuce. As it turned out, though, there was some copyright issue with the name of the place and so before they filmed the establishing shot they made a deal with the owner and replaced the original sign with one that said only BAR.

The date was going well so far. They shared drinks, talked over the jukebox, and all four of them set about forgetting a number of things. Jason and Jamie forgot that they'd been less than friendly practically all their lives. Cheryl forgot that she had thought all this through before and knew just how it would end. They all forgot they were unemployed and that so many years had passed and that they were being filmed. In the end, they got up and danced slow to a song the show couldn't get the rights to and had to replace it with another number that doesn't quite fit the rhythm.

It was the kind of date that everyone who saw it would describe as fine, which is to say no specific thing went wrong. The conversation was pleasant and never lagged. No one said the wrong thing or was offensive at any time. Cheryl couldn't help but think—this ought to be enough. She looked across the table at Tammy, wondering how she'd avoided becoming her all these years.

Then they went home, and Jamie dropped Cheryl off on her porch. He said he had a wonderful time, and she said thank you. They showed a close-up of Jamie, waiting for a kiss. They showed the door close in his face.

The very next day Cheryl was gone, moved off. We never saw her again. We wondered what happened until we saw it on television. There was Cheryl, packing, saying, "Jamie and I used to be together. But that was a whole lifetime ago. I don't think I can go back there. I just don't know what's left here for me except for bad memories." Then there's Cheryl leaving. Word around town was that she moved to Little Rock or Dallas or someplace that seems a world off but isn't but a day's drive.

Of course we had her cell phone number. Any of us could have called. She would have told us. She would have said that it had nothing to do with Jamie, nothing at all. She would have explained that the date wasn't what settled it, it was what it showed to her. She would have explained again, like she had so many times to anyone who listened, that she hadn't been missing him all this time, that really she was glad things had gone the way they had so many years ago. She had been and still was happy. She would not have said, none of you ever knew me. She would not have said that she realized when we said "fixed up" we meant corrected.

It bothered her, she told the camera before she left that next day, that she was leaving behind such an opportunity. Everybody needed money, and the money from the show was something she would sure regret. In a way, she said, it was like setting $100,000 on fire, and that scared her. But sometimes, she said, you have to give in.

But of course the truth and the story went different ways here, be that the show's story or the one we told each other. It made more sense, from either perspective, to connect the two directly chronological events. Surely the date had to cause Cheryl leaving the show, and all of us played it that way, spoke both on and off camera about the tragedy of the heartsick, how even things that are meant to be sometimes just don't happen.

All this happened in the first two weeks of filming. Cheryl was involved in less than twelve hours total. They saved Cheryl's departure to make it seem like it had happened in the middle when really it had almost been the start of things. That didn't seem to matter until later.

Season 1, Episode 6:
Steve Womack: Fish Master

Fans of the show were often surprised to learn that Steve Womack was only thirty-three. Maybe it's the way he dressed, the real tree jacket he'd worn until the pattern faded into the background and the fabric had gone shiny smooth with grease and wear. Almost certainly it had something to do with his teeth, which were tinted dark like skim milk in mottled crystal. But above all it was his hair, what was left of it, and his beard. Back in high school even, flaps of paper white were weaving their way into his fine curls; by twenty-nine he looked damn near fifty.

It should be noted, here and now, that Steve Womack was not in any way mentally incapacitated. Some excited fans have thought otherwise, have even used hateful words to describe Steve. But he wasn't stupid then and he isn't now. If anything Steve Womack might've been the smartest man in Paris, Arkansas.

But it is fair to say he had kind of a funny way of talking. Once around him for even a short while, most anyone could understand him just fine. There's even a kind of beautiful logic to it that you can catch at, the depth of meanings he packed into so few syllables. At any rate, we all could understand him, but Steve was the first of many victims of the subtitles.

In almost every conversation he participated in on camera, Steve's words are accompanied by a translation of sorts. Most of the time the subtitles were accurate enough, but more than once we noticed that when we'd been there and heard Steve say one thing, that the subtitles said something else entirely, changing conversations in sometimes drastic ways. But even when it felt strange, it was hard to read the words onscreen and not assume that was what he said. Even knowing better didn't do much to help it.

Steve for his part never seemed to mind. He was one of the easiest individuals to get along with anyone had ever met, and he seemed to take to television the way he took everything else, slowly but with a smile on his face. He did what he always did when other things weren't going in his favor. When confusion and noise overran him, he would find his way to St. Michael's pond, or Lake Dardanelle, the deep at Shoal Creek, the lake up at Mount Magazine, any body of water save the river itself. In that water, there were crappie, sunfish, brim, shadow cat, river cat, blue cat, and bass of all color and mouth size. If it swam, it spoke a language Steve understood, one he heard whispering to him through the water. He could tell where those whispers were coming from, knew the time the fish would sing, what to throw and where, and how to reel it back. When a fish was nearby, tickling at the end of his line or lurking in the shadowy roots of a tree, whoever was lucky enough to be fishing with Steve would hear him say something like, "You can smell that fish now, smell him stinking sure." We all had the decency to wait, and then to say that he sure must've smelled that fish when he yanked it from the water a few moments later. But the television crew, not at all surprisingly, were the first ones to ask Steve what exactly it was that he smelled, and to everyone's surprise he told them.

Bass, big mouth or striped, smell like the Cherrywood

his father smoked them on: sweet, sultry, tickling the nose; brim smelt like the sun in the morning, clean and sharp; catfish were the slick black earth at the bottom of deep water. The scents rose visible out of the water like mist in the night.

It seemed crazy at first, but the more anyone watched Steve call a fish and land it like he had antenna on the back of his bobber, the more they came to believe. Long after the show was in reruns, someone published a paper in a cultural studies journal arguing that Steve was synesthetic. When they asked him about it at his next press conference, Steve nodded and smiled—it was a word he'd known for some time. In high school, and really throughout his life, Steve had known that things were different for him. Sometimes, he forgot that, and would say that class was ugly today, that the colors they'd been reading in their history books didn't quite suit him. That was why fishing had meant so much to him. No one cared if it tasted sweet when the fish wriggled into the net. No one called it strange to smell a fish in the water so long as you smelled him onto the stringer.

Of course we knew about Steve's superiority at all things relating to rod and reel. But it wasn't until the cameras came that we really saw Steve's gift. We were getting enough to eat and damn sure our kids were, but it required creativity to blanch off the flavor of doing without. As one does, we found money for food—but the money we found only bought what was extremely on sale—the rawest ingredients only. And you get tired of cornpone, of cooking biscuit mix in vegetable shortening. Salt, most agreed, was vital—but many went without pepper for most of the filming of the show. Eating became a chore of sorts, one of the many things we did now instead of doing work.

All except the fish. In better seasons there might've been deer or doves or rabbits, but filming began a week after spring turkeys ended and only the water held any chance of sustenance. Everyone took their chance at the water's edge—but only Steve could produce results consistent enough to call dinner. Fish after fish, one after another—not just a few but half a dozen at least and sometimes three times that. With a few assistants, some extra poles, and a cousin for game warden, he was able to feed ten and sometimes fifteen families in a single night. He would rotate between us, making sure that everyone got something fresh at least once a week.

It had been the show's idea, sharing the fish. They had pulled Steve aside and at first hinted and then suggested, and then explained that since he was such a great fisherman, he could really help out the town by sharing his catch with everybody. Steve was used to sharing his catch, less used to explaining that he'd just thought of the idea to the camera. He smiled and said, "I reckon I ought to share these fish with everybody in town because the water belongs to everybody." The subtitles said, *I reckon I should share fish with everybody 'cause I like to be friends with everybody.* He did as he was asked, which included loading up the day's catch onto a stringer and knocking on every door in town with a wriggling chain of dinner.

After a week of oatmeal without butter or white rice flavored with paprika and ground mustard, fresh fish, seasoned by the water—fried in iron skillets or roasted in the oven—was like eating cakes of vitamins. We could feel the health and vitality coursing into us like captured magic. Steve had always been a favorite in town, always polite, smiling at children, helping folks move and reroof their houses. But the fish made Steve a celebrity. People didn't just smile at him, they waved. Women asked him to dance at BAR downtown. There were those among us who found it silly how much goodwill was being poured onto the stubby cock-toothed gear stamper, but we only thought that on nights when it wasn't our turn to get fish.

Not only was he loved, but Steve was also rich beyond everyone's current dreams. He asked for nothing for the fish that he brought, but still he found things pressed into his hand as he left or waiting on the seat of his truck or his porch. Mainly it was food—cranberry preserves put up last winter, fresh okra, one of the squirrels Mikey Plath trapped in his attic. Whatever anyone had, half of it ended up with Steve. When the extra food ran out, folks began to give him other things—videos he might could watch, whatever was on hand and that we could tell ourselves we could do without. It is truer than anyone knows that pride goes before the fall, but plenty of things go before the pride does. That summer, we paid what we owed and that way we nodded at the fish when they came, could meet whichever of Steve's eyes happened to be looking our direction.

After a time, though, the smell of fish began to fade from the lakes, the ponds, and the creeks. Some thought that Steve had lost his touch, that he really had been a fluke all along. These held their heads at the height of the vindicated. But really we all knew that Steve had fished the lakes clean. We didn't need the biology expert that appeared on the show to explain why first there were no larger fish and then no medium-sized fish and then no fish at all. We knew better than anyone that every bounty has its limits.

Down and Out

This was the first time the show taught us to sin. We all might've been a little hard on Steve. As the fish in Logan County began to dwindle, Steve kept to passing out the fish he caught but now the rotation started swinging wider and wider, no longer a dependable delivery, now an erratic thing to be craved. Our children would stand at the front window, staring hollow eyed and silent for Steve's headlights down the driveway. That became less and less, and when he did, he had less and less with him. What was once a bountiful meal was now a few morsels to a mouth.

We all learned that coming to depend on something that depended was a dangerous thing. We had loved Steve as a saint and even a savior. Now we had trouble not feeling our stomachs grumble as we passed him on the road. We had no right to those fish, no leg to stand on in resenting Steve for not bringing them around. But we were hungry.

We didn't know that Steve, for his part, felt every admonishing stare. We didn't know that our glances made his nostrils flare, willing fish to them, burning for it. We didn't know he had all but quit sleeping in his pursuit of what was certainly not there. We didn't know that Steve had long since quit keeping any of his meager catch for himself.

In mid-July, when the taste of flesh was a memory to the town, the Needleman children started screaming from the front window. He's here, the fish master is back. John Needleman was suspicious, but, sure enough, Steve Womack was pulling something from the back of his truck and sauntering towards the door.

John looked at his children, eight-year-old Shannon and four-year-old Tim. They bounced in anticipation, jiggling in a way that made him think of the prayers his wife made them say on Christmas morning before they got the toys. It made him swell with fatherly happiness just to see his children smile like that. Hearing footsteps on the porch, Shannon flung the door open, revealing Steve with one hand in knocking position, his face screwed up in confusion. Then both kids started to cry.

In his other hand Steve had his usual yellow chain stringer. Hanging from it was a single brim. The fish looked tired, the gaping and the wrinkles around the mouth made it look like a great grandparent's face lost in reverie. It couldn't have been four inches long. "I brought," said Steve and then, seeing the children, switched trains mid-thought so as to make the object of his bringing, "I'm sorry." Both of them blushed like summer tomatoes. John took the fish from Steve, put it in the kitchen, and asked the children, "What do we say?" In unison, through a veil of tears, Tim and Shannon let out, "Thank you."

Steve turned around without another word, less than sure what had just happened, certain it was his fault and that he should back away. He walked quickly back to his running vehicle.

John followed.

"Say, Steve," he said. Steve turned, and John looked him in the eye, but then looked down and addressed himself to Steve's muddy boots. "I don't want to seem ungrateful or nothing, but I mean, well, the kids are crying, you know? Maybe if there is not enough, maybe don't get them all excited. You understand, right?"

Steve nodded and got back in his truck, but the truth was that he did not understand at all. He didn't understand why a little something wasn't better than nothing at all just like he didn't understand why the blonde-headed boy and girl had cried when they'd seen his face. He didn't understand what had changed to make so many people once so proud of him now walk down the same aisle at the Walmart twice so as to avoid meeting him. He also didn't understand where all the fish had gone.

But he knew that they were gone enough, and after that he stopped coming by, stringer in hand, to the homes of the down and out. Then we heard that he quit fishing altogether, and then that he quit leaving the house entirely, which naturally left us to speculate about what exactly he might be doing in there. It turned out not much except for the television, afraid that he would upset someone else's children. When his camera crew asked him how he felt, he always said back the same thing, "Sad as there's no more fish to fish." This they translated directly.

This proved a problem for everyone, not just for Steve. Protein was harder and harder to come by, and without it we felt listless, pulled down by extra gravity, like the air had thickened up on top of us. We started moving slower, started asking to have almost every question repeated, having to fight hard to think of something to say back even then. We found things to eat, but no amount of egg noodles or cornmeal mush seemed to satisfy; we could be bloated, but never full.

Missing the fish, we missed Steve as well, which made us think of him as we thought about our hunger, and it was only during this period that we started telling the cameras those stories about Steve, about him growing up. We weren't trying to be cruel, only they kept asking about it, and in the end our civility wore away like the fat on our children's faces. We began to remember when we convinced Steve in high school to ask the history teacher to prom, or the time he tied his own shoelaces together and fell over the assembly line, causing a two-hour work stoppage. We started saying the things that the show had been asking us to say, things like Steve is sort of like Rainman 'cept Steve can't count. If you asked us even then if we meant it, if there was any truth to the things we were saying, we would have denied it, called it all a slip of the tongue. But since all of our tongues slipped together it became the truth in its own way.

If we'd thought about it, we should've paid attention to how often we were asked about our want for fish, our opinions of Steve. But it only made sense after.

One day in the last part of July, our camera crews started telling us what to do by asking questions. It was strange at first when they did this, but we had the trick by then and so when they asked us all, "Do you want to go outside to the main road for some fresh air?" we all went and weren't in the least bit surprised to find everyone else already waiting in the sun. In the distance we heard an air horn, and then saw an eighteen-wheeler painted with the show's logo. As it got closer we saw that it was a clear plastic tank, and closer still we saw that it was full of wriggling, squirming catfish, one upon another, so many that you couldn't see any one fish—so many the water looked black. The truck approached the courthouse square and stopped, and we cheered the fish wildly, surrounded the truck like some proud son who had won a state championship or been elected to the legislature. Then Steve slid out of the passenger side of the truck, his hands in his pockets as soon as it was possible. The producers explained for us, since Steve had worked for so many tiring hours, since he'd put so much time into his fishing, it was only fair, only right that that he be allowed to continue the thing that he had loved until he killed it. Since he had spread love too thin, clearly what he needed was more love, and Steve's love was wet, wriggling, and slapping audibly against the sides of the tanker truck. The tank had been built just for this occasion—normally fish are trucked in a special fish truck but the producers found this far from conducive to television, in that it didn't convey the majesty of the ten thousand fish they'd ordered. So they had an immense Lucite box built on the back of a flatbed trailer. The tank was never quite waterproof, and proved difficult to fill and nearly impossible to empty. Fish waste began to accumulate almost instantly. It took a team of three fish wranglers and a dozen production assistants twelve hours of additional work, tripling the budget of the operation, and resulting in the loss of 15 percent of the fish pre-pond due to shock. But even knowing that, when you see it, when you see Steve in the cab of the truck with his nostrils flared out and all of his teeth on display and the sun—you have to admit that it was quite the work.

The children danced around the truck shouting, "fish, fish, fish"—not realizing that they would have to be taken from here, put in the ponds, caught, and that only then could we put them on the dinner table. We all cheered and hollered when we were asked if we felt like cheering and hollering. At least a few of us were looking down, though, as we clapped for the catfish. For Steve, mind you, the looks we'd given him in the parking lots and what we'd been saying. John Needleman was biting the inside of his lip trying to look forward without seeing Steve or his children dancing around the wheels of the weeping tank.

Before they drove away the producer shook Steve's

hand and presented him with a new rod and reel. "Steve," he said, "don't catch them all this time."

With the ponds stocked, with young hungry fish fighting to eat in every creek we knew, any of us could have had our fill. But when anyone tried to head for the pond, their camera crews wondered if they shouldn't wait for Steve to bring fish. Wouldn't that make it easier to make sure the fish didn't run out? And so we waited and each in turn received his bounty.

On the part that made television, every time they showed a fish drop off it was always an early one, from before the stock truck, made sometimes to look like a late one by cutting and pinching. After the drop, we still ate it, by God, but it was never the same. No one had anything left with which to pay the fish master. Instead we accepted his catch and smiled so that we would not be asked why we weren't smiling. It tasted different too, murky and yet also tasteless—a dirty kind of stale.

But everyone had to admit that Steve looked great, and also that he deserved it. Whatever we had laid on Steve was our own ill will, and so we took it back and made a meal of it. It was lack we hated, not Steve.

When we watch the close of episode six, when Steve is caught in profile with the last hour of summer light breaking up across the water beyond him and he says in voiceover and for once without subtitles, "I just love fishing. I always wanted to fish for a job, and now I reckon I do." He deserved to say that, and to have it be true, and we deserved to watch him and to clap. All of it was only fair.

Season 1, Episode 7:
The Anniversary Miracle

By midseason, our program proudly sported recurring characters. Of course there were still new people to meet every week, always someone else to introduce, but it was clear the show had favorites. We could tell even during filming, the way that certain people seemed to always have a camera crew while others did hardly ever. And while there was some debate over how much of what footage would actually be used, it was certain even to us that Cathy and Lyle would be the stars.

The two of them had been married not ten feet from the most famous grave in Arkansas. The story goes that back when this place still lacked discovering, a team of Frenchmen had come up the Mississippi and then followed the Arkansas westward until they found mountains. A young woman, in love with the captain of this particular adventure, had disguised herself as a boy and joined the crew as a deckhand. Taking the name Little John, or Petit Jean, her ruse lasted long enough to make it deep into newfound land before she caught a colorful fever. Discovered, she died in her lover's arms, and was buried, per her own request, on the tallest mountain they'd found, looking down on the wide sweep of the river.

Her name, her real one, is lost, and so they had to name the mountain Petit Jean. Through the years, the fame of the story grew, and folks wandered up the mountain to look down a steep cliff at the pile of stones thought to mark her grave. The WPA built a railing, framed an outlook for the river by chopping out a stand of longleaf pine, and flattened a gravel parking lot. Over the years, the mountain itself became more of an attraction than the origin of its name, which through the years evolved until Petit Jean rhymed with Betty Green. Plenty of folks came from all over to camp and hike on the mountain, but in the local teenage lexicon going up to Petit Jean meant a certain and specific thing.

So Cathy wasn't surprised when Lyle asked her up the mountain on their third date. It was strange to her, however, when they parked not at the guardrail parking lot, but next to a trailhead a few hundred yards away, and when Lyle got promptly out of the car and started walking. She followed him around a few twists and down a ledge so narrow you had to point your feet one way and your everything else another, and then they came to a hollow underneath the main lookout. She could look up and just see the railing next to where the other cars were parked, and she hoped nobody saw her down there, wherever down there was. Then she turned around to see Lyle, and saw him facing a short rusting fence, and beyond it a pile of smooth white stones. "People act like the whole mountain's the place," he said, "but really this is it."

She let him take her hand and lead her to a flat spot he cleared. She wiggled a little and tried to think kissable thoughts, but she saw that Lyle was still staring at the other woman. "Think of it, Cathy. She was born in Paris, France, and she ended up here, twenty miles from Paris, Arkansas."

She looked at the grave as it was, no headstone, no plaque, just a pile of rocks that might well have been put there by anyone, and maybe by no one. If it weren't for the fence around it, and the stray beer cans that had found their way behind the fence, she might have walked right past it even if it wasn't dark. "It's so sad," she said.

"Oh," he said, and dropped her hand and looked down at his knees. After a minute, "I thought it was romantic. The way she gave everything up to be with the one she loved."

"But that's just it," she said, picking his hand back up. "She didn't get to be with him, did she? She could never reveal herself, never until she was too contagious for a kiss goodbye. She died alone, in a strange place."

"Just like all of us, I guess," he said.

She drew back a little when he said it, but only because she felt like it was expected of her.

"What I meant was that we all die, and it doesn't seem like having folks with you or being at home do much to ease the situation. But even if she didn't mean it, her death meant something. She found someone worth dying for."

And then, without even knowing why, she had kissed him, and done it with every part of her, and she felt her heart tighten up as it welcomed this new burden. It wasn't just the way the tautness of his muscles beneath his cotton shirt, or the brush of the stubble on his cheek, even if she already loved the way that his back felt square and full in her arms. This was a new sensation, and it felt like it was heavy, that it could hurt, and that made it seem, somehow, more right.

Six months later they were married on that very spot, while everyone looked down sixty feet from the outlook and Fr. William shouted their vows down to them, and they cupped their hands and hollered back I dos.

They stayed that night in a wood cabin called The Honeymooner, which came complete with a heart-shaped shower big enough for a drumline. They knew, of course, that the loft with the king-sized bed with pink and red sheets, and the wagon wheel coffee table, were ridiculous, but it seemed an appropriate time for ridiculous behavior, an event worth every doily. Their love felt rooted like the mountain, the one almost named for a girl who died a virgin in a land that could never say either of her names. They hadn't gone an hour from home, but they'd found enough of everything right there on the side of the short mountain. They loved each other like that, like finding magic right where you hoped it would be.

For nine years, they returned faithfully each October 27 and rented the same cabin, hiked out at night to the grave, once even making love under the stars. As the season turned and the date approached, they would discuss it over and over, not planning it out, but building it up, making it what it was. I can't wait till the mountain became a delicious mantra, a perfect little inside joke.

The year that the cameras came, there was no discussion whatsoever.

October approached with slow calamity, like a collision that would happen only in a telescope. She could see just from looking at him that Lyle was bearing all the weight on his windpipe, and it pained her. He started muttering into his hot water of mornings, and he kept fumbling with little motions like changing the remote or buttering a piece of bread. She caught him shaking his head coming out of the bathroom, and seeing it was like a sore tooth lodged in her ribs. She took pride in being a good enough partner to feel his suffering, liked that she was perceptive enough to hear what wasn't being said. She also liked the way that noticing him was easier than noticing herself.

But she was afraid. Every one of the last nine Octobers

had ended in the same cabin, with the same bottle of the best sparkling wine the liquor store sold, the same steaks grilled on the same fire. The loss of it seemed dangerous in a way she could never think straight about. It might just set the whole world on end. Or worse, it might mean nothing at all, that not going would turn out to be just the same as going, that all the important things would turn out to be just things, ordinary stuff piled up.

And then there was the money. She had been hearing it humming to her from the closet every time she washed clothes without detergent, or had to scrape mold from the ass of a bread loaf. But of course she'd ignored it, and it didn't hurt any at all that she was never alone, couldn't get to it if she wanted without showing it to the people it turned out she was hiding it from. But now, every time she passed the hall closet where she had it tucked behind her wedding dress, she swore she could smell the green ink. She hadn't been saving all that while to spend it, of course, but it would take so little. Even a hundred dollars would rent the cabin, buy a pair of steaks and a half a tank of gas. One single bill. And so she made a plan.

She couldn't get caught, couldn't get left with nothing but that envelope, Lyle's truck, and the mortgage they had quit paying. She thought about pretending that she had found the money hidden in a drawer or under a bed, but they'd talked her into looking all through the house for change just last week. The production team had really gone to town, having her move the couch all the way out from the wall so that they could film from behind it so everyone could watch her bend, reach, and stretch for her own nickels and dimes. In the whole house, she'd found a dollar eighty-six, and they'd filmed her walking to the Walmart to buy a can of tuna and a loaf of bread. So just finding it wouldn't do, and neither would saying it was blowing down the road, because how would she ever find a way to drop it.

Then she remembered the money dance. At every wedding, there was always at least one Yankee who, upon seeing the spectacle, would ask what exactly we were doing, and fortunately there were also always a stockpile of grandmothers to cluck their tongues at their ignorance. Hadn't they heard the DJ say money dance, and didn't they have eyes in their head? The men lined up and one by one paid good money to dance a few turns with the new bride. Some, Baptists mostly, make a special smock with pockets for the bride to wear, but for the most part, men either pin the tribute to the bride's shoulder, or tuck it into the edge of her dress. If the wine is good and there are a number of former beaus in the line, it's less than uncommon for a few bills to end up slid down the front of the bodice. Thus, when new husbands undress their brides for the first time, money spills out and cascades in piles that are rarely noticed till the following morning.

It would work, she decided, because it was just what the production crew wanted, that local flavor they kept going on about; it was strange and, even Cathy knew it, it was goddamn sad. Lyle had been keeping away lately, gone almost every morning and several afternoons, which was strange as there were so few places to go, and so little to be done. Cathy took it to mean he was sad enough that he was afraid it would slip out of him, and that his absence was for her sake.

Two days before her anniversary, she set the plan in motion. Since the dress hid the money, the logic of the whole thing was perfect. A few months ago, announcing her actions to the living room would have felt strange, but she thought little of looking at the hutch in the corner while she was filmed from both the left and the right, and saying in the voice she reserved for talking to country folks, "I'm going to try on my wedding dress now, on account of it'll be our ten-year anniversary in a couple days."

The camera crew was, as she predicted, enthusiastic, and they all filed out of the house and waited on the porch—the first time she'd been alone and not on the toilet in forty-seven days. The box that held the dress and hid the envelope was on the back shelf of the closet, and she had to stand on the suitcases to get at it. It was bigger than she remembered, and glued shut—part of the $99.95 preservation package she'd gone in for thinking that someday her daughter might want it.

She pushed the thought from her mind as she took her good kitchen knife to the fancy cardboard. Of course the dress looked small, she'd been working herself up to deal with it. She doubted severely that she could get the thing to zip, and so she'd been calming herself down, trying to mentally prepare herself to appear bloated and undressed on television. Keep Lyle in mind, she had been saying, but the dress really did look like it must have shrunk, dried maybe like a preserved flower. But even still it slid over her shoulders easily, and the zipper slid as far up her back as she could reach almost on its own. She felt it pulling against her ribs, and she knew she should have felt a little ridiculous, but all her thoughts fell back to Petit Jean and Lyle and how she'd spent the last nine October 27ths.

Mostly wearing the dress, and dragging the cathedral train as it uncoiled from the box like a lace firehose, she climbed back into the closet to retrieve the envelope. It was all the way at the back. It had been her plan to open the envelope without untaping it or scrambling down from the suitcases, but the dress added gravity to her and she tripped over herself, slipping off the pile of suitcases and falling out of the closet, bumping her head and unsettling the dress so that it hung crooked and her left breast was mashed uncomfortably against the top of the halter, threatening to spill out onto the rhinestones. And that was how the camera found her, upside down against the wall, one-eighth naked and clutching an envelope full of hundred-dollar bills.

The production crew reasoned that after five minutes, it was twenty to one she was either frantically trying to squeeze into the dress, crying, or both—and they just weren't doing their job if they didn't catch that sort of thing on film. But if she heard all five of them clamber inside, she might run into the bedroom and lock the door till she had cleaned herself up. So they sent in just one man with the hand-held. They lost audio quality that way, which was an issue since tears were so likely. But there was always post-production.

The man who was standing over Cathy had not once in the six weeks he'd been tracking mud into her kitchen and then watching her wipe it up introduced himself. Still, she'd heard his name—Trent. She wondered if it was to hide that name that he'd covered his arms in those tattoos. They were so everywhere as to be patternless at most distances, like it was a skin disorder and not a picture. But she'd noticed over the months that most of it was a series of snakes or Chinese dragons all coiled up his arms in big fat rainbow-colored sections. She'd had time to look because those were the arms she had to look at every time they stopped her from making dinner, so she could say, "I'm making dinner right now." His face, though, was always hidden in the viewfinder, and that made it eerie and unseemly when he silently put the camera down, like taking off a mask, or a belt.

His dark hair hung in long lumps all around his head, that very expensive kind of not caring what you look like. The lumps were dyed black, but his eyes had come that way, were made even more unsettling by the pasty sunless skin of his face.

Up to then, Cathy hadn't had time to feel much of anything except the bump that was rising by the moment on the back of her head. But when the cameraman put the camera down on the kitchen table and stuck out his hand to help her up, all of it came on her, not just that she was surely thrown off the show, out more money than she and Lyle had ever seen, and also, somehow more pressingly, that her tenth wedding anniversary was forty-eight hours away—that she was older than she remembered.

He pulled her up so that when she was standing he was right next to her, with only the envelope of money in between them. He held on to her free hand, and with his other he traced up the front of her dress and tucked her firmly back into the halter. Without letting go, without breaking his stare, he reached around her and forced the zipper up, squeezing the air from her chest, and they stayed like that for what felt like the longest. He reached into the envelope, took out a small handful, maybe six months of cutting her own hair, and stuffed it into the front pocket of his jeans. Then he went to put the money up, and Cathy almost let him without grabbing the hundred dollars that seemed so important ten minutes ago.

Briseño

With the envelope back where it was supposed to be, he picked up the camera and nodded at her. She shivered hard, though it was unseasonably warm even for the river valley. Then she gave the biggest smile she had and said, "I found a hundred dollars!" bouncing on the balls of feet so as to seem more excited. She explained to the camera about money dancing and how popular she had been as a bride, and how it was plausible if far from common for a loose bill to get put with the dress she had just decided to try on that day. "It's a miracle," she said to the camera.

And when she'd said it, the camera crew—not just Trent now but her usual team—believed it all, as did everyone who saw the show. Her pride in tradition, her excitement at her luck, and more than anything her love for her husband shone through her. It meant something, how excited she got over that hundred-dollar bill, how even a little comfort seemed to restore so much of what seemed broken during the previous parts of the episode—interviews with her about her anniversary where she couldn't help but look down and away when she said that it will be all right. It meant a thing, though it was hard to say what.

Through the filming, Cathy felt like part of her own audience, more impressed than anyone with the depth of emotion and sincerity she was giving off. The only thing she noticed besides herself was Trent, who was back behind the full-size camera. She couldn't see any part of his face, but she had a sense that he was smiling at something that wasn't funny, and every time her attention was directed to camera two, she caught a flash of hot dread, like this was far from a finished thing. Beyond that, she felt distant enough to see her name floating beneath her face in that special font that looked like dripping whitewash.

That disconnect floated over her as she called for and confirmed reservations at their old familiar cabin. It hung while she packed their bags. She knew that she was smiling, that her voice had the right level of excitement when she bound into Lyle's arms and said, "Honey, we're going to the mountain," but even after the confused, sad look drifted away, when he was smiling too and swinging her around like a toy, she was still wrapped in something cottony, and she could hardly feel the ground come back under her feet.

It surprised them both, but the camera crew decided that the best way to film the couple's romantic getaway was not to film it at all. They had Lyle carry Cathy across the threshold of the cabin from three or four angles, and then ended on a close-up of the heart-shaped cutout in the door, and a well-timed "ooh" they'd recorded weeks ago when Cathy had stubbed her foot, but that sounded very different out of context.

When the door closed, it was the first time they'd been alone together in so long it felt strange, like getting too much hair cut off and feeling how light your head can be. Without the buzz of the cameras, the scuffle and breath of a half a dozen extra souls, it was still-quiet. Cathy looked at Lyle, at the good man who had been beside her every day of the last decade, and for the life of her all she could think about was the head of the snake tattooed on the back of Trent's hand as it slipped into her savings. Getting robbed and groped should have hurt, but her mind was spiraling past it directly to what to her was more important—that she couldn't tell Lyle about it. In his eyes, she could see that it was a miracle and that he felt blessed to be here, and she could never ruin that by telling him where the money came from. He had his chain and his watch still, and she would be damned if she couldn't be happy for him. But she realized also that part of how she usually dealt with things was closed off to her permanently, that she could never unload this, never have Lyle hold her and say it and let it fall outside of his arms, outside of their world.

So instead she grilled steaks and baked potatoes in the coals of the fire, and didn't tell him about Trent and the real reason she'd been squeezed into her wedding dress when he got home. She couldn't tell him about the money, because she hadn't told him about saving it because she had always said what she thought he wanted to hear when he'd asked if she really wanted kids. She kept thinking of all that dishonesty and arguing against her own accusations, trying to explain to herself that all of it, all of it came from nowhere but love. But the bickering didn't stop in her head until she'd burnt the steaks on one side while the other was still red raw.

Lyle ate it anyways, ate it with a look of sheer stupid happiness papered to his face. *He loves me enough to enjoy that*, she thought, as her jaws bulged in fatigue around the ropey meat, and somehow this was the thought that broke over her and finally brought the tears that had felt inevitable all afternoon.

"I love you," she said, and Lyle came up behind her and gathered her into his arms. He quieted her and told her it was all okay, that he knew, he knew, never letting go until the tears let off, never asking what was wrong, only trying to comfort her. And she was comforted just by his closeness, but it made her wonder what problem he thought he was fixing, wonder how he sensed the gap she felt between them. When he kissed her neck and nibbled on her collarbone, she felt it in the right places, the gravity and the weight of love, but she felt something else, an eye sitting on her like somehow she was still on camera.

Lyle moved to undress her and she let it happen, tried to be in the moment and let herself enjoy it, even if she winced a little every time the bump on her skull collided with the headboard. Afterwards in the dark, she felt Lyle pull away, and the darkness hung thick without his touch, and she was more afraid than she'd been all day. She heard him pad over to his suitcase, and then the light came on and he pressed a box into her hand before she could see what was happening.

She recognized the box—a black jeweler's case worn on the corners—as coming from her own dresser drawer, and she gave him a confused look. But he wouldn't say anything to her except, "Open it." He had a familiar kind of seriousness on his face with the light shining in his eyes. Inside the box, she found not its usual contents—her mother's earrings—but a thin metal chain of three hundred tiny ovals bent one into another. Hanging down was a small misshapen something that looked polished and beaten all at once.

"The tenth anniversary is supposed to be tin," he said. She held the charm to the light, and he added, "Stuff's harder to weld than you'd think." She dangled the necklace between her fingers; it weighed just this side of a feather, and clinked against itself like a tiny wind chime. The charm that hung from it, she could see, was shaped mostly like a heart, with one side a little rounder than the other. She could see where the paint had been scraped off, and wondered what it was a can of before it was a symbol of her love and marriage.

She wanted to say, "Thank you," or maybe, "It's beautiful," but the day came back on her and she was too tired to keep thinking one thing and saying another, so what came out was, "I didn't get you anything," and it didn't sound like an apology.

"Oh, baby," he said, taking the chain from her and pulling it over her head—there wasn't a clasp. "I hope you like it," he said, looking down, and in that looking down you could see that this is where he'd been every time he'd excused himself from the house, that he wasn't sneaking off so that she wouldn't see him hurting, but so that he could show her what she meant to him even now, even like this. And she broke down again, thinking to herself that it was good that she wasn't being filmed, because they hated it when you did the same thing twice. Like the last time, Lyle came to her, like every last time, all of them, and like he would all the next times no matter how many next times there turned out to be. She thought, *It's good, this thing we've made together, damn good.* But this thought felt like it wasn't hers, like she'd just been asked what it felt like when her husband took care of her, like she was giving the answer the question implied.

And as she was thinking this, as the tears dried a second time, she and Lyle fell into each other's arms, and made love again. After, they held each other in the dark, each trying to fall asleep thinking only of the wonders of the last ten years, both, in spite of themselves, thinking only of tomorrow.

Season 1, Episode 8:
Fr. William and the Fire Sermon

Our little part of the world was settled in four distinct stages. First were the people who we named the river after, but who are long since all but gone from here. Then came the railroads, which needed a path through the mountains, between the cattle markets and St. Louis. Then came the monks because the railroad had given them land enough to build an abbey. Then came our forebears, who bought the rest of the land back from the railroads and settled near the abbey because the church had told them to. There were other houses of worship in tow, but The Church meant only one place, and in charge of The Church was one man.

Fr. William Colquit had been our priest, installed at the little church we'd named a street after just north of downtown since sometime in the middle sixties, which meant he'd given first communion to everyone in town. Taught us catechism. Married us. Buried our dead. Even way back—when his hair was the color of greased ink and his green eyes danced behind thick black glasses—he was known to mumble. He had a habit of looking down at a spot some feet in front of him, occupied by thoughts that drew him elsewhere always.

By and large, when words were not commanded by God or convention, Fr. William found that silence was the most sincere solace he had to offer. If we'd asked him about it, he might have told us that he really thought this was the most sincere love he could offer. When a child caught ill and died, when a house caught fire and took it all, what words helped anything? Presence was all one could really provide, or at least he hoped so.

Thus, it never surprised Fr. William that attendance took a slow dive year after year. People seem to get along on their own these days, and as much as he nodded along with every ain't-it-a-shame at the sacristy society meetings, he couldn't help but think that maybe this was a good thing in its own way. God might approve of a people who got along without him. It started off with a few of staying away, and then a few more.

We weren't a godless people, just the opposite, but we too needed rest. And so when there weren't enough acolytes for the morning and late masses, William started recruiting at the county jail. The men there were grateful to help, and there was always someone in holding or the drunk tank who still knew the mass by heart, usually because William had taught it to him so many years ago. Probably this was not helping attendance.

Very little surprised William, as he expected serving God to be difficult, and he was often baffled that he got by as easy as he did. Christmas and Easter were better of course, but then the church wasn't for them, the lily and poinsettia crowd. No, mass was for the everyday, the haggard few, and it was for their sake and consideration that Fr. William had quit giving homilies. It started with a few shorter attempts, which were met with no argument, and over the years, his sermons were filed down with the crowd. These days he'd say a sentence or two, or just hold still a minute and let the gospel be its own messenger. Then he'd set about working his miracle.

It reminded him of his younger days back at the abbey, when he and the other priests spent each morning whispering the mass to themselves in a series of identical chapels. Hearing the same mumblings in the walls on either side, thinking of the holy ghost's busy hand, altar by altar, bread made flesh, transubstantiation simultaneous— it was funny and it was sad and it was perfect. Prayers answered everywhere all at once, faith and purpose stacked one on another like the petals of a rose. He never talked about it with anyone, but he felt the spirit back then when he was still almost a boy—he was sure of it. Not every time, but when it happened it washed over like January creek water, like fire burning off the too-frail parts of him.

And when it was quiet enough, when words and thoughts weren't in the way, if he said little enough, he could share that with his flock. And though they never told him about it, he thought he saw the ghost in their eyes after mass sometimes, thought they moved more upright, a state closer to awe.

And then on a Tuesday Arthur Gossett's boy walked into his office. He tried to look surprised. Martin hadn't been in the church since he'd went away to college. His daughters weren't even baptized. But Arthur and Marie had their names soldered into the window they'd paid for, and church like that didn't wash off easy.

"Bless me, Father, but I tried my damnedest," he said.

Even then, Fr. William should have known better, should have asked him if he really knew what he was doing. But instead he made him back up and start over, and then he listened as Martin told him that the town was dying because the factory was dying, and that it was too late for anyone beyond God to change the course of things. But of course, Martin was there not to ask for a miracle, but for reprieve from a penance he'd imposed upon himself. Father listened to Martin as he explained the way that the town would die, block by block, support industry by service supplier, and then, after it all, explained that a producer was waiting outside to make a deal concerning filming rights in the church.

Fr. William wanted to believe that he didn't know what to think. But William knew as sure as anything that the straightforward thing to do would be to cast the producer out, just as he also knew that he was being asked more than a single question. And so, for a thirty-thousand-dollar donation to the food bank, Fr. William agreed, thinking later that it made sense at the time.

The show made good on that investment about halfway through the season. We were asked in high definition if we planned on going to mass this Sunday, and we answered the only way we could. What did it matter if driving to church meant gas we couldn't readily replace, if we thought about the electricity it took to run the iron? Truth be told, it had been on our minds as it was.

Fr. William did his level best. We all knew that that first Sunday he was looking out on more of us than he'd seen in some time. We assumed it was nerves that led him to skip the homily, the offering, the post-communion announcements that we all expected. It must have been some kind of mistake. And it should have felt strange watching the boom mic dangle above Fr. William's head as he offered the host to heaven, but it wasn't.

For his part, William felt he took it all in stride, did admirably. Why not give the mass to the faithful, say the ceremony that way that Mrs. Frauenhelder, who hadn't missed in a dozen years, expected it? When he stood on the front steps afterward, the Jeremiah Schlutermans thanked him for keeping things traditional, and so did Mrs. Mallett, several times. And that was enough for him, even if more than few of his newly reinvigorated flock found cute ways to ask him if next week's service would be as curt.

The next morning there were six messages on the machine already by the time Father walked in at quarter past nine. The Walkers noticed that the acolyte at Sunday's service—a biker type with a neck tattoo that peeked out of his cassock—was, here Mrs. Walker paused, a little rusty perhaps, and that her two boys, Aden and Spencer, would be willing and able just as soon as the next acolyte class started up. The Johnson clan wanted to know about the youth group that hadn't had cause to meet in the last eight years. What about that food bank? Did the grounds need tending? Were there catechism classes? An adult confirmation seminar? Sponsored weekend retreats. Baptisms. First communion. The Thursday night calligraphy class he taught back some years ago. When was confession.

All of these things, of course, were part of his ministry, but along with the mass they'd slipped a piece at a time until what pieces were left didn't make much whole. The church, like him, had gotten older, and it seemed that daily mass and occasional weddings and funerals were all that he and they required. Until all this.

His first most sincere and deepest response was to run, and probably that would have been the smartest of all choices. Though recruitment had been in a predictable decline, there were still younger, more ambitious priests who would love to serve the de facto most active community in the diocese. They would take him back at the monastery in a moment, welcome him with a smile and a job, letting him read to the other monks while they ate without speaking. He might work in the garden, or take reservations at the retreat house and give tours of the reliquary and the catacomb beneath the high altar. He wanted it with his bones, this even simpler life.

For years, he'd kept his coffin under his bed. He'd made it back some years ago for another priest who was thought not long for this world but then recovered, praise be to God. Though its original tenant had no immediate use for it, it seemed a shame to waste such a thing, and so he'd slid the simple pine box under his bed, and it had been there for going on twenty years now. Often at night, he imagined himself laid out in that coffin, the monks proceeding past the casket, their hoods shielding their eyes and peaking like candlewicks atop their heads, incense burning, the organ piping requiem. It was far from a nightmare.

But instead he called back Mrs. Walker and said that if she'd be willing to teach a CCD class that perhaps a youth ministry of sorts could be arranged. He called first the abbey, and then the greater diocese—and had food trucked in to fill the food bank, which was still waiting for the donation from the show. There were art classes, courtesy of a supplies donation from the Gossett boy, and a baking and knitting circle thanks to Cathy Wells, and fish fries for the whole town thanks to Steve Womack. And of course, attendance was its highest in church history, with some members of the congregation forced to sit in the loft with the newly formed choir and the camera three operator.

By three Sundays down—the 29th in Ordinary Time— the two Walker boys cantered proudly in the cassocks their mother had sewn them as they proceeded down the aisle in front of Fr. William. The organ mewled softly at "A Mighty

Down and Out

Fortress Is Our God," and we sang along in a cracked and raspy polytone that warbled around the desired pitch. Lyle Younse said the readings, and then it was another hymn and then the gospel, and then we all leaned into our pews, unsure what would happen next. We'd talked more about religion in the last few weeks than most of us had in years. And what we'd talked about most was what kind of homily Father would give us this week.

For his own part, even when he'd given these regularly, Fr. William had never been one for expansive rhetoric. But he knew that if ever one of these had to mean something, it would be this one, and so he'd decided to change the reading. Not the Gospel, of course, but the first one, the one from the Old Testament. It was a passage read at mass not a month ago, but he knew most wouldn't notice and that probably only Mrs. Frauenhelder would complain. Normally, when he'd preached in the past, he'd read word for word from a series of cards on the pulpit. Though he had those cards with him, he decided without really making a decision to close his eyes and speak.

He said, "Today you heard the story of Meshach, Shadrach, and Abednego. I remember them because they are, to my reckoning, the three most unfortunate individuals in the Old Testament.

"Now of course that's a strong statement, and you might say to me that the Lord saved them—that he protected them from the fires of the furnace, the fires so hot they claimed the lives of the would-be executioners. You could say to me that they remained, unsinged, that they walked in the fire with the Holy Ghost, and that through them God and his faith came to many. And you'd be right.

"But I say to you that first they had to get there. They

had to stand in the face of the furnace, and be asked to do a very simple thing—to pretend to be something they weren't, to deny themselves. That's a sin we've all committed. Now in the Bible, it's two sentences— Nebuchadnezzar asks them, they say throw us in the fire. But I think there's a lot that's left out here. I think you have to remember that these men were slaves stolen from their homelands, that they'd been away from home so long that even the writer of the Bible forgets their true names. You have to remember that Nebuchadnezzar had slain thousands for far, far less. You have to think about having been strangers for so long that only strangeness was familiar, and you have to think about how easy it would have been to bow, to prostrate, to tell yourself that on the inside the real you isn't the one giving in. You hate this but you are doing what you must to survive, and honestly I'm not sure even God could blame you for it—every part of you would call out to make not just the easy answer, but the logical one, the sensible of the two choices.

"But instead these three men chose faith, chose their word and their bond and their God, knowing what it meant, or at least thinking they did. They made that choice as they watched the furnace get stoked until it was like to melt. I think about how at every moment they could have changed their minds, that it was what even the king wanted. But for however long it took to prepare their death chamber, they held their faith like they were holding their breath.

"And then the miracle came. They were tied down and thrown into a kiln seven times hotter than a blacksmith knew what to do with, and as they were thrown, their executioners caught flame and burned before their eyes.

Down and Out

"I do not know, and would say that no one really can, what that next moment was like, but I'll tell you this, and it's the point I've been trying to get to—how much miracle can you ask for? Isn't even the smallest kind more than what any of us deserve?

"So when they were in that fire, God saved them, sent his own Spirit to unbind their hands, sure, but do you think that he included air conditioning? I wasn't there to know, but it seems like maybe Shadrach, Meshach, and Abednego walked out of those flames alive, yes, protected by the grace of God, certain, but that doesn't mean anything like that they didn't feel the burn. No. Rather, I expect that this miracle hurt, that it hurt quite a bit, that they felt their flesh crying to blister and pop even as God wouldn't let it. The more I think about it, the more I pray to never be given a miracle, because I'm not sure that I am man enough to be a saint. I pray that I never see the face of God in the fire—never.

"I imagine that I am not the only one here who has taken to praying of late. I wanted to talk about this reading because that's just what this is—an answered prayer. This is what deliverance looks like—this is the face of Grace and Mercy.

"So when you pray, remember to thank God for all of everything. And when you suffer, as we all suffer, we must, try, if you can, to be thankful, to wait in patience and to bite down on your faith against the sometimes searing pain. Remember that every pang might be your miracle, and that love and help must always serve not your interest, not your plans, but the greater interest, the plans of God and God alone."

He sat there, and he stared at us with a look that said

I'm sorry, and then he let out, "Amen," and we sat in silence, trying to remember if we were allowed to clap.

After the homily came the Eucharist. For everyone in the room, the host was the first thing we'd eaten that day, the wine the first spirits since our liquor cabinets ran dry. And perhaps it was that, the single sip of heavy red wine, that first morsel of the day that shook a sense of completion through the room, that made us feel something like a presence. But we were satisfied then, content with the miracles granted us.

Then it was the Prayers of the Faithful, something else we'd noticed Father had left out the week before. He gave the usual four—the Church, the Pope, the Bishop, the people—and then he offered a minute for silent intentions. And even though he said the word silent and we heard him say it, one of the Johnsons stood up and asked that for the starving children of Africa with their bellies all stuck out that they might find enough to eat, in the Lord's name we pray and we said God hear our prayer. Then Martin Gossett prayed for the health of an ailing relation in Fort Worth and Mrs. Mallett added intentions for the lost souls who would never know Christ, and then we were praying for the victims of recent natural disasters, those afflicted with cancers, with wasting diseases. It didn't take long before there was a line to stand and pray; all of us had a reason that none of us could complain, and Fr. William didn't stop us until Mrs. Mallett asked that we pray for the souls of the damned a second time.

Mass lasted longer that day than it had in two years, but it seemed like before we knew it Father was telling us to go in peace, and we filed out into the early fall sunshine, shafts of soft light breaking between the limbs of trees our parents had planted. And every one of us had a flatline for a mouth, and if we felt a thing, it was a thing like what kept your fingers out of the lathe in a double-time Christmas bonus shift. And then we found, spread out across the law and into the parking lot—an amount of food we couldn't imagine.

Fr. William explained, reading from the card the producers had handed him, that this had been donated by a local restaurant and that we all were to enjoy as much as we wanted and that we just needed to wait long enough for the film crews to get a few shots.

We watched as the cameras panned across the presentation platters of glistening chicken nuggets and pyramids of double-decker cheeseburgers, bales of fries and ponds of ketchup, mustard, mayonnaise. They even had the boneless rib sandwiches that we'd seen advertised and given up on, figuring our limited time would exceed theirs. Even when we watched it on the screen later on, it gave us hunger pangs to see them pan past all that food while we stood in our best clothes drooling like hunting dogs. By the time we actually got to eating it, the food was cold—rubbery and stiff at the same time. Still we smiled around mouthfuls of pickles and special sauce and said thank you to the camera and nodded curtly to each other, glad that our miracle was small enough to swallow.

This was for many reasons a strange episode of the show. It opens with four families—the Wilkes, the Gossetts, the Jason Johnsons, and the Jim Schlutermans, the children toddling up to their parents and asking their parents one of two questions—"Why are we going to church?" or "What's for breakfast?" Cutting from family to family, we see the answers to these questions, the blushing shame-eyed well-ums or the harsh directed go-get-dresseds, and then the bell rings and the whole town files into church.

Mass was shot with a grainy filter to compensate for the dark shadows between banks of stained glass. Fr. William's homily, which they made him call a sermon in the episode's only post-fact interview, is presented uninterrupted as the camera passes from still shots of the stations of the cross to close-ups of various parishioners captured unblinking like tintypes of the dead. Father's voice is amplified, sharpened somehow. The bells ring behind the choir as we file up to the rail where we kneel, each of us, to receive our God, and then it cuts to the hamburgers and Fr. William reading the first half of his card, and then to us eating and saying earnest thank yous to the camera, and then Little Tim Knight covers his eyes in chicken nuggets and the Gossett girls and the Johnson boys play Ring around the Rosie in the sunshine and then we see Fr. William with the crucifix behind him. He explains that religion and hard times are always kissing cousins, and that he is bound to serve the people, glad to do his small part. He says the sermon means we can survive. It means that there will be enough. It means we will, somehow, emerge unsinged—someday, we hope. The camera fades out.

What made this episode unique was that it used no footage not shot on that one particular Sunday, presented in a straight chronological order with limited editing and juxtapositional convenience. Other than the bells, which were dubbed at Fr. William's abbey, and the choir—which they replaced with a professional recording of the same song—everything else happened just like that. The forty-eight minutes of the episode condensed only 2½ hours of actual life.

For this the director and the cinematographer were both critically hailed, winning both the Golden Globe and the Emmy for Best Reality TV Episode—Dramatic. They were praised for their bold choices to show such a small thing. No weeks of condensed time. No production crew's instructions other than giving the questions to the children that started the show and teaching the kids Ring around the Rosie. It was called bold, fresh, genuine. They were praised for their originality, for their unique contribution to reality as a genre.

Fr. William was largely absent from the rest of production, but not from our lives. Though we were never seen doing so again, we continued to go to church, all of us, at least until filming ended, and William worked perhaps harder than any of us to keep the town running. He managed well overall, though he found that leaning on a cane was helpful as he made his way from catechism classes to Sacristy Society meetings to Baked Goods Bingo. The only thing he had trouble with was confession. He intentionally left it off the schedule in the weekly bulletin, but we remembered that it used to be Thursdays from three to six, and we knocked on the parsonage door and asked him if he didn't mind, if it wasn't too much trouble. But it was hard on him, absolving guilt in exchange for contrition. There is above all the burden of knowing, of hearing that Jamie Mallett dreamed of driving his mother across the state line and leaving her at one of the Indian casinos with no ID. To forgive Lucy Wilkes for falsely accusing her husband of having an affair just after forgiving Tim Wilkes for being unfaithful.

And then Lyle Younse snuck in ten minutes past once

and asked Father to assign him penance for knowing that his wife was lying to him, keeping from him a secret stash of money and some hushed business with their cameraman. Lyle wanted forgiveness for knowing these things and keeping silent about them because he was afraid of both the show and loneliness. He kept his head bowed, but William could feel the hurt in his eyes just the same. He needed something, but there was nothing in William's power to give. It was a problem not just right then, but one that haunted William as he cooked his meals listening to baseball games on the radio and tried to sleep through the rattle of the trees in the night. But then, in that moment, what he could do was look through the twine mesh at the top of Lyle's head and tell him to say a full Rosary, and to pray to St. Jude for aid in this time of need, and so he did that, and Lyle nodded deeply and asked if Father had a Rosary he could borrow.

It was late October by then, and the walk back to the parsonage seemed longer than it ought. Of late the nights were changing from crisp to flat-out cold, and there was no moon, but no clouds either. William felt his bones creak as his breath hung in front of him, shining in the starlight. As he walked into the stiff breeze, he whispered to himself, Deliver me Lord. Deliver me. But not yet.

Season 1, Episode 9:
Thanksgiving

It started off just the way you thought it would. They pulled us in one by one into those dark and private spaces they'd made for themselves in each of our homes and asked us, "What was your favorite part of Thanksgiving dinner?" Most of us thought we saw where this was going, and told them it was seeing our family, or being together, or being thoughtful, and Jason Johnson even said church though no nearby congregations had Thursday services we knew about. Tillie Mallett didn't know any better and said the truth—she hated all of it altogether.

But the ones that made the broadcast that aired in the fourth week of November were those who saw either all the way to the end, or never bothered to look ahead at all. Martin said that every year his wife made a dish called Green Beans Stefan is my Landlord, which dated to their first apartment together and an accidental application of cinnamon that had grown into an indispensable part of the holidays; it was the only preparation of green vegetables the girls would readily consume. He didn't know the recipe.

Jamie said, simply—pie.

But mostly it was the children they showed, who promptly answered the question with a tide of favorite foods, a meal so magnificent as to be impossible. Turkey, ham, steak, according to one of the Gossett girls. Mashed potatoes, sweet potatoes, stuffing and rolls and cornbread, and all manner of casseroles, layered salads of the sixth and seventh degree, gravies in a mud-colored rainbow.

Briseño

It couldn't have been the first time we heard our children ask for something we knew we couldn't give, but some pains never dull. We didn't need to wait to see ourselves on television to realize that every episode would show someone not eating. We were tired of being filmed in various outfits, looking through our pantries we knew were empty in the name of continuity. The Jim Schlutermans quit the show right then, gave up and went to live with her people in Fort Smith, and we heard he got a job working new home construction and they're doing all right.

But for the rest we hung on and did only what we could, which was nothing. Then our children explained things to us. Little Junior Johnson was in the interview chamber talking about how he thought pigs in a blanket would be an excellent addition to the Thanksgiving table and his mother broke down in tears listening from the other room. Jason climbed out of the curtain and went to his mother, climbed into her lap and said loudly, "Don't cry, Mama." And then he leaned in and whispered, "We're on TV."

At first Tammy Johnson fell deeper into her sobs as that was the one part of her troubles that hadn't been on her mind. But Junior had a smile in his eyes. "We figured it out at school," he said, whispering under the sound of her cries. "Things are going to be all right," he said, and this we heard though it was again just a whisper, and they used that image as the inside cover of the box set DVD.

And once we thought about it, we had to admit the kids had a point. They had more of a chance to talk at school than we did at home as law prevented them from filming in public schools. Which is not to say that the production crew wouldn't let us whisper or keep secrets. They in fact encouraged it to a great degree. But we were always watched, or so it came to seem. The kids had more time and opportunity for discussion, and so "We're on TV" got passed around among them like the chicken pox before we knew better. It wasn't a boast, but more like a private decade of the rosary. There was some meaning there that they weren't even sure of.

But it followed, or so all the children decided, that since we were on TV, then television rules were in play. In television, if it didn't happen on camera, it didn't happen. In television, when someone cries for something, they get that something if they've tried hard and been good. In television, the houses that still flew the confederate flag were edited right out of the landscape. Didn't the show make Mr. Gossett get a mule? Hadn't they brought a whole truckload of fish? And found a magic hundred dollars for Mrs. Younse's anniversary? In television, the children told each other and then whispered back to us, good people don't go hungry, especially not on a holiday. How could a television town go universally dissatisfied? How could their universe abide a holiday ignored? We didn't know how and we didn't dare imagine the details, but the children had a point—there had to be a Thanksgiving episode, so there had to be Thanksgiving.

But of course if it was to come, we would, we supposed, have to help it along. After all, could we expect our own personal miracle? So we talked to Fr. William and all agreed with only a minimum of whispering, almost all of it off camera, that we should all celebrate the holiday together at the Fellowship Hall. It would be a potluck; everyone would bring something. And when necessary, we could share what we had to make things come together. It was agreed that Tammy Johnson had gotten best at baking bread, and so we sent her the flour we had left. Most of the oil went to Steve Womack so as he could fry up all the fish the game warden would let him take in a week.

Cathy confided to the camera that she had nothing left to cook at all, and an hour later the cameraman Trent presented her with a Walmart sack full of fresh pig knuckles and ten pounds of grits. He stared at her, and she smiled into the middle distance until he picked the camera up and then she didn't miss a beat as she said, "All I could afford to get was grits and pig knuckles...and I don't have a clue how to cook either." She looked exasperated for long enough to make sure the shot was clear, and then went about making a grit and pig knuckle casserole, seasoned with some sage that Stacy Schluterman had sent over.

That week, children ran from house to house, distributing sugar and cans of pumpkin. Recipes held sacred for generations were passed along if they might help another. We cleaned the Fellowship Hall out, found the folding chairs. Functions at the Fellowship Hall usually used paper plates, the cheap ones most of the time, and the nice stiff ones for weddings and better funerals. But we couldn't afford to dispose, and so everyone agreed to bring plates and silver enough for their own people. We didn't see why we shouldn't use the nicer plates, that china set our mothers had left to us. It was after all a holiday. Steve Womack took a commemorative plate depicting Eureka Springs from the wall and brought it with him.

We were abuzz with life and energy. None of us talked about it because we didn't want to spoil it, but there was a tiny and thus all the more significant sense of hope. You could see it working. We were no longer former employees of a now-defunct corporation. We were more than the past tense. We had earned a now, and it was good, better than we thought. The whole town had its ovens on, damn the gas bill, and the town seemed to glow. Every house smelled like Thanksgiving.

Martin was given permission to buy two turkeys, provided he cooked them himself with no help and made it seem like that was his idea. And even though we could see how that was going, and knew certainly that among four hundred people, two turkeys was like a drop of clean water in a bucket of piss, just the thought, just the notion of turkey was enough to seal it. Goddamnit, we were excited. We couldn't help it.

And as Cathy started roasting pig knuckles and reading the instructions on the sack of grits, Lyle was outside humming. This week had been so normal. Or not even. But he could see smiles on everyone's faces. On his wife's face. He told the camera this. He said that he was glad for the holiday, because this year more than ever, they needed reminding of their blessings. It was when you had the least that you had to be the most grateful. He knew that. He said this while he was outside under the hood of his truck. The weather looked to hard freeze that night, and he faced a dilemma. The radiator in Cathy's car was full of clear water. He had replaced a hose on it in April, hadn't had any antifreeze around, figured he could get to that later on. When the show came that July it still hadn't crossed his mind. Now he didn't have eleven dollars for a jug of antifreeze.

But he wasn't angry. He didn't brood or shake his head. The editors found it hard to keep his character consistent, to cut around him whistling Christmas music as he emptied the truck's radiator, still a bright orange color, and then the car's, into a bucket, and then funneled the mixture, back into both cars. See, he told the camera. You can find a way. You can.

The morning of Thanksgiving, Martin got up early to cook the two turkeys he'd been allowed to buy. Using the kitchen was unavoidable, but he hadn't turned the ovens on since Marla had left. He thought of her as he turned them both to 350, smiling at her insistence on having the double model, even though he'd never seen her use both at the same time. He had been allowed to use a recipe, and he followed it meticulously, massaging butter under the skin and using the cooking twine he'd found in the pantry to truss the birds like he saw in the picture. He set a timer, and then looked out the window.

His mule was outside standing motionless except for his breath, which puffed rhythmically from his nose like a sourceless fountain. All around him was ice, a two-inch sheet of it, blanketing everything. He of course wanted to know how the mule had gotten out of the garage, and why the weather report had said nothing of ice, but he couldn't help but stop and take in the beauty of it, the reduction of road and ditch and lawn and ridge to a single surface, solid and gleaming in cloud-covered sunrise.

He went out and dragged the mule back into the garage, only falling once. He fed the mule, and even managed to get back inside in time for no serious damage to be done, despite the fact that the ovens had turned themselves up to 500 degrees. Several other serious potential distractions, from the girls needing his undivided attention for long periods of time to the power going out and coming back on any number of times, continued to come between Martin and his turkeys. But he persevered. Something in the way the town was feeling meant something, and he would not be the one to let us down this time.

Despite the production team's best efforts, the turkeys were beautiful. Like they'd come from a magazine. And when it came time, Martin loaded the girls into their winter coats, which didn't really fit the way they ought to, and then loaded them into the car, corralled the mule again, and then carefully lay the turkeys in the back of the SUV he'd bought when Marla had first gotten pregnant. Dinner was supposed to start at four.

There was some hope that the roads would thaw out by then, but the sun kept covered all day, and the ice was as thick as ever. Still Martin proceeded to slide down Old Military Road, past the homes of several others who were either about to make the same journey or had just now left. We fell upon the Fellowship Hall in convoys of two and three. No one was injured, and all the cars that went off the road were winched back to safety with only cosmetic damages.

Everyone brought something, whatever that had to mean. A few of us had gathered together and dusted the chairs and the folding tables, found what napkins remained, arranged the stackable furniture into designs we hoped were festive. Gina Schluterman had made four centerpieces for the twenty-five tables in the room, which were distributed more or less evenly. Along one wall nearest the kitchen were three other tables set aside for food. Those of us decorating had left our dishes there as we continued to set up.

Off to the side nearby but not so near as to be obvious were another four tables. No one talked about it. Families bundled up in other families' coats poured in, bringing with them the food that they had found.

They stopped when they arrived at the table for food. Everyone set their dishes, the grits and knuckles, the grape jelly cranberry sauce, the cream biscuits made without cream or flour, the eleven fried bass filets, the canned green beans mixed with canned corn mixed with Fritos and chili seasoning. The what we had, the make it do. Half of it was barely meant for consumption at all, but only to resemble a Thanksgiving dish. But assembled there on one table, all in one place, in a slow pan and a filter that made everything look juicy, it was impressive. There was an ugly kind of beauty in it, like the word hope scratched into the table in a prison visiting room. Fr. William stood up at one end of the table and got ready to say a blessing.

But Tammy grabbed him and said, maybe we ought to wait. Fr. William didn't know for what. But we did. We sat patiently waiting for five minutes. Then Jason Johnson went and whispered to one of the cameramen, and then whispered to his children, and within forty seconds, it was known across the room that they weren't coming. The thing we'd been hoping for so hard that it seemed like it had already happened wouldn't be happening at all. And as soon as we knew it, it felt like the most obvious thing in the world. Of course they wouldn't buy us Thanksgiving dinner. Of course they wouldn't help. What had only moments ago seemed a foregone conclusion, that a town full of hungry people couldn't be asked to eat slop on television, now seemed downright absurd. The worst part of it, spitting in our faces: we had done this to ourselves.

Just then, Martin and the girls came in. Each girl had half a turkey, while Martin held the inside rung of both pans. Though this was of course impossible, the smell of those birds filled the room instantly, and all two hundred some odd of us came to silence. It was more of a memory than a smell. It was exactly what we'd been hoping for. In the tiniest possible dose. And maybe it felt like immediate if temporary relief. Maybe it was an air bubble. But it was for then enough.

Most of it tasted terrible. What wasn't terrible was scant enough to only go around in the tiniest possible portions. Martin spent an hour and seventeen minutes diligently carving the turkey into four hundred equal servings, a bite of real thanksgiving for everyone on the show. We ate what was given to us, and did not make a face. Our children only cried a little.

The episode was one of our biggest successes. Everyone seemed to love our making do, our getting done, our community attitude. They loved Fr. William rising up after most of us were seated and had started eating, whistling at us like hogs, and saying, "Today is a day to be thankful. And all of us have plenty to say thank you for. All of us, more than we know. I might have it wrong, but it always felt to me like this was a holiday for those who have it hard, that we need thankfulness most, those who have every reason to say nothing at all. Bow your heads and say Amen."

They loved the fact that you could tell how bad the food tasted, the hollowed-eyed and practiced disinterest as the whole town pushed their jaws towards their eyes, drank water, swallowed. They loved that we had made our own miracle. That in a town where no one had had enough to eat in months, there was one day where we all went home full. We had made our own holiday from scraps and from nothing. They loved that we didn't know how good we had it.

Season 1, Episode 10:
It's a Wonderful Town

Jamie Mallett's mother, Tillie, was old enough to remember the river valley before Doyles' Gear. When the factory had opened, she was fifteen. Having seen a handbill advertising work for men and women, she had hitchhiked forty-three miles and lied about her age and started on the line the very first time it cranked into motion. To that point she had lived on her family's farm, where her father raised hogs and distilled liquor. He was a brutal man, fond of using the same kind of persuasion with his four daughters as he did his swine—a switch cut from a nearby tree. Or worse.

Tillie was happy to get away when she did and had never looked back. She and Jim Mallett had been wed in the judge's office, no service to speak of and only the secretary as a witness. Though it was unusual for someone not to have a proper wedding, it was common enough and we were polite enough only to assume we already knew why, and not ask. So no one ever asked Tillie Mallett about her family, not even Jamie, her son.

This made things difficult when she started to hear his voice. Not all the time of course, but particularly in the mornings, Tillie would wake up unsure as to just when it was, and Jamie had caught her more than once trying to drag the trash can outside to slop hogs they didn't have or fetch water for the morning wash in a coffee cup. Jamie didn't know who the He she kept saying would switch her was, and in her more lucid moments Tillie still didn't feel like explaining.

Down and Out

But every miracle starts with a tragedy. Thanksgiving had taught us that. This one started with the mailman.

Maybe not everybody knows this, but bills left on the counter have a way of ripening, turning from white to canary yellow to dog-tongue pink, to sometimes plate-special blue, and in the most extreme circumstances a red that makes it hard to read words that aren't in bold or caps, which are thankfully few. Each and every day, Gary, John Needleman's cousin who was the mailman and who we were required to wave at and thank regardless, brought more evidence of our impending financial implosion. Credit cards, electric bills, phone and gas and water. What else? Car notes, school notes, bank notes. Doctors, hospitals, vets. Most of us made deals with our landlords to pay in full with interest when the money came in, and those that owned worked out a similar deal with the First Paris bank. But how could you call the electric company and explain to them that you were part of a reality television series with payment deferred for just a little while longer so that you could pay and you would and if she'd heard that three other times today didn't that mean it was more likely to be true and not less?

But no matter how we pleaded, no matter what we said, everything went to collection. And though we didn't know it, this turned out to be a good thing in its way.

Collection agencies are like movie villains, unable to cross certain arbitrary lines of behavior, bound magically to a code of honor. Which meant that just so long as you didn't say you were you, if they couldn't prove that it was in fact Mr. James Nathan Mallett, or Mrs. Cathy Leann Younse, then they had to avoid certain topics of conversation, namely what it was that they actually called to discuss with you.

But, at the same time, they were not actually allowed to hang up. What arcane law made this so, we could never fathom, but it remained a fact that until you said goodbye and put that phone back in the cradle, they had to stay there with you. Had to.

Most of us dug through our basements and found an answer in answering machines. Good old-fashioned call screening. It was a pleasure to use a forgotten technology to foil a modern inconvenience. The Johnsons and Martin Gossett took to letting their kids answer the phones.

Jamie, however, won the heart of the town and the audience by saying hello and then handing the phone to his mother, who would assume it was some distant relation and start catching him or her up on the local news, starting with Jamie graduating from high school.

And then things got even better. It turned out that one of the big collection companies also owned one of the big production companies and as a sort of professional nod, they agreed not to film us when the calls came in. It started when Tammy and Jason had gotten into a whisper fight, trying hard not to get caught on film screaming at one another this one goddamn time, not to air their laundry in front of the whole fucking country, and the phone rang and Tammy picked it up and listened to the caller identify himself as an agent of a collection company seeking to collect payment on an outstanding debt and was this so and so or so and so, and then watched as the production assistant whose job it was to listen to all of her phone calls gave a sign to the camera crew, who turned their cameras exclusively towards her husband, and really without even knowing what it was she was doing she screamed that yes this was Tamara Jean Johnson and that she did in fact have extenuating circumstances, namely that her no-good son-of-a-bitch husband expected her to still clean the whole damn house even if he was sitting around all day. Before she was even done talking, Jason had stormed into the other room to pick up the extension and inform his wife and whoever else happened to be listening that he couldn't help it if his wife was selfish and lazy and just like her mother. They watched as the production assistant fumed at his inability to record such beautiful discord, but when he asked if they might want to have the fight again after they'd hung up, they shrugged and said they'd made up and went to do the other thing they were allowed to do off camera.

It didn't take long before the whole town took to answering every call on the first ring with their full names, just in case. There are only so many call centers. So many warm bodies to occupy the chair on the other end of the line. We weren't surprised when it became widely established in whatever circles those collectors ran in that a call to Paris, Arkansas, meant a long conversation with no return on their time, unless they wanted to know what the free clinic in Russellville had said about the boil on Terrence Terrell's foot and yes he'd had to hitchhike, even though as soon as somebody picked him up the white van followed behind like a three-legged dog.

The collectors, of course, when you came down to it, were just doing their jobs, just like we were just doing ours. Most of us understood their curtness, their desire to move on to someone who might let them collect something. But who in those overseas call centers had taught them the term hillbilly, Jamie neither knew nor took kindly to. But no matter what they said, and to be sure they said some things, it didn't really change our strategy.

Nothing they could say was worse than what we wanted to tell them. Things to just speak out and let them hang in the air. Things like, "How the hell was I ever talked into this and why won't anyone say more than six words at a piece to anybody?" or sometimes if it had been a particularly hard day, and it had, it had, we'd just ask "Why?" And some days we'd even get an answer, but if we're telling all of the truth, that's never what we wanted.

So we noticed when the calls stopped.

Not gradually, as in one call center at a time started to catch on, started to avoid all the numbers from our particular exchange, but like a wrench on a main valve. It was a Tuesday and it wasn't even ten in the morning before we were on the phone, with each other for the first time in a while, trying to explain our newfound financial freedom and the imminently ensuing loneliness. *I don't think the bill collectors will call us anymore* was perhaps rarely said so often in so small a place, and never with such wistful longing.

The most popular theory was that they'd finally given up on us as a lot. We couldn't pay, they'd decided, and so why even bother? Why not program your auto dialer around us? Other theories were similar in range, many coming to the conclusion that this too was a legal ramification of our unique situation. Tammy Johnson tried calling the number on the back of one of her credit cards and discovered that certainly her account was still in arrears and would she like to set up a payment plan. Tammy was about to ask why all of a sudden no one was bothering her on the goddamn phone when she realized that the cameramen weren't headed outside for a cigarette, but rather were framing a close-up of her silhouetted by the screen door, the phone cord wrapped through her fingers like a rosary. Apparently, calls incoming to financial institutions weren't governed by the same set of stipulations, and without even asking why what had happened happened, with the soft-spoken Bengali gentleman still explaining that her credit rating could affect her future, she hung up the phone. It seemed like somebody must have asked, must have gotten the reason. But if they'd called up a stranger they owed money to to ask why they weren't calling us anymore, the camera was instantly upon us, and the show had a giant smile. They had us. Like everything else, we wondered why, talked about it some in the little booths even, but we weren't even sure we got to complain about this one. As tight as our throats felt, we couldn't tell anyone that we couldn't tell anyone anymore, and some set about to doing whatever it was we were pretending to do for months now. All except Jamie Mallett.

For the rest of us, the collectors had been a chance to breathe our own non-telegenic issues and grievances, how we could get a chance to speak. Jamie just needed it to listen.

Probably if the factory was still open, Jamie would have had to pay a member of the Kiwanis Club to sit with his mother a few days, or maybe even found her a room at the nice home in Clarksville where he could get down to see her most weekends. But wasn't it convenient that his schedule had freed up just in time to be the one to hold his mother while she screamed, terrified of something she could no longer name. She was for the most part all together, but the bad moments kept getting worse, and her good moments became a certain kind of mediocre. It was like his momma, once she found a train of thought, was afraid to disembark and went from stop to stop until the line ran out some time later. Jamie was a patient man, patient enough to find a way where no way was, but when the collectors stopped giving his mother someone else to talk to, someone else to be with in some way, when there wasn't a place where he could find some peace—maybe it shouldn't be so easy to empathize with Jamie, so broken up because he could no longer leave his invalid mother on the telephone with a stranger for sometimes hours at a stretch. But we did understand Jamie, all of us, and not just because we knew like he did that if he'd called us and asked if we could sit with her we would have said of course and then held it against him and started screening for his phone call.

A day and a half after the calls came to a close, Jamie walked out of his house with a sense of purpose even he didn't understand. Using the gas he pretended he didn't have, he drove to Lyle's house and waited in the driveway.

Other than nods and waves the two had hardly spoken since the factory had closed. But when Lyle saw Jamie in the drive, dressed for the weather—a snow five days old— he grabbed his jacket and climbed into the passenger side of the truck. It was then 4:45 and the light was tilting off the snow at blinding angles. Jamie wouldn't make it home until after 3:00 AM, and by then his mother was dead.

Tillie, like most older folks, knew better than anyone what was happening to her mind. Most times her grasp on things was tight enough, but just now and then the used-to-be would crowd into the is and she couldn't fight her way out if it. She still knew her son, even if he did look a touch too like her departed husband to keep her sure. She knew it was him that put on the real tree jacket and said,

Down and Out

"Momma, you stay inside and I'll be back in a little while."
She had nodded then, sat down on the couch and watched
the television, which had been her routine most waking
hours since the plant had let her go. But all three channels
had talk shows, people discussing things best left unsaid. It
wouldn't do, and as she was gathering herself to get up, the
phone rang, and it kept ringing, and when she had gotten
to the phone, for the longest time she didn't hear a thing.
Dark noiselessness crackled on the line and she was about
to hang up when she heard a voice she knew. It sounded
like the sound had been a long time coming, like it had to
echo down a tube or around a tall dome. It said, Tillie go
outside. And she knew when she heard what was said that
it was her father, and that she had yet to fetch the water for
the morning's wash and that she was sure to get switched
if she didn't hurry.

As she turned the knob she saw her hands, the dark
spots, the blooming purple bruises under loose skin, the
nails gone the color of a dirty coffee cup, and she knew that
she'd buried her father in '74, before Jamie was even born.
All the same she didn't want to get switched.

Jamie found her twelve feet from the door, her feet and
hands blue and black from the cold, the phone bleating on
the floor.

Tillie Ruthie Mallett was laid to rest next to her
husband in the cemetery next to the church in a plot she'd
bought when her husband had passed. The headstone
already had her name and birthdate carved into it, only a
spot left for the year she died. Since there was no money at
the time, passersby in the graveyard may well have
assumed she still lived on for more than a year after.

The coffin was the one Fr. William had made, the one

under his bed. At first the caretaking company had refused to let Mrs. Mallett be buried without someone paying the interment fee, but when Jamie insisted that he would not only spend every penny the show ever gave him suing them but would also dig his father up and take his goddamn business elsewhere, arrangements were made. She wasn't embalmed, never visited a funeral home. After the paramedics left, Jamie found her church dress, and combed her hair, and called Father, who brought the box.

It seemed wise, considering, to convey Mrs. Mallett to her resting place as soon as possible, and so services were the following afternoon. Even still, the whole of the town was in attendance. Not just the cast, but the rest of everybody, the ones who had heretofore been avoiding us for obvious and legitimate reasons. The church was full that day, including the choir loft and the side chapel and still there were a few standing in the back trying not to lean against the stations of the cross. We sang "How Great Thou Art," and Fr. William said mass and told us all that Tillie's suffering had come to an end, and we nodded deeply because this was true.

Then because it wasn't that far and because there was no hearse to use anyways, we carried the unvarnished, unsanded pine box by its thick rope handles out across the courtyard and down the hill. The pallbearers—Jamie, of course, and Lyle, Steven Womack, Jason Johnson, Tom Schluterman, Jimmy Starling—were thankful for the cold now as it kept them from sweating through their suit coats. After one last decade of the rosary each of us came forward and spilled a shovel of earth into the grave. We knew what was coming next, and so none of us took a small shovelful. When Jamie finally came up last, there was hardly any part of the coffin left to see. And so he stared at his mother's name and didn't say anything at all, just waited until the wind's bite on his cheeks was too much to stand. Then we all went our separate ways.

We assumed because it was sad and because they had made such a goddamn point of filming each and every one of us shovel our dirt into the grave that this would be the closing image of the season, the gray snow and Jamie burying his mother. We knew from whispers that production was wrapping up, and sure enough within the week most of the vans went back to where it was they'd come from, leaving behind only a few cameras just in case something television worthy happened during the off season. Always vigilant.

Our contracts said we'd be paid on the first of the year, twenty-two days after Mrs. Mallett passed and fifteen days after the cameras retreated. We crept around unsure of how to act now that we didn't have to act like we weren't acting. And talking to each other about whatever fool thing we wanted and of course that meant the money and the show. The money was always a source of debate and serious argument, particularly among couples, trained now to start screaming when they didn't mean it. But as far as the show went, we pretty well agreed entirely regarding what a shame it was that Jamie's mother's funeral was going to be plastered all over the television. But that wasn't how it turned out at all.

The last episode of the season turned out to be about Jamie and Lyle and what happened in the woods when they were gone when Tillie walked out into the snow.

The episode started with a good deal of flashing back and talking heads, reminding everyone that Jamie and Lyle were the best of friends and that they shared their problems and joys together.

Then they showed Jamie pulling up to Lyle's place and Lyle climbing into the truck and the two of them driving off into the cold.

"Where are we going?" Lyle asked Jamie.

"I don't rightly know. They told me to get in the car, and to drive over here, and then head east." And head east they did. That part of the country had had roads laid on it for some hundred and fifty years. Back roads, side roads, farm roads, dirt roads, gravel, the black edgeless asphalt the county had put down. You can drive here in more or less the same direction for hours, idling in all the ways you can mean it, going nearly nowhere and never retracing your tracks. These roads have no names, no signs, often no maintenance at all. Here, on the back roads of the county, the difference between knowing where you're going and not is the faith that you'll see something you recognize soon enough.

Snow in Paris doesn't come every year, but it seems as though it should. The river valley takes on a quiet nobility in freshly driven cover. The quietness of the place becomes over emphasized, and the cold drives the people from the over-peopled places, lights a fire harder found in warmer days. The cameramen couldn't get enough of it, especially the way Jamie's truck looked cruising through still farm land, making him stop time and again so they could get out and film him passing and then keep on going.

The episode makes use of this footage with voice-overs of Jamie and Lyle talking. They review their friendship, how they met each other in high school, how they'd worked together for longer than either of them was old enough for.

Down and Out

They talked about the loss of the factory and how it made them both feel listless and confused and out of place. They talked about the town, and how maybe it was dying, maybe all of it was sick and there was no telling what all would happen. They worried about everyone moving away. They worried about Paris. And then they decided to go cut down Christmas trees.

Pause it right there. Do you need to even see the rest? Do you have to be told that they didn't say hardly any of that riding around in the truck, or to each other at all, that it was pieced together from other recordings, talking heads and tellbacks? The only pieces of audio recorded in that truck that made the show were the hellos, Jamie saying, "You know, I think I got an ax back here somewheres," and Lyle saying, "Well I'll be," when he saw what they found in the field.

Because when they turned some corner somewhere past Strobel Bridge, they saw a field lit up with what seemed a thousand spotlights, a copse of small pine trees full of Parisites, each of us holding an ax or a hatchet or a saw, each of us sizing up a tree. Jamie and Lyle got out, claimed and felled their own trees, and then went from neighbor to neighbor assisting as necessary until everyone had felled a tree and secured it to their vehicle as necessary.

They had filmed all of us looking at the bills on our counter. All of us worrying about where Christmas would come from, all of us saying that it wasn't presents that made Christmas, all of us saying we would make do, like we always did. They had us say it in different ways, which was advantageous as it made for a more interesting montage when they cut it all together for the show. It seemed so obviously rehearsed, especially to those of us who'd needed a few takes to be appropriately plucky. But it looked like something, all of us there together, striving in what should have been the darkness, making a point of making the best of it. Hell, it felt like something, like it and we had to be more than the sum of our parts. We knew better, knew just why we were out there in the cold and that these trees would likely rot apart in our living rooms in a week. And in spite of everything, it felt like a holiday again.

The episode closed watching families set up those Christmas trees in their front windows, dressing them in lights and ornaments, children laughing with parents, husbands holding their wives, Martin Gossett holding up Stacy to put the angel on the tree while her sister, Lane, claps and jumps. Christmas music. Willie Nelson wishing yourself a merry little Christmas. They showed more families than they had to to get the point across, let the montage extend through three verses of the song and an extra bridge. We counted—thirty-one families in total. More than half of the cast. Jamie was not among them.

Season 2: An Old Hope

Renewal

It's a word that shouldn't have a second definition. Of course there would be more. Second-season contract. Thirteen full episodes. Critical acclaim. Strong secondary market shares. High marketability. Diversification potentiation. Individualized revenue streams. Book deals. Publicity tours. We'll stop before we lose interest, but the point is this—words and hopes are the one thing you can stack as high as you need.

And that's what they did.

Ten tour buses pulled into town a week or so after shooting stopped. Buses with thick Naugahyde seats and levers to make them lean back, individual heater vents that blasted off the chill. Every bus had platters of tiny sandwiches, ice chests of beer and soda and cold wine, bowls of fun-sized candy bars—hot coffee and cocoa served in tiny paper cups with a holiday print.

Some of us were too busy relaxing to notice the hour drive and it seemed like as soon as we popped that second beer we were being ushered into the convention hall in Fort Smith. Fort Smith was a major city largely by default. The state demanded a second someplace, and since Memphis was on the other side of the river, Fort Smith had to do. The sleepy town dutifully built a mall and four exits off the interstate, and a center at which conventions might be held.

When we walked in, we saw tables finished in linen and three forks a seat, and napkins folded so as to resemble birds. Half of us looked around for something to carry and the other half wondered if they weren't being lazy. Only

Martin and everybody's children knew to sit down without prompting.

It was for us, all four courses, each a different reminder of the things we'd been doing without, and after the peach cobbler with Yarnell's ice cream in a choice of four flavors, the head producer got up and talked contract.

This season had been, by all accounts, a great success. He didn't want to bore us with a bunch of shop talk, but the test market projections and the focus group numbers looked fairly fantastic, and here was the good news—the show had been picked up for a second season.

He waited until we applauded.

Of course moving forward meant moving in a new direction. Change was a part of this, and we nodded. But this change would be exciting, it would be new. *Weren't we excited?* he asked and when we clapped some and Martin said yes and the Johnsons half nodded he said he couldn't hear us and asked us again and only when he was satisfied with our enthusiasm did he remind us that our contracts were self-renewing at the discretion of production and that not all contracts would be renewed. Some of us would be released, paid, be let back to normal more or less, and some of us would still be what he called feature families and would be guaranteed a minimum of one hundred thousand dollars per family on top of their per-episode fees and with the potential to earn far more.

We would learn if we were selected through a conspicuously large hot pink envelope with the show's logo stickered to the front to be left on our doorsteps the day after Christmas.

But the show would not start back until New Year's Eve, twelve days from then. And though he knew we wouldn't have much time to shop, they wanted us to all have a merry Christmas, and so they were giving five hundred dollars apiece to every man, woman, and child.

Then he said that we should join him in a toast and he clapped and a swarm of waiters descended upon us with trays full of champagne.

"To you," the producer said, and he raised his glass. We nodded, we drank.

And on the bus ride home the chatter alternated between what we'd do with all that Christmas money and what we'd do about next season and both topics sponsored lively debates that piled on top of each other so it was hard to keep track of who was talking about what.

Many of us just let the champagne win and let ourselves think of what all we could buy for the ones we loved. It made us want to sob to think of all the simple things we wanted to buy for each other, made us wonder at how hard it was to dream large after living so small.

But most of us focused on Season Two, talked it over in cohorts of threes and fives, wondering who exactly would be these feature families, and what Season Two would mean for them. Never mind the money, the money was more than Martin made in two years, was enough to put any two kids through the University, enough to buy four houses and rent three of them out to pay the bills on the fourth one. And any fool with sense in his head could see that Season Two meant Season Three, meant who knows what and for how long? Suddenly employment that we'd dreaded and hated for as long as we'd known it became not only lucrative but eminently desirable, if only because it was made clear that some among us would soon be denied it.

Briseño

We used words like gravy train and cash cow and honey hole to talk about the show. We talked some of us loudly and others in hushed whispers while the buses slipped down Highway 22.

The greatest shopping season Logan county had ever known began the very next day. It was the twenty-third of December and scant snow left over from weeks past clung to the shade of the ridge. We marched out into the cold.

We descended upon the Walmart and bought practically everything inside it. Ours was one of the first Walmarts ever built, the smallest still in operation. Tiles set in the floor commemorated employees with twenty-five or more years of service. Its aisles were relatively narrow, its stockpiles less than other establishments, which was likely the start of the problem. But really it came down to this. When there were only so many of a thing, and this thing was something you had not been able to think of owning for so long it made your jaw suck in, you found yourself feeling entitled to that particular thing, and should someone else express interest in the same thing, you took that interest as a personal insult. There were no real fistfights to speak of, but certainly shoves were exchanged, particularly at the hunting counter, where the short supply of firearms was causing no small amount of flaring tempers. Mothers fought with mothers, and fathers with fathers. Children banded together and attacked each other and single adults.

It didn't seem like a riot at the time, but the store afterward told a different story. There was little left on the shelves and the racks, almost everything deemed a special present for someone else.

Down and Out

Martin drove down to Little Rock, four hours either way. Five hundred dollars is just enough to make an eight-year-old's dreams come exactly true and that's just what he did. Two handmade dolls with honest human hair and authentic-looking birth certificates. American Girls. He had hoped to get them a Latin version, something to remind them and him of their mother, but he was told that particular model had been discontinued. When Christmas morning fell his daughters among many had a Christmas they would never forget. And the reason they never forgot it is that six days later, per a stipulation in their new contract, they packed that Christmas up in specially marked *Down 'N' Out* Boxes and put it in the specifically designated storage center next to the Durkee coin laundry, north of downtown.

It was largely agreed that those were the best twenty-six hours of Christmas any of us had ever had. By now we had learned the hard way about happiness, that it is a fruit in season rarely in the wild world, and that when it comes you should eat what you can. What does that mean? It meant that when Jason forgot the batteries that were never ever included, Junior only looked at his Mighty Morphin Zord with more admiration and said dead-eyed to his father, "I can make better noises anyway," and proceeded to do just that.

That year we had that rarest and most un-purchasable of gifts. Perspective. It was the best Christmas ever and everyone knew it. Nostalgia is a powerful thing in the present tense.

Ours had been a row too tough to hoe, and each of us in turn had broken. Fell apart. In spite of ourselves and with high definition testimony to prove it. And yes, even later that day when Jamie Mallett knocked on every door in town with an airplane bottle of the nicest scotch he could find for every household in town, we knew we had plenty to be happy for.

Due to some insensitive miracle, Jamie had received two portions of Christmas, a full thousand dollars, half in an envelope with his name, the other half in another tucked inside that one which said "Tillie." His mother had been gone at that point for sixteen days.

How much of what happened was premeditated was a topic of debate for some time, but it was certainly the case that Jamie drove to the liquor store before he went to the church and dropped one of envelopes into the offertory box in the church vestibule. It was also clear that he drove himself home and called the first taxi anyone could remember seeing in town. What was less clear is where and how he procured the Santa suit. When the taxi finally arrived from Fort Smith, Jamie had squeezed himself into the red velvet and had a trash bag full of the finest individual portions of liquor somebody else's money could buy. The cab driver's lips worked around words he never found as Jamie climbed in and said, "Take me everywhere."

Jamie proceeded to drop by every occupied residence in the town of Paris, Arkansas, and bequeath to every man, woman, and permitted child 187 milliliters of fine Christmas cheer. By the time he reached his own home on the deep east side of town, every part of the Santa suit had settled in a different direction. His cheeks were unnaturally red in a way only the youngest children wouldn't recognize as wrong. Yet with his hair gone to salt at the temples and sixteen days beard, he looked more than a little like a drunk St. Nick. Lyle and Cathy and Jason and Tammy and everybody else should have pulled him in and said that it was late, that he could sleep it off on the couch and make good in the morning. But they didn't—none of us did—and maybe it was the cab and maybe it was all that solid nasty hurt hanging off his back that made that other lighter burden more reasonable. Who could say Jamie couldn't have a Christmas?

It didn't take much to know that it was this or not much, and so all of us pulled off the stapled bow and drank a pull with Jamie and swallowed down hard like it was bitter and salty, which it wasn't. Who could say that Jamie's Christmas was less honest, less important than the rest of ours? And didn't he have a point that there wasn't a point in it, wasn't a reason to watch it right now because after all it wasn't like there would be a damn drop to drink come day after tomorrow. We felt like reminding him that maybe he wouldn't be picked, that maybe his part in this was over and that maybe there was a thing worth hoping for. But he didn't seem to be without hope, just hoping for all the wrong things.

But as Jamie reported to everyone that night, he knew, he just knew. Not because he'd been told, but just because he knew, the way everyone says that after something they couldn't have known about occurs. He said he didn't need to see inside the envelope that was to be left on his porch the next morning. He wouldn't even look at it.

But the rest of us did. And that morning was one of the quietest we'd had since the furnace burnt out. Not that anyone noticed but the cameras, who drove around town filming establishing shots and an extended sequence of Horsey the Mule chasing his tail in the snow, which they used as background when they ran the credits.

Briseño

That day we weren't so much a town but one hundred seventeen households united only by this common task. Our lottery was a private thing, the sort of news one might need space to cry over or fight about.

Dear Down 'N' Outers,

*Congratulations! Y'ALL have been selected as a featured family for Season Two. Season One is scheduled to start airing in the fall and all signs point to a big success—*Down 'N' Out *might be the next *SURVIVOR*!*

For the most part, this means things will continue as normal. We'll be back tomorrow to start filming again, and like always all we want is for you to do what you normally do. Every success that we have achieved starts with you, with Paris, with the honest American struggles that you've shared with us and that we have tried to faithfully convey to our waiting audience.

Also starting tomorrow we're enacting our new bonus program. In addition to your established compensation, you may also be eligible to up to an extra $250,000 just for taking on certain individualized tasks that will help us show the world a new and continuously fascinating side of the community. Of course, to maintain authenticity, all bonus payments will be delayed until the end of taping, and any mention of the bonus system, explicit or implied, is strictly forbidden on camera. But remember that no matter what— it's y'all that are the cornerstone of our success, y'all who we want to see. Just be yourselves, like we know you know how.

Here's to the future,
Your Production Team

Down and Out

Dear Down 'N' Outers,

First we want to say thank you. Without the hard work and sacrifice of every former Doyles' employee, this show could never be the success we believe it will become. Below, you'll find your family's check. The Paris bank has asked us to ask you not to cash it directly—there might not be enough money to go around!

This means that your time as a featured family has come to close. We will no longer be filming directly from your home.

But that doesn't mean that your chance to help us make television history is over. This began as one of the most ambitious reality shows ever created, and to continue with those lofty goals, we need help from everyone. It's about realism and continuity. If our viewers see things that don't add up it cheapens their viewing experience. So if half the town is still struggling to buy groceries and the other half has clearly received a significant financial windfall, then it could cause confusion to our viewers. So to help keep things feeling authentic, here are a few guidelines.

New purchases of size (cars, boats, livestock, farm machinery, etc.) may not be displayed or used in such a way that they might appear on camera. If you do decide to purchase large items, they must not be visible from the street at any time.

You are now more than welcome to seek employment. However, you may not, without special permission (see attached application), seek employment in a business within the Paris city limits or a surrounding thirty-mile radius.

You may now go about your lives as you normally would and of course that will naturally involve interacting *with the* Down 'N' Out *Feature Families. But because these families are so heavily involved in helping us make great television, at times we may limit access to these individuals and the parts of the city that they are currently using.*

Again we want to thank you for sharing your lives with us and with America. Since your time on the show has now come to a close, it's only natural to miss the spotlight. But please refrain from trying to place yourself on camera. If you appear in too many shots, we'll ask you to change your patterns to not distract our audience.

Naturally, many of you will consider moving away, and others will find themselves in new and interesting situations and we wanted to let you know that we'd love to hear from you! In fact, every episode in Season Two will feature a Spotlight on Success ninety-second feature (see attached application). Even as we move along, remember that this is and will always be your story that we are all telling.

Good luck,
The Down 'N' Out *Team*

And so the stage was reset, the opening credits re-shot, catching Paris roiled in filthy January slush, and this time they added still shots of those soon-to-be famous faces of the stars of the show. Martin and the girls. Obviously. The Jason Johnsons—his wife, Tammy, and the three boys. Again it made sense. Lyle and Cathy. Really none of them surprised us. These were the pretty ones and that's what mattered in the end, wasn't it. Or else they were, if we were to say it where it wouldn't be repeated, the trashiest. Wasn't Tammy Johnson always showing a little more than kindness to everybody who would look, or at least that was the whisper at the beauty parlor. Or maybe they picked them because they were the ones most willing to be the clowns they wanted. Surely that had to be why they picked Martin. Hell, that goddamn mule was the real star of the show.

But in either case, those were the choices that made sense to us and to the ones they picked. They all expected it and nodded to each with a tight-lipped acceptance normally seen outside of hospital waiting rooms. They understood the producers' choices just like we did. And we wished them the best.

The other two selections, both single men, caused a more varied response.

Jamie, for instance. We could already see him in the opening credits, standing on his mother's porch glaring at the camera with the last of his Christmas whiskey in his hand, label conspicuously faced forward. Jamie was notoriously hard to film and we didn't expect he'd been in the first season hardly at all. And yet now he was going to make a life of this, living on god knows how much money he'd make. It didn't seem right—we'd all tried harder.

And if Jamie was hard to understand, then the last choice was downright mystifying. We instinctively felt like Steve Womack needed our protection, that the show was playing a cruel joke. Steve, who was as decent a man as you could find but who couldn't talk about things that weren't fishing or pressing gears.

We gathered on our porches, those among us who could now assemble as we saw fit, and so we ended up in clumps of eight and ten confirming our own results and calling around to figure out who wasn't answering the phone.

Briseño

They filmed us this way, gathered in half dozens breathing fog and keeping our hands in pockets. They used it as the opening for the first episode of Season Two: "Home Burial." As they showed it, a banjo played a requiem and the announcer said, "The people of Paris, Arkansas, are gathering to grieve the passing of one of their elders."

With the word *Earlier* and a collection of ellipses, they cut to footage of the night Mrs. Mallett died. They showed more of it than we thought had been filmed, used some older footage to fill it out. It is a tough thing for us to watch.

They followed Jamie as he went and saw the cemetery caretaker, caught the fight they'd had when Jamie had insisted on digging the hole himself as he couldn't afford to have it dug. But they didn't show the end where Mr. Crawford said they'll take care of it no charge, because it was the right thing to do. Instead they cut right after Jamie said, "Dammit, I can't pay to have you dig it, and by God if you don't let me bury her here I'll take her home and do it my damn self."

The next shot was Jamie and Lyle digging a hole behind Jamie's' house. It was a meaningless hole, one they filled as soon as they were done digging it. It was the first thing on both of their bonus lists—ten thousand to dig a large hole in Jamie's yard. They added a talking head of Lyle saying friendship means being there, no matter what.

And they showed the funeral and Fr. William praying over the grave, except all the workers are gone, covered up in the same gray snow that surrounded them. If you paused it, you could tell from the pixels where they edited out the other gravestones and left behind only the ridge that's behind everything in town. It really did look like he was burying her right in his own yard.

Down and Out

They showed Jamie planting the wooden cross they'd provided him in the fresh earth he and Lyle had just turned over and closed with Jamie crying into a solo cup and shaking his head and then a picture of Mrs. Mallett and a note indicating that Season Two is to be dedicated to her memory.

When tourists come and ask for Mrs. Mallett's Grave, which you wouldn't think they would be so ugly as just to come out and do, but they do, they never believe us. And they often go poking back behind where Jamie's place was no matter how big of a No Trespassing sign there is. They all wonder, out loud, if perhaps the marker had blown away.

Season 2, Episode 2:
Down 'N' Out at the Pawnshop

Dear everyone,
As you may have noticed a new business has come to town. The Paris Pawn 'N' Loan is pleased to be joining the greater Paris community.

It came up like a weed, or maybe it descended like a swarm, fell altogether like hail over rain. Like it was sped up, a goddamn camera trick. We all talked about it different, and there was some disagreement as to just what specifically had happened. But this much was certain. On January 9 there was a parking lot where the old laundromat had burned down but no building to speak of, just an empty field where sometimes the high school kids would stand and smoke. On January 11 there was a pawnshop.

And that alone we were fine with. We wouldn't have minded the construction work that went exclusively to out-of-towners, as we understood that maybe it took a special set of skills to do work that slipshod. That they built it like an Amish barn we could understand. Time is money and all. But what we couldn't understand, what had us having our children ask the Johnson boys and the Gossett girls what those on the inside knew, was that it all seemed to make so much sense. Two days old, and you'd bet anything the place had been there since you were in high school. The bricks looked storm washed and sun baked. That Paris Pawn 'N' Loan sign had all the lowercase Ns burnt out so it said Paw 'N' Loa after dark. Maybe all pawnshops open this way, but it seemed strange that a new place would open without unoccupied space on its shelves. And those shelves, along with the walls they were screwed into, and the tin roof those walls held up, all looked like they'd been here since Tillie Mallett was running a drill press. It was like someone'd color-matched the gutter rust to the barn roof you could see just behind the place. And of course someone had.

It took a team of set designers months of work to create a new old part of the city. Concept design began shortly after production on Season One. The producers made it a primary priority to investigate how to get around the problem of the standard rate of expansion.

If a thing is good there must be more of it. You and us all would like to pretend that this is a thing we don't believe, but maybe it's deeper than thinking or maybe it's just tradition. Season Two has to mean new characters, new locations, new scenarios. The house is in another city this time or this time the eligible gentleman is pretending he isn't rich. More is the law of America. New ice road truckers and one more generation on the fishing boat. And of course here that was a problem.

Being clever never goes unrewarded, and having already optioned the entire population of the factory and anyone else in town who seemed even remotely interesting there were simply no maneuvers to instigate this natural course of things, or at least none presented themselves in several rounds of brainstorming. Besides, conducting cast calls would lead to unwarranted internal social pressure— the producers were concerned that this would lead people to act interesting intentionally, which was for the most part undesirable. So instead they brought in a tested concept that made thematic sense and that also provided much needed merchandising opportunities.

There were three teams of antique archaeologists who were responsible for acquiring the necessary fixtures and decorations, along with six visual artists and a surface preservationist, not to mention an untold crew of production assistants provided through an internship program affiliated with the nearest art institution.

And anyone would have to admit, they did a flawless job. Without photographic proof to the contrary, it was impossible to say the lot between the town center and the old vacuum emporium that would someday become a video rental store hadn't always been the Paris pawnshop.

When the announcer came on at the beginning of episode two and said that "The Paris Pawn 'N' Loan and its owner Bobby LaDue have been helping out folks around here for years now," who were we to argue? We found ourselves waving our two fingers at LaDue as we drove by even before we'd been told how we knew him.

Maybe it was the faded Paris Eagles hat he wore (found in a barn behind the Schriver property) or the truck he drove (sourced locally, one your cousin had bought and sold some years ago). Maybe it was the way he stood like us, the way he made eye contact with our noses, or maybe it was how he sounded like another boy from the valley. Some of us were never sure he wasn't from around here, kept saying wasn't there a LaDue from over by Scranton and maybe wasn't he kin to them.

What we're getting at is that it was a good job they had done, that brand new or not the place was as much a part of Paris as anything. It maybe bothered us that it didn't bother us, but that was why we all went down there so often. Of course it helped, the rest of that note they sent out.

Please join us in welcoming the newest citizen of Paris, Arkansas—Bobby LaDue. Bobby brought with him his own family tradition—the pawn and loan business.

To help welcome Bobby and to get the shop off to a good start, we're giving a special bonus to anyone in town during this season of filming. Anyone who sells an item to the Paris Pawn 'N' Loan will receive double the price they agree to— what a deal!

Happy bargaining!

The Down 'N' Out *Team*

And the thing was, you knew it was a pawnshop. You could sell it and then buy it back on credit, walk out with 80 percent of 20 percent of what you'd agreed it might be worth. Or maybe we just wanted something to show for it. Maybe when everyone else was turning in whatever gold and jewelry they managed to keep through the unquestionably hard times of the first season, then maybe you too thought you and yours deserved something nice even if you didn't want to leave the town your grandparents had founded. What did we know then?

And yes, it should be noted, we did know what we were getting into, and yes, we did it anyways, and why not? Why not take your mother's china set, the one her grandmother had received on her wedding day back so long ago, pack it up carefully in used Walmart circulars, and cart it down to some stranger who looked for all the world like a cousin you didn't remember having, and have him tell in you front of God and everybody that these plates wasn't worth the clay they's fired from?

That was the first thing you noticed about Bobby, the way he talked—or maybe it was only the first thing we noticed. More likely you didn't pick it up, concluding that all of us rednecks sound the same, and of course you'd be right in that we were too poor to afford a hat at the moment and that, yes, we know we talk funny. But we knew that and that was what was off about Bobby. We all knew how we must sound and we knew to watch it so you won't catch us on camera saying acoustical, can't never, ain't got, doggone. Unless they asked us to, we made a point to say that we were tired and not, as Bobby mentioned in the opening of the episode, that it felt like a wolf done et me and expletive-deleted me off a cliff.

Episode Two opened on the trailer they'd drug from God knows where and set at a right angle to goddamn nothing. Bobby came out in boxers and a white shirt holding a quart of Miller High Life and announcing proudly to the camera, "Yee-haw. Time to get up! It's another beautiful day in Paris, Arkansas, and somebody's got to make some money." And then that's what he went and did. Needless to say we were doing our part to make sure that Paris's newest business venture was a success, but we were only the tip of the knife. From a hundred miles round and more folks came just so Bobby could beat them down and offer an amount lower than the reservoir and then watch him point at the sign above his head, the one we never read clearly that said, "Incomplete transactions will not be part of the show." To come all that way, to wear all of your mother's jewelry that you weren't trying to hock, well, it was defeatist. And the river valley is not full of quitters. This led many to attempt to pawn things they reckoned not to lack, which made for great material to show while the credits rolled—somebody in the real tree hat they'd given him at the door trying to pawn a bottle of whiskey in the shape of Elvis Presley, insisting adamantly that a premium was due on account of the thing ain't but half empty.

Through the course of the rest of filming, the pawnshop continued to do brisk business. The partially imaginary business was turning an entirely real profit, so much in fact that the producers felt it only made sense to consider adding pawnshop elements to several of their other properties.

Yes, pawning was a regular part of almost every episode, even after the feature at the beginning. You can probably guess what happened next, what with Cathy and Lyle and the wedding rings and all. It was their first truly nasty fight in some ten years. It started with the overdue pink envelope tucked in the screen door. Though the shots were never used, the crew had the feature family in the habit of gathering together to read the missives and to act like they hoped to find good news inside.

Cathy and Lyle!

Last season your anniversary was a huge success and one we hope to repeat this year. Unfortunately, filming won't continue through the fall, and besides, people like a change. So this time it's Cathy's birthday! And you cannot wait to go camping in the Ozark mountains (see included map)! For this adventure, you'll need $200 (see included shopping list). Of course for the sake of authenticity this must be money that makes sense, so don't use EITHER of your savings accounts.

Briseño

For a $5,000 bonus, pawn both of them.
But first turn to the camera and explain why going on this trip is so important to you.

Cathy had always been a quick read. She was already finished and on her way down the hall before Lyle got to that EITHER and had processed what it might mean, those ambiguously obvious capital letters. By the time he went looking for Cathy she was staring up at the closet shelf. She looked beautiful that way with the tilt in her neck making her face look younger than it might have and her soft brown hair left to grow like a Pentecostal child's, spilling down her back like a cataract. He joined her, put his arms around her, held her tenderly, one hand on her hip, the other on her shoulder, leaned into her ear, and whispered, "You've done us a good one here, you know that, right?"

They both stared up at the boxes right where they'd both left them. Nothing was changed. If anything it looked too much like just how they'd left it. "But how?" whispered Cathy.

What he wanted to say was that it was eerie. That only now did it occur to him that strangers wandered his house while he slept. Only now did so many other coincidental happenings take on the proper ominous shading. He meant to tell all that to Cathy.

"Well, I figure your boyfriend told them," said Lyle, and the two of them looked deeply at each other and each could see the pain in the other, that deep hurt, all caused by things well beyond their control now backing up, clogging till it concentrated, blackened, became that look that couples normally never share. Lyle might have said, *Don't deny it*, and Cathy might have told him to go right straight to hell, but that didn't make the show. All they needed was that stare and the fifteen years of cashed-in *It's okay*s and *I'm not mad*s that went behind it. They needed that stare, but not the fight that came after it, and that's what they used. Of course Lyle and Cathy didn't know that then and didn't want all of their dirtiest secrets so unsecret, so they conducted their fight in whispers too quiet for the camera even to pick up.

While Lyle was asking in dear earnest just how stupid his wife thought he was, if she really thought a lie that big could ever stay hidden for long and she whispered back that overreacting was just the start of it and that she thought he was plenty damn stupid if he thought she would ever cheat on him. Which was not to say that the cameraman hadn't been trying. Every chance he could find to be alone with her, where alone meant a good excuse to put the camera down, he moved towards her, pulled by she didn't know what, some inexplicable shit-head gravity right into her personal space. He almost never said anything, just pushed against the air she thought hers, breathing it up through his tattooed neck. And because he was always there, and so often too close, in spite of herself she thought about it, and because she'd thought about it and not wanted to, she thought of it all the time. And when you think of something so long, no matter how hideous, you think of liking it, and it also meant that look of guilt had a grain of truth behind it, and it was that he saw, the non-filter over honest subconscious admission.

It can be dangerous to know everything about a person. It wasn't even a twitch, but Lyle saw it and knowing what it was, assumed what it meant and so he leveled a stare at Cathy that she'd never seen and whispered, "You and that money," which of course wasn't what he was mad about at all.

She quivered in shame, knowing what it meant that he couldn't even say the thing on his mind, only think the most of it. They said more, sure, but it was those first few shared glances and whispered accusations that psychologists claimed they could use to map the conversation, decode the squints and eyebrow raises and cheek muscle twitches. But you didn't need a degree or a facial tomography scanner to see what it was that was happening—two people very much in love torn apart by shit luck and random chance, a couple that could blame it on anything except who they were blaming it on—each other.

But of course they couldn't have Lyle and Cathy arguing about things the show didn't know, so instead they added a cut-in scene of Lyle turning up the stereo that they shot some weeks later on, and they spliced in a country music soundtrack. So the audience mostly heard some cowboy bemoaning the loss of his truck and then read a dialogue in subtitles that explained that Lyle wanted very much to keep their tradition of camping for his wife's birthday, that broke or not broke some things still had to happen. They even added a goddamnit at the end, bleeping out the words money jar and even blurring his lips, so as to make it safe for consumption by the hearing impaired.

At the end of the fight without benefit of subtitles or soundtrack, Lyle stormed outside so no one could see him cry, though of course camera two was prepared for this and got an awesome close-up just as he stormed by on his way to the woodpile. The wood was split and chopped and stacked and the cold had broke besides, but Lyle re-split it and re-stacked it until it was damn near dark. Work had

the same opposite of healing effect it always did. Inside
Cathy was flitting around pretending she was looking for
something to do and she kept pacing until her heels started
to burn.

The show skipped all that and picked up at the
inevitable truck ride downtown. They showed a full fifteen
seconds of the couple sitting flat mouthed and silent as Lyle
drove, which was largely accurate. And then there was the
pawnshop. They sat in the cab for what seemed a long time,
even on television. Lyle sucked his finger into his mouth
and bit down, trapping the wedding ring behind his teeth
and then pulling his hand free. Off his finger it looked
fragile, a tiny hoop no wider than a two-penny nail. In the
ring's wake, a thin white brand, a tiny reverse scar of pink-
white skin on his callous-brown hand. Into the shot comes
Cathy's hand, not as tanned but just as marked, her
wedding bands and engagement rings pinched between
her first and second fingers. All three rings fit between the
heart and the head lines in his palm, and then his fingers
closed around them and the two kissed. They said they
were sorry. They swore everything would be okay.

And then the rings were under a jeweler's loop and
Bobby was saying, "These have quite a bit of wear to them.
I know y'all need the money and all, but the best I could do
for the pair is a hundred and a half." The show cut out the
part where Lyle said, "Goddamnit, you know as well as I do
that I have to get two hundred to go on this damn fool
camping trip in the middle of February, you miserable
carpet-bagging piece of trash. So..." They left in, "You'll just
have to do better, mister, you'll just have to," along with the
blank stare that both he and Cathy gave to the pawnbroker.
And though the script actually called for him to refuse to

raise his offer until Cathy cried or Lyle broke something, he flinched, and without an inkle of twang said, "Two hundred then," and walked to the cash register.

The next scene is the Mt. Nebo campgrounds. We see the sign for the state park, we see Lyle paying out for the spot, the pale stain where his ring should have been accentuated in post-production. We see the tent go up, the hot dogs hit the fire. They eat and wash the one fork and plate between them. They say nothing. This was no trick of the camera. Whether out of protest to the cold damp conditions, the absurd situation, or lingering pisstivity due to any of the things that had happened in the last few days— it was impossible to tell. But the silence hung like fog, like blackout curtains in a bomb raid, like candle smoke— invisible until the oxygen's gone and freezing is the least of your problems.

But the show spliced in a clip from the first season, one of the gems they'd caught in those rare moments where we really did forget about the cameras. Cathy said, "I love Lyle so much it hurts, sometimes it burns like, and just being with him makes me feel like the luckiest woman in history." Lyle said, "When you been together ten good years you don't have to say it all the time or go around acting like teenagers. We know and that's plenty. And that we don't have to say it, that's almost the best part."

And that's what it took. When they climbed into that tent and the lantern went out, with those thoughts in mind it made the scene sparse but romantic even in a way that was simple, and in the darkness that stood where the tent had been Lyle said, "Love isn't what keeps us going. Love is the keeping going." Roll credits.

Down and Out

As soon as the camera crew yelled clear, Lyle and Cathy relit the lantern and started breaking camp in the kerosene glow. The cameras were off, pointed down, but the crew still watched, the flicker of the lantern glinting off their eyes and lenses.

Back on Old Military Road everything felt wrong. Lyle checked the pilot light and the gas line but the heat was still humming predictably against the chill that had sprung up. Cathy opened every cabinet thinking a possum might have snuck in and started breathing up their air.

What it was was that the cameras were gone. And when they figured it out, they met in the living room, fell into each other's arms, and started crying, both of them, and stood there like that until it seemed they had to do something else and so they went to bed. They again didn't say anything. They fell into bed too tired to make love, too beat down not to cling to each other. And maybe their thoughts went back to the fight they'd whispered earlier, that if they talked now with the cameras gone they could really talk, get it out there. They both knew that was what they ought to do. It didn't make them do it.

Trent was sitting across the street. He had his camera running and pointed at Lyle and Cathy's silhouette in the window, but he wasn't paying attention to the footage he was filming. In fact, he wasn't scheduled to be shooting at all; the production schedule called for a night off for everybody. They had learned the hard way that reality stars need time to regenerate the emotions the cameras were here to harvest. We didn't know why it was that Trent had decided not to go to the bar in Clarksville with the rest of the crew, or why he didn't head back to the hotel like he'd said he would. We didn't know why he parked at the end of the long driveway, when being watched was a given by then. We didn't know why he watched and we didn't know why he stayed long into the night, long after the silhouettes and the light that cast them had blinked away, until the braying of Horsey the Mule told the roosters to start the morning's business.

Season 2, Episode 3:
The Fishmaster Goes on Tour

Season Two Trailer Script. In white letters, no sound, black background. Next season on *Down 'N' Out*—[Cast member] eating questionable food source. [Cast member] Voice Over: "We been keeping going for a while now—seems like nothing much comes our way—nothing much at all." In silent letters: The struggle continues. Country guitar fades in very slowly. Black and white footage of Jamie drunk in public. In white on black, The Pressure Rises. Guitar music builds, humming breaks in—a spiritual, something you've heard but can't place, but a fresh version. Footage of Jason-Tammy/Lyle-Cathy having marital dispute. Text: Some stumble. Footage of [Cast member] being arrested. Music rises. It's "Amazing Grace," the first bar repeated three times. One voice, the man who was humming. Two voices, a woman joining in. A choir. Text: A community comes together. Footage of the church on Easter Sunday from the balcony. Text: Miracles can happen. Footage of TBD. Jamie: "Hard times aren't what we suffer through, they're what we are." Close on Jamie's face. Was blind but now I see. This August.

When he'd gotten the yes letter, Steve Womack had immediately gone to Lyle and Cathy's for explanation and advice. But one of the show people was watching outside and waved him off and at the next house he could hear the fight before he even got out of his truck. At the third house he stopped at, he finally got some kind of plainspoken English regarding what his life had become, but not before the person who answered the door read his letter twice, compared it to theirs and said "You?" some number of times. We couldn't blame them—even if they should have known better—it was what we all were thinking.

You? was a fair thing to think if not a fair thing to say, and in fairness Steve didn't really notice. But everything else aside, what do you tell him? How do you explain what you can't explain? All we could say was you're rich and you're still on television.

And so he managed a smile when the cameras came back and knocked on his door and introduced him to his new favorite bowler.

The bowler was a tie-in. The Professional Bowling Association saw a lot they liked in our demographic. The bowler was far from a pretty man with a head the shape of a mason jar and hair like a pilot's helmet. But he looked damn American and damned hardworking, with a neck that looked like it jutted proudly from a blue collar. He smiled all the way back to his molars and explained to the camera that naturally he was a huge fan of the show. "I was watching at home and, well, the story just sort of spoke to me." Then the bowler told about how he worked at a factory until there wasn't a factory anymore, that he'd gone home with a pink slip and a thank you. And so, he said, when I saw Paris I knew I had to do something. Anyone who's been through what this town has been through, what I've been through, can't sit by and watch others suffer. Of course I can't help everyone but I can do something, and watching the show I couldn't help but notice someone who seemed to be—he squinted meaningfully at the cue card—a kindred spirit—you know, a story like mine. Cut to a brief montage of pictures of the bowler, who used to work at a factory and who took a chance on himself when he got laid off.

"Steve," said the bowler, "I know you have a dream. And today—we're going to make that dream come true." Steve looked down. He rubbed his head, too terrified to think about what might come next.

"You have a gift," said the bowler, "and it's time you shared it with the world." Steve still didn't know what to say—hadn't he been sharing enough? He hardly kept any of the fish at all. Of course he knew people needed to eat and he was happy to share. But what more could they want part of except himself? But before he had thought that much, the bowler went on.

"Steve," said the bowler, sponsored by Storm and Foot Joy, "you're going on the BASSmasters World Tour!" The bowler knew he sounded like a game show host when he said it. But why not? Here the bowler was, living a dream. Maybe not the dream, probably not his dream. Here he was getting paid to pretend to give a boat to some other poor son of a bitch who would also get to live a dream. *Why not be happy?* he told himself. Why not smile about it?

They showed Steve picking out and admiring the new boat, a wicked state of the art everything brought to you by Evinrude—the power you can rely on—a name you can trust—seventy-five years of boating excellence. They showed him meeting his sponsors at Spiderwire—purveyors of fine fishing line, Johnston tackle boxes—when you need the best, and of course Monster Energy Drinks and Walmart—always low prices, always a sponsor of the tour. There was even a montage of someone sewing the brightly colored patches of his new sponsors to the old fishing vest Steve had had for as long as anyone had known him.

We saw the boat. They stopped the river bridge for three hours both ways to hang a camera from the girders that could catch footage of the boat, but really that was unnecessary. We would have noticed it even if he never took the cover off. But of course, it didn't have a cover, as that would defeat the purpose. There was Steve's face, blown up to the size of a windshield, and in huge letters "Steve the Fishmaster Womack," and under that in letters a good deal smaller "Paris, Arkansas."

We knew not to begrudge another his fortune. But hell, we didn't even know if Steve could drive the thing.

Steve knew he could drive it—that was no problem. Like all the men and women and a good deal of the children in Paris, he could drive most things with a steering wheel. What he wasn't so sure about was how he was supposed to fish from it or for that matter stand up on the thing. It was the latest and greatest in bass hunting technology—which meant that its ultra-light carbon-fiber body slid across the water like butter in a hot skillet. He never quit casting from his knees.

And then there were the rules. Only so many fish, only certain kinds of fish, must be so long, must be so old. No trot lines, no trolling, no stink bait, no crickets, stay in the designated area, avoid interfering with other fishermen who were no longer fishermen but anglers.

That was just one of the new words Steve had to learn for this new life. DQ'd for instance meant disqualified, which is what Steve was the first tournament when he submitted a thirty-pound blue catfish he'd smelt lurking in a dammed-up lake north of Dallas. DFL meant dead fucking last, which was the finishing position he'd achieved in his second and third tournaments. These were terms he heard whispered behind him in line at the weigh in. Of course by the end of the season, Steve was consistently in the top twenty-five, and finished third in the last event of the year. But his sponsors chose not to extend his contract. Though his skill was unquestionable, he was determined to be a less-than-successful spokesperson. And further, BASS-masters leadership felt that there was a real danger that Steve would continue to improve and become a frequent winner on tour, and their fanbase didn't respond positively to that idea.

When he'd won third place, he'd been invited to drive his truck onstage and weigh his fish in the big plexiglass tank scale. The other anglers waited for their names to be called and then reached into their live wells and produced champion fish one at a time, and let the crowd ooh at them as their final weigh ins climbed ounce by ounce. When Steve's turn came, he dutifully walked up and waved, reached in his bag and pulled out a sixteen-pound large-mouth bass—easily a lake record and maybe even the state. The fish glistened under the lights, majestic and perfect. It'd taken Steve two hours to coax the thing into his boat. A cheer started to grow as the crowd whispered about the near-mythical beast in front of them.

But before it could gather steam Steve threw the fish into the tank and walked back to his seat. The crowd ended up golf-clapping as the announcer read his name. For Steve's part it was simple, he hadn't won, and so it shouldn't have mattered. Five four-pound bass beat his one any day and he knew it. Later when the fishing media did their level best to swarm him and ask him where he'd found that monster fish, he'd shrugged and said in the water and walked away as soon as they made space for him. Or maybe that's just the joke we told each other, which seemed funnier at the time.

Long story short, Steve came home to the trailer behind his mother's house, dragging the boat behind him. He took four cans of black spray paint to his own face, and once the boat was painted solid black, never touched it again.

But Steve came home to a town that knew him all too well—for here was our ambassador, the one who had gone out and spoke on our behalf—the face of Paris, Arkansas, our miracle.

We stayed inside and watched as they filmed him driving slowly back into the only place he'd ever known, back to us, the only family Steve'd had to speak of since his momma had passed away. We ought to have lined the streets to welcome home our fishmaster, our longtime friend and former provider.

But while he was on tour, the lone television ad that Steve shot ran during daytime and prime time on all four networks. In the ad, Steve didn't mention his affiliation with BASSmasters, *Down 'N' Out*, or even his last name. He looked somewhere left of camera and said, "I'm Steve from Paris, Paris, Arkansas, and I use Paulson lures." Then Steve cast, got a bite, and hauled in an old tire, the announcer proclaiming, "Even Steve knows that Paulson lures are built to last, made to mimic wildlife as accurately as possible, and in the hand of the right fisherman, they can catch almost anything." Steve turned away from the campfire where he was cooking his catch, wearing a bib with a picture of a fish and holding up a knife and a fork— because he's going to eat the tire, get it?—and said, "All you gotta to do is reel 'em in." The screen closed to a tiny circle around Steve's head—he was almost smiling like he did when you make him take a picture.

That was our first taste—the first time any of us had seen any of us on television, long before the show itself started airing. It felt like picking a scab three days too soon. This is what we were—what would be made of us, anyways. We ought to've known, to've seen it coming. And truthfully we did, knew from the beginning it's what was meant by local flavor.

But there is a difference in the seeing and the knowing and it's not always the one you think that gets at you. There Steve was, speaking for us. So maybe we didn't speak much to him after. Because maybe when we saw Steve we saw the way they see us up here in the valley off the mountains, in the place where nothing and nobody comes from. From the dark tooth Doc Spratley had begged to let him pull, to the stained plaid shirt, to the complete and utter complicity in our own intentional ruination—that was us, and seeing it in Steve should have made it easier on us, or done nothing at all, or led to a general feeling of misgiving not directed at any one place, but none of that, none of it happened. Instead we blamed Steve without blaming him. He was making us look bad—did he have to be such a goddamn redneck about it?

We measured us against Steve—and measuring means finding lack in each of us and lack never was hard to find.

And, yes, we knew. We knew the whole time from the start. That this is what they wanted—why they'd shown us him again and again and what they wanted us to say when they asked us how we thought about the ads, about Steve, about his so-called professional fishing career, they being the ones so-calling it. We knew what we were supposed to say, what they were leading us to—the base response of dark-hearted envy and selfish difference-making—and we obliged, all of us in our way. Maybe we were tired and maybe a lifetime of holding tongue about Steve has a weight to it. But really it was that we liked it, that it felt like taking off too-tight shoes. Mr. Director, you can roll the cameras now, the girl is crying. We the people have finally stopped being polite and started being something else. They were right. After a while the cameras don't even matter. They weren't even watching except from the corners when we went to their pawnshop or their family's houses. Yet there we were.

Season 2, Episode 4:
Martin's Résumé

The Outpost was fifteen miles outside of Paris at the crossing of a road that led nowhere and the bridge over the river. Whether the filling station was named after the town or the other way around, what kept both afloat was precisely how far from anything they were. For rural folks in a fifteen-mile radius, the Outpost was the closest place at which money could regularly be spent, always just a little closer than town was far away. As a result, the Outpost sold the wrong kind of almost everything, just enough cold meat and preserved baked goods to cobble together a meal. The Outpost was the property of Davidinia Montgomery, only daughter of David Montgomery, founder of the gas stations and the town's only recorded mayor. Miss Montgomery had inherited her father's business acumen and distrust of generally everyone, and since no one had the sense to need things after reasonable hours or during mass on Sundays, the Outpost had never had an employee in its thirty-nine-year history.

We expected, of course, that like everything else that changed around here, this was futile or sinister or both. But the Outpost was offering the sort of chance we knew wasn't coming around again all that often. It was just outside the radius set by the show as the limits of the authenticity zone, so we could work there, spend whatever money we wanted there, and generally act like whatever we were when we weren't just acting like ourselves. Further, the Outpost was paying eight dollars an hour, less than we had made at the factory and certainly with fewer hours—but more than we could have made at Walmart if we could have even got that job. Eight an hour could keep the lights on and your children fed. And this could be more than stopgap, more than getting by till taping stopped—you could make that work. And never mind those future issues you can see so clearly without even trying to—Old Lady Montgomery needing more and more help—you investing your show money in the store, buying in as a partner. Owning your own business, owning your own labor. Husbands didn't even have to tell wives. Everyone put on their Sunday jeans and drove out to where 22 meets 197.

There was a line out and around the door and cars lined up a quarter mile up the highway, and passersby looked toward the fields for a revival tent. County fair was closer. There was one job and three hundred unemployed Parisites. The odds stood stacked against us in an oddly familiar way. But still there was that tiny sliver of hope. Somebody was getting hired anyways. Someone was getting back on track. It might even be you. And besides, nowhere in the growing train of vehicles stretched down Route 22 was there a single white van, nowhere a camera and boom.

Always the crafty businesswoman, Mrs. Montgomery put up a sign announcing that purchase was required to either pick up or drop off an application. Most of us grabbed a coke or a candy bar the first time through, but as the line grew and started to relax and curl into itself, we spent a little more freely. Why not buy a loaf of bread and a pack of bologna and a block of cheese and make a few sandwiches? Why not pick up the self-contained charcoal picnic grill and some hot dogs? Why not fill up the ice chest in the back of your truck with thirty cold beers and a bottle of that candy-flavored wine you used to like so much in high school? By the close of business, the Outpost was depleted in a way Mrs. Montgomery had seen before only once, after a tornado had struck not far off some years ago and everything potable or portable had been carted off by or for those in need. What had been three notebooks of letters of application was now a stack of loose papers four inches thick held down with a roll of pennies.

Outside, even with our applications turned in, we lingered, let the feeling of the day's sun shine on us, passing around the mosquito repellent, eating what we'd bought and sharing it around. It was like a spring thaw, like a return to something we wanted so bad to believe we used to have.

Old Mrs. Montgomery looked out at the whole town crowded along the shoulder of the highway, and shrugged. She wondered what she'd gotten herself into, and then took down the now hiring sign, turned it over, and wrote, "No longer accepting applications." And outside we cheered.

We had been there all day, which meant that one of us had gotten the job. We'd filled out every application there was, and while we knew better than to count our blessings before they hatched, each of us looked around at the others in the applicant pool and found two that looked wanting. It was a hop skip and a jump to *Why not me?*

And then Martin drove up, which is to say Martin and a van of cameramen trundled slowly around the bend and into the parking lot. He walked past our picnic grounds with a sheet of not white paper in his hands, his hair combed neatly, wearing the suit he used to wear when he was trying to sell something, the one he'd had on when the producers had first come here, when he'd sold Paris. Martin walked through us to the Outpost, where he went inside, smiled at Mrs. Montgomery and added his piece of paper to the stack of applications and walked out, back to his vehicle. We all watched saying nothing, angering irrationally that he hadn't been asked to buy anything. Then we heard a production assistant explain over a bullhorn that they'd been held up unexpectedly, but that they wanted a shot of us in line to turn in our applications and that they would pay twenty dollars to anyone who participated. We didn't protest or share knowing glances or whispered I-knew-its. We only lined up and another PA distributed applications back to us. We each ended up with someone else's form, and most of us couldn't help but notice how similar they all were. Education—Paris High School. Experience—Welder, Stamper, Office Clerk, Doyles' Gear, sometime long ago to very recently. They filmed us waiting in line and started the episode that way with the announcer explaining, "Job opportunities don't come around too often and when they do, there tend to be a fair number of applicants." The shots did not show the picnic at all.

The announcer continued with, "That's why one Paris resident has a plan up his sleeve," and there's Martin in the mirror, brushing his teeth and eyeballing himself. He looked less than pleased.

There was a hot purple envelope on his porch that morning. It offered free childcare and a $5,000 bonus if Martin could secure employment at the Outpost. So Martin washed up, cooked lunch for his daughters, tended their mule, washed up again, and headed outside of town. It was three weeks into the second taping by then and Martin had been waiting for thunder having seen the lightning. He'd spent every day with the girls like he was on his way to prison, sticking with them to the point they began to chafe at his constant attention and started to ask what was wrong and when that yielded no change, where their mother was.

When the envelope came, the thought he was trying to have was, *This isn't so bad.* But it wouldn't come. Something else entirely started to build within him as he loaded the good paper into the printer and adjusted the dates on his resume, switched duties from present to past tense. They filmed him doing so and had him explain that he figured that he would probably be the only one to apply with a résumé. We assumed that the résumé was the show's idea, but it wasn't. That was Martin—even without meaning to he was thinking two steps ahead of us, one ahead of himself.

When we saw him walking up to the door with that piece of paper in his hand we knew what it was. And if we'd gotten a look at it, we would have seen what amounted to another identical application—yes, he had one more listing in the education department, but he still had just one line filled under work experience.

And maybe that's why we kept looking at the spot where the door swung shut long after Martin had gone inside and came back out. The difference was a question of paper and ink, presentation and not merit. That's what set him apart. And it didn't seem right. Which isn't to say that it was anything other than what we expected. Martin was no better than any of us, he'd told us so himself at more safety meetings than we could remember. But we would have picked him over us too.

So no, we weren't surprised that Martin was the one

who got the job. More surprising if we'd noticed was the way our daily movements began to accommodate going out that way. Though it was on the way to precisely nowhere and had nothing you could be said to want, we surprised ourselves by driving out to the Outpost time and again. Part of it was that the store had the distinction of being the closest place that sold beer and wasn't on camera. And of course as you bought the beer, you ought to at least say hello to Martin, might ask him how much several bottles of wine were and then buy not much at all, in fact might more than casually mention that you thought the bathrooms could use some attention. Maybe you kept thinking of one thing or another to drop back by for, or maybe you bought your beers one at a time in tall, fat cans and drank them in the parking lot just so the cashier formerly known as Mr. Gossett would say, "Thank you, sir. Come again," each and every time.

It is a hollow pleasure being on the receiving end of a professional smile or watching a just man get what a lot of others had coming to them. It's not that we were so vindictive that we wanted to hurt Martin, or anybody, really. We just got the hang quickly of not being quite at the bottom of the pile.

Martin, too, seemed to fall into this new role without much prompting. For him, it was a kind of penance. Every moment that he manned the semi-electronic cash register without a functioning 4 key, every one of the three times a day that Mrs. Montgomery did her level best to barge in on him trying to catch him stealing chewing tobacco and ice cream sandwiches, he saw his wife—ex-wife by her count, he was certain. He saw Marla's face.

The face, like the woman it belonged to, never said, "I

told you so." She never had to. Instead she would just smile at him in two-faced benevolence.

When we came in and asked him to look in the back for fresher milk, he saw her face in the door to the walk-in. When we pulled up to the gas pump clearly marked as self-service and honked until he came out and filled our tanks for us and then tipped him a quarter just to watch him jump to catch it, he saw her eyes in ours, nodding as he scurried. And even in his imagination she still wouldn't say it. She wouldn't tell him a second time what she'd already told him once. He had wanted to save this town. He'd made a choice to give this town all he could, and what he got for it was taking shit from people who had been happy to work for him for their whole goddamned lives.

And then how could Martin blame the town for blaming him? As if the money from the show was enough to compensate for two years of being homeless in the town you'd grown up in. As if this, his final solution, was anything but a long and in the end painful severance package with more strings than attachment. He had failed us, and he knew it as well as we did, as well as Marla must have.

We tried, after a while, not to take it out too hard on Martin. We took to smiling at him, and pumping our gas and not going quite so far out of our way to see him in his new post. They showed us keeping after it like dogs on pork chops, but all that was filmed in the first few weeks. By the third month of his employment, we even took to calling him boss again, even if now it sounded like a polite term for a stranger. We learned to accept it because it was what we knew how to do. All except Jamie.

It started that first week when Mrs. Montgomery still

sat on a cushioned stool in the corner watching Martin to make sure he wasn't miscounting change. Jamie walked in flushed pink from either whiskey or hard exercise, thick rings like brake fluid around his eyes, filthy everywhere. He ignored all the merchandise and walked up to Martin and said, "I heard you was working out here," and then waited for a response and got anxious when one didn't come.

"Why you gotta make this hard?" asked Jamie, swaying from side to side and they showed that, but not when Martin asked, "Make what hard?"

And Jamie answered, "My envelope said get drunk and fight you. So come on."

Martin looked at the register and said, "Call me College Boy."

Martin was, in that moment, trying to be decent. He had a good handle, or thought he did, on what it was the show wanted to see and figured that if he could just get it over with, if he could just feed Jamie the line and get him to move on, then it made both of their days a little easier. It worked about as well as any of Martin's other recent attempts to help. Jamie looked at him and something broke loose.

"You are a college boy, ain't you?" said Jamie, his lips curling back. "A college boy on a cash register," he said and laughed full and hard once and walked out shaking his head. They showed that part too. And they showed the next week when Jamie went back and shouted at Martin for the better part of half an hour. And the time a week later when he did about the same thing, but this time took his tire iron into the station with him, not doing anything with it, just carrying it around while he screamed at Martin about how proud his alma mater had to be. It kept up.

Down and Out

Most of us figured that it was the show, that they got good mileage out of Jamie's class rage and that they sent him up there every time they didn't have some other catastrophe to immortalize. But Gus Johnson from across the road said that there weren't any more pink envelopes on Jamie's porch for some time, that maybe he was doing what he was doing for some other reason.

So maybe it was the show, or maybe it was because of Jamie and not our conscience that we quit treating Martin like he worked at a gas station. Maybe it was easier to let Jamie say it, easier than saying it ourselves or admitting that it shouldn't be said. Maybe that's always easier. Maybe that's what went wrong.

Season 2, Episode 5:
Keeping On

It wasn't the space in Jamie's house that bothered him, or the meals he ate standing over the stove out of the pot he'd cooked them in. It was the sound. You wouldn't think that one tiny old woman could dampen so many echoes. Jamie hadn't realized it, but he'd never lived alone before.

Of course he wasn't alone now as they kept the camera on him just about constantly. But it was a still quiet. Intentionally so.

Since before he had found the pink envelope on selection day, he'd been wondering how the show was going to use him. Of course it was possible that they just needed him so they could show his mother's funeral, that they were really after Tillie and that Jamie was only collecting the checks. But if that were the case then the twenty-four-hour recording of his every thought and motion would be far less necessary. And then there was the booze.

It was left out every night like the news—a paper bag full of airplane bottles and a twelve pack of Busch light, which was not his brand but which did a purchase large number of advertisements during Seasons One and Two. He tried telling the cameraman that they were daily dropping off more booze than he'd drink in a month, but they wouldn't respond except to remind him that his contract required he not mention the show. If he left the shit out on the porch, willfully ignored it, they would stack up the next day's shipment right next to it. He thought

Down and Out

about trying to sell it or give it away, but figured that might be their angle, so instead he brought it inside and let it accumulate, twelve packs and paper sacks scattered across most every surface for a time.

He tried calling folks over, or having a party, but all the other current cast members had gotten a note offering them ten thousand dollars not to share a drink with Jamie, and the rest of us had at that point had enough of things that were supposed to be free. And if we were being honest, after the Christmas episode, it didn't sound like much fun. Of course we were all as nice as we could be about it, told him that we'd love to have him over once the filming came to an end, but that for now, partner, we'd have to pass.

So Jamie forcefully kept to himself and took to stacking up the booze in the room that used to be his mother's. He walked the neighborhood a few times, changed the oil in his truck even though it didn't need it, and tried to only drink the beers he would have drank anyways.

And then the note came. It said: If you get arrested at the Outpost we'll give you seventy-five thousand dollars and cover your legal expenses.

Now of course the first thought is always, *I would never do that*. The second thought is always, *That is a lot of money*. The kind of money, on top of all the rest, that would mean never thinking about money ever again. And in the end you have to have a lot of money to say no to a lot of money and Jamie like most of us only had some. And if it played out any other way, then maybe Jamie doesn't do it. If maybe there had been some way to answer no. But there wasn't. Jamie could only say yes.

So he sat down with a tiny bottle of liquor and set about to make a plan. Stealing was of course the obvious choice.

But Jamie was averse to the thought and besides, how many times would he have to do it before he got caught and then if he made it too obvious trying to get caught then of course the show wouldn't pay him and he'd go to jail for nothing. Worse yet, Mrs. Montgomery might try to pity him, thinking that if he had to steal it then he must need it or some such bullshit and Jamie wouldn't be pitied. He also considered simply bringing a firearm in with him, not to do anything with, just to have, but armed robbery was a little too serious of a crime and besides it was a poor waste of a good weapon.

And then, scanning his mind for any sort of good way to get arrested he lighted up the idea of just showing up drunk. Drunk and disorderly. It was a crime, he was certain, and one he was almost committing just standing there as it was. Besides, he had liquor stacked up in most of his corners, ammunition for a battle he hadn't known he'd be fighting. And then of course it occurred to him that this is what the show had in mind all along. Why else the daily shipment, what else could they want him to do with it? What other purpose might it serve?

So Jamie went out and tried to get arrested, which it turned out he wasn't much good at. The first time ought to really have taken care of things. He'd sat outside the gas station choking on cheap scotch and nodding friendly like to everyone that drove by. When he was sure he was drunk enough to qualify as a public nuisance he sauntered inside and went up to Martin and the counter and stopped. That was as far as his plan had taken him. Step one, drink. Step two, go inside. Step three, get arrested. It didn't seem like it should be difficult.

But there stood Martin with that doe-eyed expression

Down and Out

he'd taken on ever since his wife had grown some sense, and the two of them stood there waiting for what seemed like forever.

"Why you gotta make this hard?" asked Jamie.

"Make what hard?" said Martin.

"My envelope said..." He stopped there. In case Martin had gotten one too and was too busy pretending to get the damn show on the road. Jamie had looked it up and he needed a .10 to get taken to jail and if Martin didn't hurry up he'd have to have another drink, which really he wanted nothing to do with. When it was clear and probably it should have been already that Martin didn't know what he was supposed to do, Jamie turned around and eyed his camera crew. He knew they would make him start over if he said the plan out loud, or worse yet disqualify him for doing it the wrong way and then take him off to jail anyways. But one of them was giving him the keep going sign, so Jamie plowed forward. "Envelope said to come here and fight you." He figured that if anybody would call the law to settle his differences he'd found him. But no. Martin was too damn busy being righteous to do the right thing. Instead he hung his head and came up with, "Call me College Boy."

And it was probably the whiskey. It was probably the stress. But really it was how little time it had taken Martin to come up with his answer. He had it there on his tongue tip just waiting to be gracious enough to give someone a way to knock him down. What did that even mean?

Well—damn sure if he wanted to get called College Boy, well, Jamie reckoned he might oblige, which was more redneck than he liked talking, but when you get mad and drunk, it's less easy to be in charge of the words coming out of your mouth. And so that was the first time Jamie went into the Outpost, his pockets tinkling with empty single-serving scotches, trying hard to get arrested. But Martin just couldn't be made to cooperate. Jamie called him names for five straight minutes, and then he ran out of hateful things to say. The silence that followed was too much for him to stand still in, and so he walked out and sat in his car for half an hour before driving home.

He tried the same things about every third day. Jamie'd go out there and call Martin all the hateful things he could think to and Martin would just hang his head. If there were too many of us they would shoo us out before Jamie made his entrance, but if it were just enough to look natural we could stay and watch.

Martin could have done any number of things and instead he did nothing. And it seemed like it was that that kept Jamie going. Of course we didn't know that Jamie was trying to get paid for it; we figured he was just as bored as the rest of us. Some of us even argued that it was for our sake as much as the show's that he kept making the appearances. It is, for the most part, always better to let somebody else do your breaking down for you.

Yes, we were grateful for Jamie, and even grateful for Martin. Grateful for a sacrifice not our own. By then we'd pretty much decided not to be on the second season, except of course for when we decided the opposite. These were decisions none of us regretted. They who were on the show could have it to themselves. We were happy to be closer to fine, pleased to be trying to be all right again. This was our new routine. We were back to a kind of normal.

And so too did the show crave consistency. It is a valuable commodity. When people tune in, they want familiarity. Yes, it breeds contempt, but only after a while. There is always too much of a good thing, but there is never enough. The fifth episode of the second season was just that pleasant reminder. There were new laughs in old places, several outpours of emotion, and a healthy cry.

It was a lull in a storm, as it turned out. The last moment anybody who had anything to do with the show could remember as peaceful, calm, like it used to be. This was a false nostalgia—already things were miserable and had been for some time. But this was the last moment anybody ever wished they could go back to.

Season 2, Episode 6: Sweeps

Let's get to the point—halfway through the second season and the show was going nowhere. No, that wasn't it. It was going the same place over and over again. The kids were eating cornstarch and Jamie and Martin were still trying unsuccessfully to hurt each other's feelings. But how many times do you see the face of a hungry towheaded baby and still tune in next week. It's not a question. Halfway through and the plot wasn't so much arcing as trailing off like so many overwrought figures of speech.

And it could be said, hey, it's reality—that's the idea. There's no script. Anything could happen. But something was supposed to be moving by now, we could feel it, and just how much late push would it take to undo all this inaction? And on a related note—did it have to be so goddamned sad? Who'd want to watch a town full of simple people get kicked in the teeth every Tuesday at 9/8c? How would that compete with the attractive drunken stereotypes swapping DNA and throwing drinks at each other when we weren't even shooting alligators or driving down particularly dangerous roads? Tragedy hasn't been showing well at the focus groups and what I mean by that, by all of this is that, yes, I know, it has been moving slow and I have the emotional pallet of a daguerreotype. And I am not proud.

I'm not tired either. We. We weren't, tired that is.

And this week was Sweeps.

And Sweeps are always in a way magical. Once a year a few thousand families deemed exemplary of America record what shows they watch, which members of the family joined them on the couch, but not whether they liked it. Those numbers are tabulated and formulated and from this data shows are ranked time slot by time slot, demographic by demographic. If a show's rank goes up, ads on that show cost more. If its rank goes down, the show gets canceled.

At first reality was resistant to sweeping because they were afraid they'd tip their hand. But you can't be the only show in your time slot that doesn't sweep. We had to follow the rules like everybody else. And those rules were older than us, dated back to a time before the fourth wall had been put up, older even than television.

Rule #1: Up the Ante, Load the Gun

The featured families woke up and found their houses empty of food. This hadn't taken a lot of work as they'd gotten damn good at hungry, but there was a surgical precision to what the production assistants did this time. They took the mustard from the Younse's fridge; they took the gum from Tammy Johnson's purse. They emptied the seasoning cabinets that Jamie and Martin had hardly opened since last season.

Lyle and Cathy stared each other down, trying to figure out how to blame this on one another. Tammy Johnson nodded at her husband and they went to dress the children without saying much at all—they'd been planning for this for weeks. Martin packed the girls into the car and took them up to the Outpost to get week-old white bread and cherry slush puppies for breakfast. Jamie said, "Well, at least they left the beer."

Cathy and Lyle quit making meaningful eye contact, but it took a while. They'd made up since the last fight, were back to a kind of normal, they were telling each other, but it felt like the coffee pot had been left on, a nagging kind of nothing that didn't mean anything unless it burnt the house down. Cathy said, "Well, I guess we're just supposed to starve?" It was a question of strategy, not desperation.

Lyle assumed the opposite, "You're awful a fan of giving up on things these days." He got up and stormed off. He didn't know where he was going exactly, but he knew he'd need his tall boots. When he went outside it was hot again, the first day of the year that the sun could bake shimmer out of the asphalt. The camera caught him stretching and looking down, got close enough to see him biting at the inside of his lip. Cathy was waiting in the truck.

They drove through town. School had let out for the summer last week, and Paris was flocked with children, some with their parents, others pedaling around in twos and threes, the teenagers who could afford gas dutifully cruising from Walmart to Steve's IGA and back again. Lyle knew that seeing the children tore at Cathy, and a year ago he would have told her that their time would come, that it would work out, just wait and see, or he would have reached out and at least grabbed her hand, but he didn't want to have to explain himself to the camera later, didn't want to share his wife's pain with everyone, so he didn't say anything and neither did she. They drove to the Grapevine. It had been reopened again and this time there was a big sign announcing as much. The owners had taken out a loan, figuring that any moment now the town would become a hotbed of television-fueled tourism, and so they were covering the walls in old Doyles' Gear memorabilia and a mount of the twelve-pound catfish that cost Steve his first fishing tournament.

Down and Out

"What are we doing here?" asked Cathy.

"Hell if I know," said Lyle, pointing at the camera crew that was filming for an approach shot, the production assistant waving him into the lot. They cut that. They cut them directing Lyle to park around back behind the restaurant. They used a tight angle lens to show the truck settle down in front of the dumpster, so as not to show the cameraman perched on scaffolding aiming for a shot directly above.

Rule #2: Find Something New to Aim at

Of course Jason Johnson and his wife, Tammy, and their three boys, Junior, Dale, and Ricky, had been on the show. They were always a part of everything, there in the background, smiling around a free cheeseburger or offering an opinion on what someone or everyone was up to. But for a feature family, they had been largely left alone. We couldn't help but wonder what part they had to play in all of this. It turned out the show was waiting, holding the Johnsons like the queen of spades.

Jason Johnson came to the show believing that all reality shows were competitions, even—no, especially—the ones that didn't offer a cash prize or a five-digit number that America can text its vote to. Thirty-five people had equal claim to the title True Survivor and there were fifteen Top Chefs, twenty-three America's Next Top Models, seventeen Biggest Losers, and ten Ink Masters. But there was only one Honey Boo Boo, and who could argue the fact that Kate had clearly bested John and taken the Plus Eight as her spoils in victory.

Say what you want, Jason Johnson wasn't stupid, and so he and his family held a meeting early on where they discussed character continuity and the importance of lying honestly. They tried on a series of prototype catch phrases before settling on "Aww, Bubba," which the family said in moments of both excitement and pain as well as in place of most swear words and which became available on t-shirts and coffee mugs and which featured prominently in the *Down 'N' Out* Official Drinking Game—if anyone says *Aww, Bubba*, take a drink. Double if it's during a fight or while throwing something.

The boys were remarkably obedient, sweetly willing to curse their mother for not having better clothes to send them to school in, prepared without notice to fight each other for the last taste of an unappealing dinner, and just as good at shedding a poignant tear after a meaningful talk from Dad that made it all okay. And before you start thinking that the Johnsons had it coming, that you can judge these people, remember that this was the opportunity they were given, this their chance to work hard and make something of themselves. What could be more American. It's not a question.

You couldn't help but like Jason and the family if you met them off camera, without all the chairs and the shouting. The boys were well mannered, Tammy a polite and Christian woman, Jason surprisingly eloquent without the accent. Even when we could hardly think about the features and their gravy-train lifestyle—getting paid for doing the same things we all were doing for free—even still we had to admit that the Johnsons were earning it. All that squabbling couldn't be an easy row to hoe, and so we smiled at the Johnsons when we saw them.

With the food gone, the Johnsons loaded up into the minivan and Jason took a deep breath and looked just left of camera on account of Tammy had told him that was his good side.

"Boys," he said, "is it right to steal?"

"No, sir." It was all of them together and little Dale shook his head vigorously.

"But is it right to starve?"

The boys had no easy answer. Junior said, "I don't know, Pa."

"Well, it ain't right, boys, it just ain't," said Tammy. She said it again, and then added, "Sometimes life gives you choices where there ain't a right answer." It took a lot more practice than you'd think not to flinch when she said *ain't* in front of her children. Her own mother had slapped her when she was seven for saying it, told her it was a filthy word for filthy people.

They cut Jason telling the family, "So it goes just like we talked about, and don't forget to look guilty."

Earlier that week the show had installed a series of robot cameras in Steve's IGA so that they could have the camera crew follow Tammy as she begged for a job and then begged for rotting produce. She begged well, offered in entirely uncertain terms to do whatever it took to keep her family fed. She is better looking than she has a right to be, even with the dye job grown out and only enough makeup to look like she wasn't wearing any—still the queen of the prom all these years later. She reached out and touched the manager's hand, asked, *Please, isn't there anything you can do?*

While the manager told her that he couldn't help, that he was sorry, her husband and sons robbed the supermarket of everything they could fit down their overalls. With double-time banjo music in the background

Briseño

they slid down aisle by aisle, quietly filling the extra pockets Tammy had sewn into their clothes. It was over almost before it started, Jason and the boys were back in the car waiting in front of the store as Tammy strolled only a little too fast on her way out, looked only a little too nervous when the manager called out her name, turned around only a little too slowly. Cut to commercial.

Tammy walked out of the manager's office again. The announcer said that Tammy is the decoy while her husband and sons take a dangerous chance to survive. She walked only a little too fast on her way out, looked only a little too nervous when the manager called her name. She wanted to run, but she turned around slowly and he held out a paper sack full of black bananas and razor-sharp longhorn cheese. "I'm sorry we can't give more," said the manager.

"You've given plenty," she said.

Back at home, Jason and his family joined hands around the table with their hard-stolen vittles piled up. Canned hams and bags of rice and beans and, thanks to Dale, a wide and colorful array of sugary cereal, snack-sized puddings, and Little Debbies. Also a large bottle of Kikkoman soy sauce, which they hadn't stolen but that production assistants had added to the pile for marketing reasons. Jason said, "In the name of the Father, the Son, and the Holy Spirit. Bless us, O Lord, and these our gifts which are about to recede through Christ our Lord, Amen." He felt his way through the prayer, making sure to say it wrong. Cut to Jason, in a talking head, saying that God helps those who help themselves. Yes, he knows it's wrong, and he hates doing it with the boys watching, never mind helping, but he didn't have no other way. And they only took what they needed.

Down and Out

Cut back to the boys putting away their supplies. Ricky showed Junior something in his pocket, just a peek, couldn't even see what it was. Jason's hand crashed into the shot, attached itself to his middle son's arm, retracted it from the pocket and with it a deck of playing cards still in the cellophane wrapping. You can read the price tag. $1.49.

The hair on Jason Johnson's neck stood up and his cheeks flushed.

"Aww, Bubba," said Little Dale.

"I said it clear—no toys, no nothing—just food. How dare you disobey me?" he said, and he raised his hand back and Tammy said, "Honey, no." But his hand stayed there a spell all the same before he let go of the boy's arm and said, "Go to your room," and the boy ran off, tears streaming down his throat. They cut out, Jason asking if they need another take.

Rule #3: Pull the Trigger
Back at the dumpster Lyle looked up and mumbled but it was probably not a prayer. Cathy looked at his back, hoping that there was some misunderstanding.

You go keep watch around the corner, said the director. "I'll go keep watch around the corner," said Cathy. She added, "I love you, baby," but maybe Lyle didn't hear over the sounds of his OSHA-approved safety boots scraping against the green metal.

He just looked back at her, damn well knowing that this wasn't her fault, but when you're about to climb into hot garbage looking for a meal, you don't have nice things to say. Much sense as it made, he was mad she'd come along, and just as mad that she was to be spared this. He couldn't help but think that there was more than enough room for two.

Dumpsters are a one-way street, meaning that's it's easy to get in and all but impossible to get back out. To prove the point and for those all-important close-ups, Trent jumped in right after Lyle, knocked him off balance so they fell into each other and then into the garbage. They flailed like drowning sailors and nearly got in a fist fight trying to stand back up.

They cut Lyle opening the second, third, fourth, and fifth sacks. They cut when Trent dropped the camera to wretch over the side of the dumpster. They kept Lyle wallowing through garbage he'd spilt everywhere and finding a sack filled with days-old brown bread, the little loaves they would set on the table with honey butter, double if you ordered the new signature dish—chicken 'n' dumplings. He brushed off the more-than-days-old bratwurst potato salad and a few receipts and stood to climb out of the garbage.

But you can't climb out of a dumpster—you either jump or you fall. And as he fell, the bread spilt out on the ground, and he picked it up, dusted it off. He started to take it back to the truck. He looked down at it, shook his head. It had indeed come to this. They cut the director saying, "Eat it."

They cut Lyle saying, "You go right to hell."

They cut the producer nodding at Lyle and waiting through the cuss with an expectant look on his face, and they cut Lyle flipping him off, but kept when he turned to stare at the camera like it had stolen from him. They kept when he bit into the loaf like it was the only thing he'd had to eat since breakfast yesterday, which it was, and they kept when he choked back a tear and a stale wad of brown crumbs all at once.

Down and Out

And then Cathy came around the corner with a white plastic sack that said Thank You Thank You Thank You Thank You. She explained that the manager saw them and took pity. They cut when she added that he wouldn't give her the food until after they knew for sure that Lyle had taken the bite, wouldn't let her leave the store until he was done outside, she'd even tried to steal it, she swore to God. They kept when they cried into each other's arms, and when Cathy said, "Let's get you a shower."

With a few choice talking heads they played it as a real coming together. Lyle said, "It's the dark times that make you see what you have." Cathy said, "He'd do anything for me. Anything. And I'd do anything for him." Both of these were recorded early in Season One. They cut the drenching silence that lasted through the ride home, through the chicken fried steaks and through the evening news and on past tomorrow, when they ate the rest of the bread they found in the dumpster, though they showed that last part next week.

While they were at it, they cut Jason apologizing to his son for getting angry, reminding him that they were all actors now, that he would never really hit him. They kept Jason watching as Ricky ripped every card in half one by one and let them float into the trash.

Rule #4: Reload for Bear
Martin said, "These girls can't live on gas station food alone, and I think about their mother all the time."

Jamie woke up the next morning with his brain wrapped in fur and his pants nowhere in sight. He said nothing at all.

Jason told his family that they'd have to keep traveling

further and further away to find stores where they won't be recognized and it's only a matter of time before they get caught.

The camera showed Cathy washing dishes and Lyle said, "I love her to death, but sometimes I wonder if she really knows what love is about." This is not a recording from a previous season. It should be a non sequitur, but it isn't.

Stay tuned for scenes from next week's episode, when maybe someone finds hope and maybe a family finds love, but definitely the action will be thoroughly fast and hopefully furious. Trouble's abrewing in Paris, Arkansas— eight out of ten focus group participants agreed or agreed strongly.

We moved up to second in our time slot among basic cable reality dramas, showing particularly well among women with more than two children, the self-identified very religious, and college students engaged in pregaming. The most likely reason listed for *Would you watch again, why or why not?* was a strong desire to see if things got a little bit better or much, much worse. Investors were pleased. Aww, Bubba.

Season 2, Episode 7:
The Gun on Stage

Jason Johnson was cleaning his gun, a Winchester 30/30 single bolt dual action with a walnut stock, and—he wanted us to see this—a specially designed double-fail-safe trigger lock. You could give this to the boys, let them play soldiers and terrorists, couldn't harm a thing, Jason said. They cut him making it clear he would never do that. They kept him saying nobody gets shot with this gun lest he says so. Aww, Bubba. Cue the fucking banjos.

Little-known fact: prior to filming there were no banjos within Paris city limits. The theme song was performed by Champagne Hayseed, a quartet of college students from New York who took up mountain music after an elective in Musical Appalachia.

More widely known fact: Cathy and Lyle were having trouble. Not the kind that all of us had, or the kind that we tried to stay out of, but the kind we got to whispering about, the sort we not so secretly indulged ourselves in.

It started with little things. She couldn't find this, he had forgotten to do that. It didn't matter that he had done it and that it had come undone, or that she hadn't forgotten but that others had come behind and lost it for her. None of this came into the equation. It is easier than you imagine to make people resent each other. Hate and love cannot be contrived but annoyance is an easy button to mash. We couldn't tell you what they were fighting about that day, but we knew as sure as the announcer's voice on this one: "Lyle and Cathy were fighting again," and Lyle decided it was time to take a drive.

He and Cathy had lately been trying to avoid the fights, but it was like avoiding cow patties in a dark field—a feat of dead reckoning, with at most limited success. It was such a raw thing, a blister right on the easy spot between them. The greatest evidence of their love had always been how little they had to say between the two of them. He hated liking leaving, but here he was all the same, on his way to no place, feeling angry for leaving himself open to a situation with too many possibilities.

And still, the four o'clock sunshine was bright as anything and felt good enough to be stolen, breaking up high clouds and spattering silver linings all over. He was driving down Old Military Road through the corn patch that somebody had leased to ConAgra as long ago as he could remember, and the light picked out a single stalk of corn and set the thing on fire. He heard the road crunching under his tires, and was about to start smelling for the honeysuckle that was sure to be laced among the barbed wire, but then he saw the creature and he had to swerve to miss it and nearly plowed through a ditch.

There in the middle of the road was Martin's mule, staring at him, chewing idly at a sugar cube as if he'd been waiting on Lyle all day. Of course it could have been someone else's mule, or even someone else's donkey for what Lyle knew about it, but he didn't figure anyone else's animal would be wearing a dog collar.

Breathing deeply, Lyle considered his options. He could drive around the mule and thus the whole problem, hope it sorted itself out. But things around here had a way of not being ignored. He could call Martin, which maybe was the idea, but probably he was at work and he'd have to sit here with the mule until Martin could arrive and then the two of them would have to figure it out together, which was awkward enough when Lyle was paid good money to listen.

So instead he leaned his head out the window and looked ahead at the animal, then headed back into the cab of the truck and said, "Well, I suppose there's only one thing to do." Thinking of the two better ideas he already had, he pulled the truck upside against the mule. While the mule looked on him with what could never be mistaken for curiosity or respect, Lyle dug behind him into the half back seat. The animal stood his ground, and that made it easy for Lyle to slip the jumper cables around his neck.

Throughout the operation, the mule eyed Lyle with no emotion. When he eased his foot off the brake and started shuffling the truck forward, for a moment the mule stood still as a woodpile. The animal waited until the cables were stretched out, as if to prove a point to the truck. Only then did the mule move. But once its feet were moving, the mule began to lope along more or less agreeably.

"Now you can see when there's no use to fighting something," Lyle said appreciatively. "You know that goddamn clouds mean goddamn rain. Don't you?" He got that far before he realized he was talking to a mule but the cameraman, not the usual guy, who knew why, was waving at him to keep going. Lyle gave a look like he wished he hadn't thought anything all day. "I just don't understand why it keeps going this way." What had kept going on was Cathy, he told the mule.

It had started when they were at the Walmart. The production assistants had insinuated that they might be able to get a discount on dented cans, then insinuated that they might drive to Walmart, then asked forthright if they would just head to the vegetable aisle. Lyle looked at Cathy, confused. It fell to her to explain things to him more often than either of them would have talked about out loud. She was the smart one, it was a thing they'd both known for some time. And so he looked to her, quizzical, unsure. Hoping for reassurance or at least some kind of a way forward.

Cathy had said nothing. She just reached out to the shelf without watching what she was grabbing—a silver can of Italian Style Green Beans—and threw it as hard as she could at the floor, where it flopped and dawdled in a weak semicircle. Then she reached to the shelf and grabbed another can—beets in their juice this time—and repeated, this one bouncing toward the camera.

And Lyle reached to stop her, but instead found himself holding a white and blue can of Great Value Black-Eyed Peas. He didn't know why he threw it, why he picked up another and threw that one, why neither of them stopped until the stock boy and the meat clerk and the manager had a hold of them, and by then there were cans rolling all over the aisle. At forty-nine cents a can, they'd done more than a hundred dollars in damage, and Lyle still didn't know why, and Cathy had still not said a word about any of it.

Finally, this very morning, he cornered her in the empty pantry, too small for the cameraman to get behind her. She put her hand on his breast bone and said in an incongruously sweet tone, "I don't care what they want. I won't give them the satisfaction." But the subtitles they added to her whisper said you and not they. And so today, when they asked the two of them to do the can routine again Cathy wouldn't even respond, wouldn't be bothered to turn her head and that's what led to all that unpleasantness and him leaving.

The mule made a noise in his throat, halfway between a foghorn and a giggle, and Lyle realized he was about to miss the turn into the Gossett place. As he made his way up the driveway, the two little girls came out onto the porch holding hands. They were both covered in patches of dirt and what looked like forgotten bread dough, with streaks of mud and maybe strawberry Kool-Aid through their golden hair. "You brought back Horsey!" said the older one.

"We're pretending we're home alone!" said the younger.

They cut "we're pretending."

Lyle stopped the truck and led the mule to the pen the show had built so as to get approval from the animal ethics folks. Then he came back to the porch where the girls were watching him.

The narrator's voice boomed, "Earlier that day at the Gossett house."

In the episode, Martin woke up and microwaved three frozen burritos that expired four days before. The girls swung their legs as they picked at the beans and ground-lowest-common-denominator with cheese. Martin, who needed to shave but broke his last razor three days before, went outside to tend to Horsey, and found a pink envelope on his porch.

The letter inside explained that, should Martin choose to leave his girls alone, the production staff included several trained child care enthusiasts who would be happy to watch the girls, that if a situation arose in which he had little choice but to leave the girls alone for a short period of time, the girls' safety could be absolutely guaranteed. As soon as he turned the letter over, the phone rang. It was

Mrs. Montgomery, and a situation had arisen, one that required Martin to come immediately into work even though it was his one day off, even though he didn't have a sitter, and, no, he couldn't bring the girls with him, didn't matter who had done what.

What got to him was that they didn't even ask. They wouldn't even say, *Would you mind pretending to abandon your five- and seven-year-old so we can film it?* That would have somehow been all right, if they had at least asked and made it someone else's idea. But with Martin they didn't, because they knew they didn't have to.

And so, unprompted, Martin got down at eye level with his young ladies and explained that they were going to pretend to be home alone because Daddy had to go to work. They would be just fine. But they had to be good. "Take care of each other," he said and found himself gasping and clutching them both to him until he felt them start to squirm.

He left and then only after extreme coaxing and insistence that it's what Daddy had meant, Layne and Stacy timidly wrecked their home while the production staff let the mule out of the yard and fed him sugar cubes in the middle of the road until they heard Lyle coming up.

Lyle looked at the mess, at the strewn-about dish detergent, gluey white footprints, and then at the two little girls.

"The camera people said it would be fun, but I'm sticky," said the younger with a frump in her chin.

Lyle thought about it and asked the girls if they knew where their swimsuits were, and sent them upstairs to get changed.

Down and Out

He had spotted the hose while putting the mule away, and he went looking for towels and shampoo, wandering into the master bedroom.

The girls' onslaught hadn't reached here, leaving things eerily intact in the face of all that havoc. One wall was a sapphire blue, and the whole room had a put-together feeling, those proper dashes of color, the interlocking vases and picture frames. All of it spoke of Martin's wife.

Lyle hadn't thought of her since she had left last season. It was funny how easy things were to move away from. The longer he stood there, the more he could feel her presence, or rather the absence of it, a Marla-shaped hole in the air. He saw that the bed was unmade, but just on the left side.

When he came back out the girls were waiting patiently at the foot of the stairs in matching suits, both of them one year too small.

Lyle used the hose to rinse the pink Kool-Aid powder from Stacy's hair while Layne played in the puddle they were making, then they switched. When the girls were clean enough, he put the hose back where he found it, and then reconsidered and put it back where the thought it should go. He started to set things right in the yard and on the porch. The girls saw and began to help. Slowly and deliberately the three of them cleaned up the mess two of them had made. The cameras ate it up like the last plate of rolls at the Sunday buffet. None of them noticed the hour pass by before Martin finally got home.

He even drove tired, and when he spilt out of his SUV, he took in the scene like it was written in some language that not only he but no one understood. Here was his former employee sweeping flour off his porch, his girls dutifully folding towels, still wearing their swimsuits. It would have been funny, or strange to look at, but Martin wasn't really looking at anything. Nor did he hear Lyle when he said, "The mule was in the road. When I got him back here, looks like the girls had spilt a few things, and so I figured I'd hose them off some. Then we started cleaning up."

It was then that Lyle saw that Martin had a black eye. Not a bad one, but the swelling seemed to restrict the rest of his face, make it look numb. Martin's expression didn't change and he kept looking right through the side of the house as he said, "Girls, what do you say to Mr. Younse?"

"Thank you, Mr. Younse," the girls chorused.

"Listen, there's still a pretty bad mess in there. Do you want some help cleaning all that up?" said Lyle more enthusiastically than he'd meant. It was the first time he'd felt sorry for anyone else in a long time.

Martin kept surveying the house like he saw the mess through the brickwork, and then finally said, "No, I guess I can manage. But thanks."

Lyle stood there thinking about whether he ought to just start helping anyways when the replacement cameraman said, "Don't you think you ought to ask Martin why he left those two little girls alone?"

Without knowing why he turned around and looked at the camera and said, "I reckon I know." And before they could ask again with different words, ask over and again until he lost his will to be indignant about it, he got in his truck and drove home, the girls waving until he was long out of sight.

On the drive home, he kept thinking of that half-slept-in bed. It was a taste of something more bitter than he was used to. Cathy was a part of his life like the heart was part of breathing. Folks often say things like they couldn't imagine living without this or that. No longer could Lyle take refuge in such a lie.

On the way home, he knew for certain what was valuable to him. He knew where and how his bread was buttered, knew further just what being wrong would look like. He made up his mind to say he was sorry, and to take a good long turn being wrong even if he didn't know what it was that had to be his fault.

But when he got home he knew everything was broken even before the truck's engine dieseled out.

Cathy sat on the front porch not moving. He thought something was wrong with her at first, and then figured she was mad at him. He looked at her face, unmoving. He smiled, thinking he knew and understood. Then he launched into the most heartfelt and honest apology of his ten years of marriage. He apologized for having to say he was sorry, for not knowing what he was sorry about exactly, and for everything, everything he'd ever done that was even close to wrong or made her sad or angry.

She didn't move. She didn't turn his way. He wasn't sure at first that she was blinking. And then he noticed that she wasn't wearing a bra, and then that she had something in her hand, something she started rubbing between her thumb and forefinger during the second time he swore he'd change.

In that hand was a pink sheet of paper in a pink envelope. When Lyle reached for it, she let him take it but didn't move it any closer. He started reading, saying the first few words, a mumble dissolving to a whisper dissolving to a prayer. Then he finished and was looking at her, begging for an explanation.

Briseño

Finally, after all that, she exhaled but didn't turn to him and said, "We might as well just get along with it. Sooner or later, they always get what they want." She spat and went inside. Lyle took her place on the porch steps, reading the pink letter over and over again. Just a few tears dripping from his crooked nose. And then for the second time that day he got in his truck going no one knows where, and just as soon as his taillights faded into the distance, some other headlights started to bounce up the driveway.

Season 2, Episode 8:
The Gun on Stage, Part 2

The producers had something special in mind. They wanted to use the whole town, every featured family (excepting Steve, who was still on tour) in a single story arc. It turned out to be the toughest segment to edit of the whole season. Not just to make it entertaining, but just to make it understandable, make it clear. The first episode was cut from different parts of the day, and the second meant to fill in those holes. The idea was that viewers would get a deep sense of satisfaction from the way it all braided together. Focus groups were unenthusiastic at first, but adding the time of day helped a great deal.

So just before Cathy refused to go have another fight in Walmart (9:00 AM) and an hour after Martin got called into work (8:00 AM), they sent around one of the camera operators to deliver the little pink envelopes with the show's logo on the front. He had started at Jamie Mallet's place, leaving two envelopes remaining, both addressed to "The Younses or the Johnsons (Parents only)." Lyle and Cathy's place was a quarter mile up the road, but the operator drove directly past it to get the Johnsons their letter first (10:00 AM).

Trent, the camera operator, had gone over to the Johnson house and found the boys hunting a theoretical gopher with pointed sticks while Jason watched from the porch, cleaning his gun. He hadn't owned a gun before the show began, had never fired one even. But after a little practice he was more than capable of breaking down the drive spring rod assembly from the bolt from the receiver assembly in little enough time to seem, he hoped, authentic. He had just finished telling his own camera that with the safety on, his gun was safe enough the boys could play with it, not that he would ever do such a thing, of course.

Unlike the other cast members, Jason accepted his envelopes with a whoop and even though he was pretty sure they couldn't use it, he made a scene of taking the envelope and running it through his mustache, saying, "Smells like money to me." He even thanked Trent and waved as the white van drove off, before he set to reading his and Tammy's copy of the letter Cathy would get to open two miles down the road.

When Jason finished reading he called his boys to him, gave each a long hug and a kiss on the cheek, told them he loved them, told them he wanted only what was best for them, that he hoped to God he was making the right choices.

Then he sent them to their room and asked his wife to join him so as they could figure out their next move. They talked it through and cried and told each other how much they loved each other, made sure they had done all they could to heal before the wound even came, and then they went outside and had a picnic with their children. They spent the whole day as a family, and even the boys could sense that it was a time not to act out but to act right. Then, around 6:30 when the sun started to set, Jason took the gun and the truck and headed to Lyle's while Tammy started walking down the road the other way.

By 9:00 AM, Martin had made it to work at the Outpost,

discovered that the emergency was a bingo promotion at the Choctaw Casino across the Oklahoma border. He thought about calling the girls to see if they were okay, but the PAs cued a customer to walk in every time Martin picked the phone up, so he resigned himself to selling beer and waiting for Jamie.

By noon normally only a dozen or so of us would have dropped by the Outpost. But the PAs had been passing out free muscadine wine and letting it publicly be known that something worth seeing was about to occur at the gas station, so there were about forty of us on hand and we were calling friends and swilling the greasy sweet wine they were handing out. After all, it wasn't like we could have jobs, or freely spend the money they gave us, or walk around our own goddamn streets.

So, yes, there were a few of us, and when they put us back on camera and asked what we'd been drinking we did, in more or less unison, shout out "homemade musky-dine wine." And when Jamie weaved up to the gas pump and climbed out of the truck cab, we did scream and holler.

But no matter what the announcer said, it is not a Paris tradition to taste the new wine in the first week of July. Nor was it the case that Jamie had "happened upon us and joined the festivities." He was drunk when he got there, like always, and as soon as he was out of the cab he marched right into the Outpost, came back to us only when the camera crew insisted.

"Hello, boys, I understand y'all got some wine for me to drink?" We were told to holler in approval and we did. A PA handed Jamie a jug of wine made to look homemade. He drank right from the bottle. After several seconds of watching his adam's apple dip up and down like an oil well, he threw down the bottle and said, "Keep it lighthearted, boys—nothing too depressing, am I right?" and he held out a hand for a high five. We were told to high five him back and to again hoot in approval, and we did both.

With his crew satisfied, Jamie set back to his original goal and walked to the Outpost. Martin didn't even look up until Jamie was right on him, looking down at the Marlboro place mat between them and then throwing down an envelope. "Reckon you got one of these today too, didn't you?" he said.

Martin looked up at Jamie, and both men thought the other had aged too many years in too short a time. Both wondered how it had gotten like that.

"I sure did, but mine didn't have anything to do with you."

"Read this," said Jamie, and so Martin did.

Jamie,

It's time for a serious conversation about you and this show. While we respect you as an individual, we quite frankly don't believe you're giving us your full effort. We have invested hundreds of thousands of dollars in you and in this town so that we can tell the true and honest story of America and you're making that difficult. Your task, simple as it is, has eluded you for far too long, but more than that you lack conviction, spirit, grace. Even your listlessness is unconvincing. There have been discussions that perhaps we should write you out, that maybe we were wrong to make you a featured part of the show and pay you a not insubstantial sum of money just to be yourself. When we chose you, we saw you as a reassuring source of quiet hope, a bright spot in the lives of those around you. We thought that you could keep this light hearted, funny, in other words not so depressing.

And you know what, Jamie, we still think that. This can be your moment. Years from now, we may look back on this moment and laugh at just how far you've come.

So to close: Go get arrested! Today! And have fun doing it!

Best,
The Producers

"So I bet you're right, Martin," Jamie said when he finally looked up at him. "I'm betting a kiss ass like you didn't get a letter much like that one at all."

Since Jamie had taken to coming into the Outpost, Martin and Jamie were certainly enemies, though probably neither would have used that word. Still Martin hadn't anybody else to talk to, and so he found himself blurting out, "They made me leave the girls alone. They were already letting the mule out before I pulled out the driveway."

Martin was on the verge of a breakdown, and drunk as he was, even Jamie could see it. And like any good Arkansan, his natural impulse was to solve problems, his or anybody else's. And so without a lot of thought behind it, Jamie said, "Can't your wife take them?"

Martin felt like most of what he recognized as himself was melting away like rice paper touched to flame. Even before he could catch his breath, he had debated, considered, and then decided to kill Jamie Mallett, and if it wasn't for the fact that Martin had never thrown a punch in his life, he might well have succeeded. Even still he managed to knock Jamie's feet out from under him with a single slack-wristed right cross, sending Jamie spinning into a rack of fried pies and cinnamon cake doughnuts. Jamie came up bleeding but quickened by the pain, and might well have done serious damage to Martin had it not been for all the drinking he'd been up to as of recent. Still he got in one half-clean shot to the cheekbone, enough to raise a black eye. Still no amount of clever editing could render anything but what happened: two mildly overweight men, both wearing plaid, grappling each other and taking the occasional half-hearted swing, but basically just slow dancing without music. It was a slow angry hug, and they held that position for a while, hating each other even as they were certain there wasn't much they could do about it.

And then the police were there. They'd been instructed to check up on the Outpost today, and were there in time to pull the two sweating sacks of thirty-nine away from each other. Martin, upon seeing the police, panicked and started verbally expectorating all over everyone in distance. It was an accident and he didn't mean it and it was just a giant misunderstanding. He begged not to be taken to jail, that he had two daughters at home and they needed him because their mother was far away.

Jamie was thinking clearly for the first time in recent memory and was struck by the oddity of the situation, and he thought about fishing and why they hadn't made anyone go to church in quite some while.

Neither of them seemed to have their thoughts interrupted by Jamie's brisk arrest. The two officers handcuffed Jamie, hauled him off the floor and had him in the squad car almost before Martin quit swearing at his wife. The arrest report said 1:00 PM. Martin didn't get to

Down and Out

leave work for three more hours.

At 1:00 PM, Cathy was on her porch trying to think of a good reason to cry. Halfway she wasn't even aware she was doing it, halfway it was like sticking your finger down your throat when you knew you were getting sick sooner or later. She wanted it over with, whatever that meant. She had to admit she didn't have a clue as to what she would be crying about or what crying had to do with anything. The reaction felt simpler than that, and if she'd been thinking about it, she would have thought instinct.

The white van approached and like everything else in Paris, you had to see it coming. Streaming down the long gravel drive with purposefulness. There will always be drama kicked up along with the clouds of dust, and it didn't help that she could watch the driver watching her even from this great distance.

Trent got out of the van tattoos first with a smirk wide enough to dam the river, like he'd done a thing worth doing. He didn't say a word, only walked up at a pace that Cathy expected he thought was intense and handed her the note.

The note. There had been dozens of pink embossed envelopes stuffed with fun-oriented ideas and instructions. They even put our paychecks in them. Like the bells at the abbey or the flies at the lake, they had largely become an unnoticed nuisance, the sort of thing you didn't remember yourself resenting. And yet for all that, anyone in town knew what note The Note was.

We never saw it or one like it, but we figured it had to say something like this,

Briseño

Greetings, Jason and Tammy / Lyle and Cathy,

As Season Two begins to draw to a close, it becomes in all of our best interest to start thinking about what we can do to make the show that much more outstanding. This show is proud to be American, and few things are more important to America than families. Families are the building blocks of this nation. We love to watch families build, grow, and prosper. We also love the drama inherent in every American family and part of our goal is to share that drama with the world.

And some of that drama comes from secrets. Everyone has them. And the fact is, plain and simple, secrets—and the revealing of secrets—make great television. For that reason, we want to make our final bonus offer of the season—and this time the offer is only available to our married featured families (that's you!). Anyone who truthfully confesses to his or her spouse that he has been unfaithful will receive $125,000.

Please understand, we can neither pay you for nor wish to encourage marital infidelity in any manner. We are offering this bonus only if you choose to reveal preexisting infidelities or those you choose to engage in naturally. Checks can be made to one or both marital partners at the discretion of the bonus earner.

We're sure that with your help, we can continue to produce exciting, heartwarming television.

Best,
The Producers

Cathy read the note through three times before she remembered she wasn't alone. There was Trent, the camera operator, a delicate balance between practiced nonchalance and a shit-eating grin. "If you don't come, I'll double it," he said.

Now if you think that you know right now how you'd answer that question, you're a sanctimonious asshole or a fool or both. Your morals are far less concrete than you'd like to think, of that much be assured. The moment that this scenario becomes more than a conversation over happy-hour peanuts, once you find yourself in a situation that all of us can only imagine, you will find that the rules are quite different in this new and foreign land.

You will think, first and foremost, about the money: $125,000 solves a lot of problems, doesn't matter who you are; $125,000 dollars, the sound of it, the way it drips all too quickly from the sides of your tongue. You will then, in spite of yourself, think about how your husband has it coming to him, his self-righteous insistence on not giving up but always giving in. You will think that he would forgive you, this will always cross your mind, as will that if he didn't, it wouldn't be the end of everything not by a damn sight.

You will think about the other times you'd thought about it, about being with someone else—someone new— what it would be like, a new set of pressure points, a new way to touch everything, to use bodies. You will think about the tempting ghost of sex without love, of the freedom of no guaranteed tomorrow.

You will think that you are growing older, that what remains of your looks sublimate daily without so much as a smoke trail. You will remember, in spite of yourself, only the excitement of what happened before, only that breathless notion of expectation comes back. The rest of it is there but no more real than a soap bubble.

You will have each and every one of those thoughts and most likely you will have time to hate yourself just for thinking them as well.

Cathy shrugged into and out of every one of those thoughts like a used coat. Had she a camera to peer into, she might have confessed for the first time in her life that she had no idea what to do.

In spite of himself, Trent couldn't help but notice how beautiful a shot she would make now. It caused his face to turn, to soften, and it was that that saved her, as Cathy had the fortunate accident of mistaking that look for pity.

"You know what you can do, you can go right to hell and don't you spare gas on the fucking way."

He was supposed to be taken aback, but he moved in, taking her anger like a cue he'd been waiting for. He halved the distance between them, then halved the distance again.

She couldn't believe him, the goddamn nerve. She couldn't believe this asshole for a single second. But she could smell him and her body set to work preparing her to make the wrong decision. One hundred. Twenty-five. Thousand dollars.

Promises. The one word was all she thought.

"Get the fuck away from me or I will end you." She thought she was whispering it, but it came out like straight-line wind. She screamed at him to just go in her lowest, angriest, most lip-curled voice, propelling him away and back into his van with wave after wave of simple, nasty hate. He tried for one last moment of meaningful eye contact, but he couldn't find it in him. And he drove away, thinking about how much of his time he'd wasted, already blaming her for all of it.

Long after he was out of sight, after the road dust had

settled itself and the whippoorwill had gone back to its standard complaint, Cathy sat still in the same seat. She knew she should move or at least close her mouth but none of it, none of anything made sense, so that's how it was when Lyle found her, as close to dead as one could get with nothing wrong on you.

It was far from the first time she felt as if she were watching herself from the middle distance, but it might have been the first time she watched herself stand so still. Not saying anything when four hours (5:00 PM) later Lyle approached her on the porch, came up asking first what was wrong, not saying anything when he broke down in tears and grabbed her empty hand, told her how sorry he was just for everything, how he knew she deserved more, how he could try harder, how he would find a way, find anything, find something. She didn't move while he cried and the tears cut channels in the sweat-stuck grit on his face. She watched herself stay there just to the left of catatonic while he held her and himself all the way from apologetic and regretful to spiteful and palpably alone. She was unable to respond to his question of concern, those of worry, those of distinct accusation. When he pulled the letter from her hand, they both heard a tiny snap as her fingers rejoined against her palm.

For his own part, Lyle was never more in love with his wife, never. Having seen Martin's house, and of lesser importance, Martin, he felt armed to the teeth with new knowledge, like Scrooge on Christmas day. He was ready to cry and ready to mean it.

And when he saw her he was moved to awe, loved her deeper. And that made it hurt, made it hurt like nothing else, like a toothache just under his solar plexus, like his whole insides were a throbbing bruise. But once he'd asked her too many times not to have to look on his own, once he'd read the note himself, had read it through twice and looked at Cathy, looked at the note, looked back at Cathy and cried out, "Oh, hell," all the love and readiness for what had to come next seeped out and what was left in its place was a simple overriding question.

And then she said that they might was well get it over with, that the show gets what it wants anyway. And she walked inside, and this part is new, reserved from last week's broadcast, a new wrinkle. He followed her in, and asked her the only word that was left in him.

"Who?" he asked in a low growl.

"Who?" He said it was an honest, fair question he deserved an answer to.

"Who?" he hollered not just at her, but at the blue gray ridge a thousand yards beyond the window and at the sweet gum tree and the lawn tractor he hadn't had gas for in sixteen episodes.

Who, he said to the creases in his palms and the flattened spot where his wedding ring ought to have been. *Who*, he said as he reached to touch her arm. *Who*, as he felt his fingers tighten around the thin bones of her arm as she twisted away from him for the first time ever. *Who*, as he recoiled in shame at what he'd almost done. *Who*, as he climbed back into his truck, spun around in the driveway and took off down Old Military Road with no particular notion as to where he might be headed.

By then it was 6:30, a shade past dusk, only the faintest purple light giving shape to the world. Had it been earlier he and Jason Johnson would have seen each other, and in spite of it all, Lyle would have waved. Jason would have waved back and then probably pulled Lyle over so as to point a rifle in his face. But unfortunately for everyone that didn't happen.

Jason Johnson arrived at Lyle's house at 6:45. After having sat there for much of the afternoon, no one was more surprised than Cathy that she'd gotten up and took to sweeping clean every inch of the house the broom could touch. It wasn't something she was thinking about, the same as whatever had made her sit there and let Lyle drive off misinformed and desperate. But after long enough, everything reverses itself, and it happened that long enough for Cathy was just long enough to ignore the man she pledged her love to eternally, but just short enough to come outside with a broom held in a defensive stance and to scream at Jason Johnson as soon as the truck slid into the gravel driveway, "Well, I reckon you think you can fuck me too, is that right?" Her teeth showed purple white in the blooming dark. Her breath came in spasms and heaves— dry, red-eyed, furious. She was beautiful. Watch it yourself.

Jason calmly assessed the situation, decided to bring the gun anyways for continuity's sake. But he walked with it held by the stock, pointed down and away. "This ain't for you now, I don't want no trouble. I just come to threaten to shoot Lyle, but I can see he ain't here. So I'll just go then." He didn't go.

She thought it would be far from rude to ask what in hell he was talking about. But somehow she felt compelled by decorum to let him finish or not as he saw fit, driven by what you'd call pity if pity made you feel like an asshole. Jason took three false starts and four ums to come up with, "Got anything to drink?" It wasn't so much a question, because of course that was all any of them had.

She brought out two plastic glasses of brown liquor and sat on the porch clutching her knees and keeping her eyes on Jason, thoroughly unsure he wasn't about to try something. But Jason kept his distance and only looked her way when it would have been rude not to. He said, "You know, Tammy and us, we been admiring y'all's work for a while."

He waited for a non-delivered thank you.

"Honest. That bit with the trash and the takeout container? Aww, Bubba that was something else. Can't wait to see it, I almost cried hearing about it."

Cathy sized him up, took his measure, and couldn't come up with anything to say except, "What the hell are you?"

"Oh, come on now," said Jason, the accent falling back as his eyes tilted down. "You're not going to try and tell me you're all innocent, are you? Like you weren't making up all of that shit with the wedding dress last season? Like you don't know any better? We all play dumb, all right, but don't tell me you aren't gaming this show the same as us." He stopped and took a contemplative gulp from his drink. "You're good, but you're not that good," and then, just then, like he'd only now thought of it, "are you?"

And of course the truth was—she wasn't. She'd been playing the role of herself for a long time now, for maybe longer than anyone. Thinking that made the talk go slack, until after a while it dawned on Jason that he was the expert here. His role more clarified in his mind, he proceeded with some confidence.

"Tammy and me, we have a four-year plan. It's hard now, sure, but this is just year two. Next year the show has to either renegotiate or let us loose. We figure our names will keep us in work for another year or so, local talk shows, mall openings, casino appearances. We figure we get more as a family. One more year as a has-been—Big Brother 2.0, Dr. Phil Celebrity Intervention—and anyway, you do the math, all three boys go to University and Tammy and me don't have to work except to go on vacation. It's a plan. I know that now every day feels like a car alarm that won't turn off, and it's bound to get a touch worse before it gets any better but it'll all turn out. And you know, if you and Lyle play right, might be there's room for all of us. This always was a group thing, an us."

For an answer Cathy went back inside and came back with the bottle, poured herself another, set the bottle far enough away from her so she didn't have to offer it to Jason, only nod when he took it up himself.

A calm settled between them. There was an understanding. If they weren't being filmed, if a production assistant hadn't briefly stepped from behind the camera to adjust the bottle so as to make the label read in the shot, they might have been becoming friends. Cathy began to think more normal thoughts, and then she asked, "So why were you gonna shoot Lyle?"

"I wasn't gonna—Tammy's on her way over to...to um...We got one of them pink letters. We figure that it plays best, it uh, it makes better television if while she's...with Jamie...if I come over here thinking it's Lyle, and then, you know."

At first she was in awe of him, of how well planned out the two of them had it, that it was so certain to work, not in spite of but specifically because it was a story you'd sworn you'd heard a thousand times before. And then she looked at him again. "You really love her." And then, "But don't you get the bonus all the same? Why even bother coming over here? And don't tell me it's the show 'cause that's bullshit. Hell, they ain't even taking audio on this shit." It was true, the film crew had backed up some one hundred yards, and had adapted their lenses so as to make it seem as though they were even farther off. "Why even come here? What's the point?"

"Do you reckon I ought to have hung around and done the laundry while she was at it?" He took one of the two rifle shells out of his pocket and twirled it across the back of his knuckles without noticing he was doing it. "No, sir," he said, but it looked like he didn't know he said it.

After a while he stood and dusted himself off, and with it went every trace of the last half hour's conversation. By now the sun was gone and a heavy crescent moon had come up behind First Ridge, revealing hidden blues and purples in the half-light, just at 8:00. Jason walked back to his truck firearm in one hand, ammunition in the other. Afterward Cathy would find it strange that he said nothing, not one word. He just walked back to his truck, opened the door with the hand holding the shell, climbed inside and shut it hard behind him. The headlights came on, blocking sight of every other thing. Cathy waited for the lights to flicker, for the starter to turn the engine, for the first roar of sound and moving air.

Instead she heard the windshield shatter, she felt the ground pulse, and then felt her ears start to clang with the unmistakable racket of a gun going off.

Season 2, Episode 9:
The Shot Heard Down the Road

Most of us didn't hear it at all. The echo of a gunshot can travel a dozen miles in the right conditions, but between the trees and the brick downtown, and the dry night air, and the way the town is put together, Cathy and Lyle's place is just far enough down Old Military Road that just about everything south of the courthouse—the Walmart and the Outpost and the stretch of businesses treading water in twos and threes down Route 22—was too far away to hear anything for sure. For most of those a touch closer, they were watching TV or fighting over bills or listening to the radio.

Jamie, however, was in the jail cell on the south side of the courthouse, staring out the window at the old hospital with its boarded windows. He heard the sound carry on the wind. He hoped that he'd just imagined it, though he was certain he hadn't. He looked to check the time, because being in jail put him in mind of cop shows and he thought it might be useful to an investigation to know when the shot was fired, but jails have only one thing in common with Vegas—no clocks to be seen, and if he'd had a watch, they would have taken it when they'd taken his shoelaces.

Twenty minutes after he'd been incarcerated, Jamie had done a fair amount of sobering up, and was fairly certain he'd made some mistakes. Forty minutes later, he was convinced that none of it was really his fault, that in some strange way he'd been a great success, or at least a team player. He had after all accomplished a difficult goal in most senses of the words. He looked around the four off-white cinder block walls, the solid door with a window too small to bother looking out of, and felt an inkling of pride, like when you fold the last towel in the load of laundry. *Yessir*, he said, *even when what I was supposed to do was get thrown in jail, I did what I was supposed to. Pops would be proud.* It was just then that his moment of clarity gave way to a mountainous craggy hangover, the likes of which most will blessedly never know. It occurred to him that the hadn't been quite sober in some amount of time, and he thought making himself sick might help, but it didn't. Then he thought he might sleep it off, but he couldn't. And so there he was, in a cell, alone in the jail except for the guard at the end of the hall, and all of America looking in from the surveillance camera recently installed on the ceiling.

How does it feel to spend six hours alone, trembling in spite of yourself, waiting for the sake of waiting? To illustrate this painful reality, they cut together a montage of thirty-five seconds of Jamie pacing, tossing on the skinny sweat-soaked mattress, standing up, sitting down. For every second of that montage, Jamie spent twelve minutes alone; all focus groups agreed that the scene dragged on too long, and in post they reduced the montage by half, for the sake of flow. For the sake of continuity.

About halfway through, Jamie started thinking about the necessity of movement, how motion was the only certain thing, whether you were talking people or television shows or the goddamn ground beneath you. Actions were unavoidable and every action led to another. Where his actions were to lead him was monumentally uncertain. In the real world, he was fairly certain he would have at least gotten to call somebody by now, but then he wasn't sure who he'd call, and he was fairly certain that whomever he thought to hassle, they'd either already know about it or be too busy doing whatever it is that their pink letters had told them to do. Like most things now, it was well out of his control. He sat and wondered who they'd send. Lyle, probably. That made sense. Which is why it wouldn't be Lyle. Maybe Cathy or the Johnsons. Probably Martin. But he never considered the first visitor he ended up receiving.

The first visitor walked in without an introduction, bringing a folding chair with him, opening it, and sitting down. Jamie had seen him before, someplace, but for most of the first minute, it wouldn't come. Then, all at once, "You're the one from the pawnshop," he said, and just saying it made him tired.

Bobby LaDue nodded. "That's right. But who I am right now is the man who can help you out. You might not know it, but you're in trouble, Jamie, a lot of trouble. You know Martin's pressing charges, right? You know the Outpost is pressing charges, right? You're going to owe a lot of money. A lot. And if you're not careful you're going to spend a lot of time." He did not see it necessary to motion at the walls, only to pause, "In here."

"They must have sent you here to cheer me up," said Jamie, and though he thought he was being sarcastic, he really wasn't. There is something in those of us who know what it is to be kicked that won't wake up until we see the bottom of a boot, and this is the worst part about being down and out. Jamie found himself snarling, "You know I got some money, or I will, anyhow. And the kind of snake-ass lawyer that could handle all that is the same kind that would be willing to wait on money he was sure to get a piece of."

Bobby tried to smirk. "You don't get it yet, do you? You signed off your rights months ago. The show retains the right to hire your legal counsel for you. And if you think you can outsmart us, think again. You got no way out, redneck, no way out at all. We didn't even put you in here, we had you put yourself in here, and we'll let you out if and when it suits us." He left that to set in for a spell. "You can be as smart as you want, Jamie, but," he stopped to give a signal to the camera in the ceiling, "you're either going to play ball, you're going to get out of here, and when I say I need something you're going to get it done, plain and simple, or you're going to rot your ass in here for longer than you'll care to think about."

With no further communication, he swung the door open, walked out, and left Jamie wondering if the door had been unlocked this whole time. He was still in the middle of being confused when the door opened again and the second visitor walked in.

"Father William," Jamie heard himself saying.

"Hello, Mallett," said Father, taking the seat Bobby had left.

"You're short an altar boy, I reckon."

The priest took a deep breath and settled his head into his craggled hands. "You're a goddamn jackass and a moron to boot. And don't you try to tell me about your whys, you done got yourself sent to jail and if half those assholes had their way, you'd be sent down river as quick as next week and that would be that. And wipe that look off your face, son, don't you know the difference between danger and trouble? Your ass is this close to plain on fire and you're giggling like the boys at the reformatory."

A deep-set switch had been flipped in Jamie and what

Down and Out

was only a second ago detached bemusement and a hateful glare melted into simple contrition. He was instantly sorry for sins he hadn't understood committing. And yet still he heard himself say, "But you don't understand. I was told to do it."

"Oh, I understand plenty, you damn jackass. Somebody told you they'd give you a bunch of money to do something you damn well knew better than and you went right ahead and did it, and now you're wondering how it is that nobody's shaking your hand. Son, you were always the smart one. Don't tell me they paid you to stop thinking while they were at it."

"Enough," said Jamie, with a touch of hardwood in his voice. "I don't need anybody to yell at me anymore."

Fr. William looked down on him, as benevolent as Fr. William ever got. "Oh, hell, son, don't get soft on me yet. You're going to take a hell of a lot more than an ass chewing if you expect to find a way out of this mess. But," and Father stopped, sighed, begged God's forgiveness, and then made a sign at the camera he barely understood. "But if you're willing to work at it, willing to sober up and fly right and do good by this town, then I can find a way to get you out of here. If not, well, hell, I'll pray for you, son, I will."

And with that, the second visitation was over, and Fr. William went back through the door and Jamie was alone again. Alone long enough for it to be what he was doing again, alone enough to not be waiting as waiting implies a coming change, long enough even that he actually had imagined the third visitor before he walked in, which was in itself an impressive thing as he'd seen the man who walked through the door three times at most.

He came in, sat down, lit a fresh cigarette from the nub

of the one he walked in with, didn't say anything, let the whole of the day hang like the trails of blue fading smoke. Only after things had settled in a way that was far from restful did he speak. "Don't let them lie to you, you've done good today." He looked right at Jamie as he said it, the first time anyone had done that since Martin had punched him in the face. It felt about the same. "You know who I am. right?"

Jamie nodded, "You're the HMFC."

The man smiled, which made him look more dangerous. "The way you people talk, I swear it's the whole reason we're here. We could have done this easy in the Midwest, out closer to L.A., but no—the whole thing doesn't work without all the y'alls and the reckons and the what was that, HMFC? The head motherfucker in charge, right? Yeah, that's me."

Jamie waited, and only after a spell, "So what's your pitch?"

The producer told him to repeat himself.

"First the pawnshop owner, then the priest, low road, high road. What are you here to tell me?"

The producer nodded, lit a third cigarette from the butt of the second, but as he did it, you could tell he didn't want to, couldn't make himself want it any more than he could make himself stop from lighting it.

"You're smarter than I give you credit for, all of you. They always are, really, but everyone in this fucking town has got this whole damn thing figured out. You're all just too fucking clever to be on television." Jamie didn't know which way he meant anything. "Mr. Mallett, I'm not going to bullshit you. We don't know what you're good for yet. I picked you myself, out of the whole town, because you're the only one who doesn't listen to the others. The one who doesn't just look to Lyle and Martin, who doesn't run their mouth and then change their mind like a herd of chickens."

"Flock," Jamie said automatically.

"Herd," said the producer and went on. "I picked you because I know you're going to be good for something. I just haven't figured out what. So I'm hedging my bets, Jamie. Maybe we'll need a new villain. Mr. LaDue is a longtime employee of mine and he has an idea—and well, bottom line, somebody has to go find out what's under rock bottom. Hell, you and I both know you been eating misery and shitting out thank-you-sirs for long enough, years now, really. And of course we'll pay you. We won't go into specifics now, but I can be plain enough and say that there is a much greater path downward than you might expect, lower lows." It came out so hopeful. "Jail can just be the start of something really spectacular.

"Or maybe you want to be the hero. Maybe you want to be the one we all admire, want to go on talk shows and tell them how you saw the light, came to, moment of clarity, all that yackety yack. Personally, I've seen it done and it looks to taste like absolute shit, but the truth is that tragedy and miracles trade even money.

"We don't do this all the time, and I'd be lying if I said my collaborators all agreed with this decision, but literally and actually, the choice is yours. Hero or villain, we don't care. That's why the two little outros."

Jamie said, "So on the show, if I go one way, the priest bails me out, if I go the other, it's Bobby or whatever at the pawnshop."

"You got it," said the producer, and then he sat there and waited.

Briseño

Jamie knew what he was supposed to ask, and just to see what happened, he decided to say nothing. The producer knew he was defying him and so he sat there unmoving except for his smoking hand, blinking every three seconds, and they sat that way for seven full minutes. By the time one of them spoke, Jamie didn't believe it was him that said, "So tell me why you're here."

The producer smiled. "Like you've figured, a backup plan. Another one. As I mentioned, my colleagues don't all see you as the asset that I do, and while I'm far from giving up, I play by a well-defined set of rules." He stopped and gave the signal to the camera. "Jamie, I'm sorry, but based on your behavior as of late we have no choice but to ask you to leave the program. We cannot tolerate violence on *Down 'N' Out*. We can't and we won't. I'm very sorry." And with that he walked out and left Jamie to sit there replaying the last half hour in his mind once and then again and again. He was still at it when the guards told him he was free to go and gave him a ride to the impound lot so he could pick his truck up. It wasn't until he was almost home that Jamie thought about the shot again when he saw the flashing lights and the county sheriff standing on the side of the road keeping passersby from getting any closer. Though he wanted nothing to do with this commotion, it still took Jamie twenty minutes to get past the roadblock and make it to his own front door.

An hour before the shot went off, Lyle was knocking on Jamie's front door, not knowing that Jamie had finally managed to get himself arrested. He hadn't talked to Jamie hardly at all since the funeral. The show pushed them apart, sure, but it was more than that. In the factory they stood shoulder to shoulder, sometimes for twelve hours out of a day. Now their work, such as it was, called for a great deal less interaction. Lyle was on his way over to talk to Jamie about his troubles with Cathy, which was strange not because of the lack of contact but because it had likely never happened before. Not their talking of course, but Lyle's problems to this point had been thankfully few. Those that he had, if they were simple, he chose not to bother others with, and if they were complicated they were usually too private to talk about.

This problem that his wife had likely slept with another man, that clearly went in the second category—thing you just weren't supposed to talk about. And yet here he was, propelled more by a lack of a clear other choice in destination than anything else.

When he saw that Jamie's truck was gone, he ought to have turned around and found something else to do with himself. When he got no answer to a loud and consistent knock, he should have climbed back into the cab and gone any place else. But some instinct for bad ideas told him to have a load off on Mrs. Mallett's porch swing and the production assistant offered him a drink, which he couldn't think of a reason to say no to.

He sat there, thinking back to high school, when he and Jamie had been all but best friends, had talked to each other quite a bit. About how if Cathy would marry him, then the rest wasn't all that big of a deal. About how anything, anything was better than being here forever, or was it? They talked a fair bit sitting in that very swing, drinking beer they'd stolen from Jamie's father. He figured he could sit there and wait for Jamie, relive some of that.

Tammy Johnson was wearing the outfit you'd suppose

she'd be, cut-off shorts and a low-scooped top. Her tan matched the golden-hour light, and as she approached she was almost camouflaged by the last of the evening, so Lyle didn't see her until she was level with his truck. By then she was close enough to inspire thoughts in Lyle he hadn't felt in twelve years.

Lyle had, to this point, never given serious thought to the idea of cheating on his wife. This was less a great accomplishment of will and more a product of circumstance. In a town that size, there is precious little opportunity to make certain kinds of mistakes, blessed be. At the sight of Tammy swaying up the gravel drive in an old Paris High t-shirt caught up around her waist in such a way, he in that moment formed a plan that filled him with dread and that he knew he would go through with all the same.

"Lyle?" she said, and she was asking what he was doing here.

"Jamie ain't here."

Tammy came up to the porch, sat across from him on the steps, a good four feet away. He mumbled, "I thought I'd talk to him some myself, but he hadn't been home."

She looked at him and he had no idea what that look might mean. "So why're you still here?"

Lyle held up his drink as a response, and the production assistant brought him a new one and one for Tammy besides.

After a while he said that he and Cathy had gotten one of those letters again. Then it was Tammy's turn to make a plan, or rather to adjust the one she'd already had. Did it make her feel like a whore, just to switch from one to the next? Of course, but she felt that way just the same. It was an ugly word, one she never even thought if she could help it. But it had been forcing its way into her mind and often enough out her mouth. Every time she said it, it felt like dry heaving and she, unlike Lyle, had been given every opportunity to be unfaithful. She had been tempted, and had every time up to now chosen family, chosen Jason. She told herself that's what she was choosing now.

She stood up, went to the swing, and sat down next to Lyle and said, "We got that letter too."

Lyle turned to look at her, and she looked back at him and they shared the sudden intimacy of close quarters with a new person. They didn't say anything, just stayed like that until all at once they fell into each other. Fingers and lips first, no rhythm to any of it. The transition from simple conversation was so sudden the editor spliced in a shot of Tammy with Lyle's voice saying, "You know I've always thought you were beautiful," and then a shot of Lyle with Tammy's voice, "You aren't so bad looking yourself." The audio was recorded some time ago and originally referred to different people.

Lyle was as wracked with guilt as he was sure he wanted this, and both led him to a frantic pace. He pawed at her breasts, ripped at her jeans, fumbled with the clasp of her bra like he hadn't done this before. Tammy was surprised by his hunger, surprised as well that she responded to it.

When he pushed into her with little preparation and no warning, she dug her nails into his back because it felt good and more importantly it drove other thoughts from her mind.

For Lyle, her passion had the opposite effect, made the moment tragically more real, but he kept at it just the same, trying to empty his mind, already wondering what was wrong with him. He was right then certain that he was ruining his life. And somehow that only made it more important to come, at least until they heard the gunshot.

They both turned instantly in that direction towards Lyle and Cathy's house further down Old Military Road. And thus right into the camera crew still filming them, on a porch neither of them owned, in the very last shades of twilight.

And of course, more clearly than anyone else, Cathy heard the shot. Jason's truck wasn't more than twenty feet away when the gun went off.

The back glass shattered almost before the sound ripped through the air and for longer than felt right nothing at all seemed allowed to move. Then she started running to the car. The door opened and Jason fell out. Blood was trickling from both of his ears and his nose. He looked confused and lost and stupid, and all of it seemed to hurt so bad. "I didn't—I didn't—that wasn't even."

Cathy grabbed him and pulled him into her lap unsure of what else was required of her. And they were so arranged when four minutes later Lyle squealed into the driveway, Tammy beside him in the cab. Tammy went immediately to Jason, took him carefully from Cathy and took to comforting him, and asking him repeatedly if he was all right, to which he responded alternately, "My ears are ringing," or, "I just don't know what happened. I just don't know."

Cathy stood up, went to stand by Lyle. Her hand slipped into his, purely on instinct, a reaction she didn't even bother to make sense of. He said, "I saw her walking and I gave her a ride."

Down and Out

She didn't know how she knew, but she knew. As soon as he said it, she pulled her hand from his, and they stood there together and alone while Tammy cradled Jason's bleeding head and it took longer than it ought to have for anyone to call an ambulance.

Season 2, Episode 10:
You Can Never Go Back

Martin was thoroughly prepared to think deep and meaningful thoughts about what he was in the middle of. But he found it far easier to think nothing, never mind that it wasn't but another few hours to Fort Worth. Behind him the girls slept peacefully in their booster seats, both dreaming gape-mouthed like magnificent catfish, and behind them, the bags he'd packed without knowing exactly what he was doing, and behind that the mule staring right back at him re-chewing the grass he'd plucked from beside the road in Poteau, bouncing in the rickety trailer, and behind him the white van trailing with a cameraman lunging out the passenger window.

It had all made so much more sense when he'd got started.

Yes, it was the day he'd had—getting Jamie sent off to jail, Lyle and the mule, and all of it. But if it was anything it was the peanut butter sandwich. After Lyle had left, after the mule had his ASPSCA-mandated full serving of oats, it was dinnertime. Since the job, he hadn't had to go hungry to feed the girls, and, God, wasn't he thankful for that. But it didn't mean that there was much in the way of choice. Tonight it would be very large glasses of milk, packaged pre-sliced apples that had expired not twenty-four hours ago, and peanut butter sandwiches. There were precisely six slices of bread, two of which were the shriveled end pieces—the heel and the ass. Without hesitating but not without regretting it, he made the girls' sandwiches from the four standard slices and then made his from the two puckered remnants.

He set the table, and looked down at the tattered excuse of a sandwich in front of him. The spongy white bread was so flimsy the peanut butter had torn through, little globs the color of mud blooming through pond water. He had had worse, certainly, but there was something about the way it sat there on the plate. He watched the film crew get a close-up of the sandwich, frame him up to watch him eat it, and he realized that they were not going to make the sandwich seem symbolic in any way, and that was the part he found sad.

He called the girls to dinner, and when they came and sat and looked to him, he caught himself starting to say grace. He remembered the way Marla used to tease him for things like that, crossing himself when the ambulance passed him, reflexive Catholicism, she called it. But of course she wasn't here to make fun of him anymore, and so what the hell. He raised his hand in the sign of the cross and said, "In the name of the Father and the Son and the Holy Spirit. Bless us, O Lord, and these our gifts," and then he stopped, partially to make sure he still had the words right, and partially because both of the girls were staring at him confused and even a little worried. He let his hands open and his head fall into them and he sobbed openly and loudly, not looking at anything even after Stacy came up and wrapped herself around his right side and then Layne came to join on his left.

"It's okay, Daddy," said Stacy and hearing her say it was the first time he realized it wasn't and wouldn't be. She was only seven, for everything's sake.

Briseño

"She'll come back," said Layne. "Sissy promised," and then it was right there in front of him. An answer. Plain and simple. And so he kissed his daughters and told them he loved them for just long enough to feel like he was the one comforting them, but not long enough to change his mind. Then he packed everything that was clean—a medium-small pile on the loveseat—and told the girls to get into the car. They walked outside obediently but Layne's steps got shorter, and as she approached the porch steps she grabbed her sister's hand. Stacy looked at Layne and then off to Layne's left. She wrapped her arm around her sister. Martin saw this happen and was dumbfounded, struck stupid at how much it had turned out he had missed. He was so proud of his children for leaning on each other, so aghast that they had to.

"What about Horsey?" said Layne.

It is easier to forget about your mule than you'd imagine. He figured of course that the thing would be fine on its own, that the show was required to tend to it. But he could see from the quivering lip of his younger daughter that this would cause tears, and of that he had enough already. And so Martin hitched up the trailer and much to his surprise its passenger trotted in without so much as a please or a thank you. The girls supervised the loading procedure and, completely satisfied, climbed into the back seat where Stacey buckled Layne and then herself into their boosters.

For the first time in a very long time, he looked right into the camera. He was going to say something, to explain where they were going or why. But no words came. He just looked at his convex reflection, losing hair and dressed like he worked at a gas station, and eventually he just climbed in and started to drive away. Fifty miles down the road he wanted very much to climb into the talking head booth and explain himself. Not being able to explain himself left him feeling physically burdened. He wanted very much to tell someone, but even the girls seemed already to know, like it was all a bit too obvious and Martin had been the last one to figure it out. All the same he wanted to say it out loud just to hear the sound of it, I'm going to find my wife and bring her.

He had her address and her phone number and knew she wouldn't refuse to see him—knew it. He knew that if he said he was sorry, if he meant it when he told her how right she was, that he had made so many mistakes, so many, and that the only things that had ever mattered were now here together, where they ought to have been all along. That togetherness would be enough.

Every once in a while he caught the girls in the rear view, dozing, and he wondered how long it would be until they decided most things were his fault, and how wrong or right they would be. But by and large he stared forward, drawn onward by a force he pretended he didn't have time to contemplate.

But as the miles poured away, one thing hung in Martin's rearview mirrors, peeking out behind the trailer. Even when all he could see were headlights he could feel the camera boring into the back of his mule, his truck, his mind. It made for dangerously simple math. Marla had left him over the show. She wouldn't be a party to this, her words. And equally stupid was the wording of his contract, which it seemed foolish and unfair to remember so clearly, which said any attempt to avoid film crews was subject to forfeiture and cancellation. There really wasn't a choice to be made.

He pulled off for fuel, got out, put the filler in the tank. The film crew stopped beside him, and got out, sleepily, stretching into the cool night air, shuffled inside to use the facilities. As soon as two of the three were inside and occupied, he pulled the filler from the tank, hung it up, and scrambled back into the car, drove away as fast as six cylinders and a mule would allow.

For the next hundred miles, he looked more at the rear view then he did at the road, and if it weren't the very middle of the night he might easily have killed himself and others just by looking for ominous headlights in the background. But they never came, no matter how far behind he looked, and before it seemed fair, Fort Worth was right in front of him.

Jamie woke up and tried on several aphorisms akin to *Today is the first day of the rest of my life*, none of which did much for him. So he got up still uninspired, had coffee instead of a Pabst, burnt three eggs, and then headed on down to the church.

He found Fr. William in the sacristy, mopping while a film crew studied him intently, closing in on his face and vein-bound hands, another watching the room and the floor get cleaner.

"Well, it's about goddamn time," said Fr. William.

Jamie looked behind, and then asked, "Am I late?"

"These," Father stopped to complain with his hands, "friends of yours said you were coming by and wouldn't leave until you got here, so what took you so long?"

Jamie looked at his feet, "Well, um, Father, I'm here to do good."

Down and Out

The priest looked him over surprised but not for very long before he shrugged and handed him the mop. "Do the chapel next."

And so he did. And when the floor was as clean as he could get it, he found a rag and dusted everything he could reach, made the church, those parts of it he was certain he could touch, glow like a tongue of fire.

Jamie looked at the work he'd done, and felt a simple satisfaction in spite of what would turn out to be a three-day hangover. It meant little, but it was done, and he went to find Fr. William.

He was in his study, a second, larger pair of glasses trembling at the edge of his profound nose. Jamie walked in and looked at his shoes and waited. Then he made a noise, and then a larger noise, and then said, "Um," to which Father finally responded to with, "Well, what now?"

Jamie was hoping for an answer to that very question, so getting asked it was more than a touch unsettling. Father looked up and took off the second pair of glasses, and Jamie started, "Well, sir, you went and came and talked to me last night and I—"

The priest interrupted him with a gesture. "They told me they'd only let you out if I came and chewed your ass out. I figured I owed your ma at least that." This was true; a production assistant had stopped by the church and explained that Jamie had been arrested, and that they would arrange his release, but that for continuity's sake they had to make it look like the priest had done it, and they could only do it if he would yell at Jamie and then read whatever it is that card had said. It was not at all the first time he'd bailed out a parishioner, but it was the first time it had required memorizing lines. The priest thought this explanation should have settled the matter, but Jamie went on.

"The man who came after you, he said I had a choice."

Father thought to ask what the hell he was talking about, but decided it was all about the same most ways. "I suppose we all do, son. But I don't know what it is you thought I could do for you."

Jamie shrugged into his hands. Mopping the floor, he had the mistaken sense that everything was just starting to work out. He was getting less sure by the minute. "The man said I could pick to be good or be evil, but I had to pick one."

"And you figured I was in charge of being good, is that it? If all you had to do was say yes to it, don't you think heaven would be a touch crowded? A better priest might tell you to pray over it—but why don't you do what I do? When it comes to two things, do the harder one—and hope that that's enough."

Jamie wanted to say more, a whole lot more, but what words would you choose and how would you say it? Can you tell a priest you need better answers than he's given? And what did Fr. William know about hard choices? Not a day went by that Jamie didn't think of the day his mother had called him at the university, or of the funeral—her crying in thanks at the sacrifice he was making. But he'd done it, left behind God knows what and made a sacrifice, one so deep he never even had to think about it. Leaving came natural, as he'd known what he was expected to do.

He figured there wasn't much else to say, so Jamie walked through the church and toward his truck. Before he got there, two more vehicles sped into the parking lot. First was the white production van which emptied quickly, a second production crew spilling out and taking form with all the precision of a pit crew. Then before any more of the surprise could wear off came the second van, the door opened and pawnshop Bobby stuck his head out and yelled, "Get in!"

Jamie started a step in that direction because it was his nature to do what he was told, but he stopped to think about what Father had just told him, wondered how much of his life had been shaped by forces such as this, and for how long.

There was a choice in front of him. One choice was easy, the other murky and unclear and doubtful. And he thought of every choice he'd ever made and thought maybe, for once, he ought to make the hard choice. It was, then and now, probably what his mother would have wanted. And so he gritted his teeth, and nodded, and climbed into the van.

Fort Worth was, as it turned out, almost too close. Before Martin had come to grips with much of anything he was swinging the trailer off the interstate and into the gridded streets. Marla's neighborhood was on the Southside of the town, tucked up against the freeway, under the shadow of grain silos and what used to be a steel mill. Martin had been here of course. Marla had taken him to her home, introduced him to the few relatives she talked to. But that, he realized, had been ten years ago.

He drove down Hemphill Street towards downtown, looked at the panaderías, the carnicerías, the botánica, the fried chicken places. It was bright and alive and it made him feel lost and all the way out of place. He felt like he was supposed to be afraid here. He had never seen so many, he knew he wasn't supposed to say Mexicans but couldn't think of the other word, in one place together. It made him turn and look at his own daughters, see them as part of something he knew nothing of. He had never seen so many streetlights or trash cans or windows or curbs either, but somehow it was the beautiful faces of old women that stuck in his mind.

He found the place easy enough. It was an older house on the corner of Jones and Bolt, white with blue trim and a stoop, exactly the kind of place you would picture when you said *big city*, rickety with a yard full of weeds. As luck would have it, there was a parking space right in front of her house, big enough even for the trailer.

Martin hadn't slept since early in the morning before, knew what he and for that matter the girls must look like. But at this point, he thought, it almost argued for him, and he and the girls clambered up the stairs feeling curiously unburdened and not realizing why.

If he had been asked, Martin would have been unable to describe his feelings, had no words in his head or his mouth, no will or way to articulate what he thought would happen next. All he saw when he closed his eyes was her face. Marla, ageless, perfect, kinder than he deserved.

He knocked on the door, heard shuffling but no answer.

He knocked again, and the shuffling grew more frantic. Someone was trying to get somewhere fast. He reached to knock again, but the door swung open in front of his fist, just like he'd knocked only once.

"Martin!" he heard her say, and her voice offered acceptance and forgiveness and warmth and love and everything he wanted but knew he didn't deserve. But he was staring at his own distorted face, blinking back in the convex face of a camera lens.

Season 2, Episode 11:
Right in the Eye

Sometimes making reality television is easy. Sometimes a prominent character experiences a traumatic injury, and in those instances all you have to do is be there. Sometimes all it takes is a tripod and a hospital waiting room and Tammy Johnson holding her kids, yes, all of them, her eyes batting worriedly between the door where she thought the doctor would come from and Lyle, posted hangdog in the corner of the room trying not to notice himself. You don't need an establishing shot of the squat building known as the Paris Hospital, or even an explanation as to why exactly the gun had gone off. No, in the best of scenarios, you just need to be there when the doctor comes out and sighs, heavily and wearily and like he wishes better news for everyone in the room, most of all himself. And when that doctor says, "Mrs. Johnson," and everyone in the room starts to listen, all you have to do is be present. She will cry, good news or bad.

Whether you're telling the story of a miracle or a tragedy remains to be unfolded, but something worth watching is going down. And that is in its own way beautiful. Beautiful like Tammy clutching three boys in two hands of joy chased by unsureness and confusion. And yes, as it turned out, Jason would be just fine. The cartridge was a blank, no shrapnel had been found. The ringing in his ears, a tone just shy of a b-flat, was likely permanent, but he would go on. The wife and the children rushed into the private room the show had paid for.

They crowded into Jason's lap, pressing against him as

if to spread out the burden amongst them. Jason pressed back, their caresses each a tactile explosion of love made only slightly more intense by the morphine and the sweet bouncing tone that seemed like the whisper of the universe. It felt good, better than good. Right.

Outside in the waiting room Lyle waited, steeped in quiet and his thoughts. He had never felt more alone in his life. Now the shot widened. Cathy was a single hard orange plastic armrest away, likewise quiet and thoughtful, likewise alone. Neither knew what they were waiting for. Both were aware of everything they weren't talking about.

He kept sneaking an eye at her, tilting only the smallest part of his neck, hoping to catch her glimpsing back. She only stares ahead, only sees the backwards written TIXE on the window of the door they could hear Tammy thanking Jesus through. Long after it became clear that no one needed them here, they got up and walked to the truck. The ride home was seven miles, and took them past downtown, the two stoplights now retired for the evening, past the factory cold and dead and easy to miss, past the Johnsons' place where Jason's truck had been towed to. The moonlight glares off the blue cloth bench seat. And they drove past Jamie's house, only recently reoccupied. Both noted that the light was on, watched until it was no longer safe or possible, respectively.

They entered their home with no discussion, went about their business with no interaction, made it to bed, and woke up and cooked and ate what they had for breakfast, and went in search of more and came home and cooked and ate and cleaned after that. And they said nothing, not to each other and not to the camera. It was all anybody could talk about

Down and Out

Their house was a little over nine hundred square feet with a single bathroom. Their movement required a certain unspoken level of coordination, like a ballet set to a funeral mass.

There was a simple desperate beat to this mating dance in reverse, the energy it took to maintain a commendation in its own right. Two different editors were relieved from duty for being unable to cut a sequence of these events lasting less than four minutes. There is a limit to how long one can watch someone not do something. But Lyle and Cathy stayed at it, burdened by a mystery, silenced by we knew just what. To our knowledge, they hadn't so much as shared a word since just before Lyle left Cathy sitting on the front porch. For three days, it remained just the same. They had literally nothing but time. Which is always true until of course it isn't.

They let Jason go home the morning after he'd got there. He would be fine, more or less, the doctor explained, and it wasn't as if he had insurance to cover the recommended psychiatric evaluation. The boys had picked flowers from the beds in front of the hospital, and made a card with crayons and paper the nurses had given them. It said, "Get well soon, Dad." It was decorated with stock cars and deer and red razorback pigs. Though he kept insisting he was fine, Tammy took him upstairs and put him in bed with the television remote. Jason let himself be led to bed, kissed the boys when they came one at a time to hope he felt better and to say goodnight. When Tammy came to bed, he left her to read while he pretended to doze and then after they said goodnight and after the lights were off and things had stilled, after she closed her eyes and just before her breathing settled, he whispered loud enough to be heard in the next room, "Don't move."

She was awake instantly. Ready, in spite of his advice, to pounce or to run to the boy's room. "Be still," said Jason. "I think we might finally be done. But I have to listen. Please." For forty seconds she froze and thought of dreads too vague for shape and then out of the dark almost startling her. "I don't hear them. But we might not have long."

"You don't hear what?"

"Cameras, microphones, electronic surveillance devices. I figured it out—they're always watching." She needed to see his face to understand why he thought that was a secret, and so she reached for the lamp. Through the darkness his hand found her wrist, wrapped around it with a sound they both could hear. "I didn't fire that weapon in the truck, and it wasn't no accident neither."

He paused like he expected a response. None came and so he went on. "I damn sure didn't squeeze the trigger, even the cops know that. But I left the safety on, I know I did, I always do. I know, I checked it, I'm absolutely certain."

"It's the show," he said, too loud for his own liking and so he corrected himself, said it again softer, "It's the show."

She didn't understand.

"They made the gun go off, they rigged it."

"Baby, they said it was an accident. Accidents happen to everybody."

By now their eyes had adjusted and she could see him staring at her cold and clear-eyed. "When was the last time anything was an accident around here?" he said.

She didn't have an answer. She wanted to say that it had been their plan, their plan all along, but it hadn't.

"But they didn't shoot you—they couldn't. They wouldn't—"

"Ruin our lives?"

She didn't know what to say, and so that was all they said. They settled into each other's arms, not at all clear who was comforting whom or from what.

Jamie had gotten into the van. For an appreciable moment it was quite the buzz throughout camp. Bobby spoke into the radio in a tone he hoped vainly Jamie couldn't hear—"He, um...he got in the van." He clicked the channel closed, heard it open on the other end but only heard the half-shaped static. And then, "Come back."

Bobby came back, repeated himself, clarified—Jamie was certainly and absolutely in the van. Jamie chose that moment to notice that the cameras—all of them—were off. The camera operators set down their burdens and rose up looking all too foreign, their whole frames unused to light and space like the scalp of a third baseman. They lit cigarettes and touched their skin where the camera was and would be, looked at each other, saw themselves.

"Did he see the priest?" asked the box Bobby was talking into. He had seen the priest. "Did he clean the church?" He had cleaned the church. "But he got in the van." This one was a statement, not a question. Bobby confirmed just the same—he had in fact got in the van.

"Well, why the hell did he do that?"

Bobby turned and looked at Jamie and then back towards the non-direction they were headed in. "You want me to ask him?"

Jamie didn't know whether to laugh or get nervous. Because of course he didn't quite know himself. Part of it was Father's advice. He knew for certain that it would have been easier to just go home, to let it all just slide away. The producer had said it—do good, do bad, do nothing. Jamie was dead certain at this point that he had eliminated choice three. Good or bad—indifferent was off the table. Like it or not his role in all this was likely set. All that was left was to figure out what all that might mean.

We could only imagine a quiet squabbling, a hasty call back at headquarters. Scripted is the wrong word for what they did. Scripted doesn't do justice to it. More like making a clock using only kittens as the moving parts. It was like forecasting the weather down to the raindrop. They sculpted time, set forth a path not insisted upon, only hinted at. They had domesticated reality. But every shaping hand is bitten, all of them always. To say that they were unprepared, however, would be to overstep it a touch.

It took only a few minutes before the voice on the other end of the radio crackled back into the lack of conversation. "Roger that. You are clear to proceed with LCR. Proceed to location fifteen. Rendezvous in thirty."

Bobby widened his eyes and smiled and asked the other end to repeat themselves even though it was clear he'd heard the first time. He put down the radio and said, "Gentlemen, we're about to all get famous." The crew all knew what he was talking about. A tiny cheer went up. Jamie wondered if now was the best time to ask what the hell he'd done, but decided against it.

Location fifteen turned out to be the old Double Deuce, now faithfully identified only as BAR. It was at that point eleven in the morning, and Jamie was unsure if the place was even open. But when the crew pushed on the door it swung in, and Jamie walked in with them. Inside it was darker than it had any right to be. The sun outside was cut off in a way that would be almost magical if it weren't so menacing. Jamie looked around and realized they weren't alone. Three or four other souls were already at the bar even this early, men and a woman Jamie had seen all his life but never looked at.

"Sit at the bar and order a beer," Bobby said, and Jamie sat down. The barkeeper came over and Jamie hesitated. Part of it was of course the hour, but more it was the location and the company and everything that had happened in the last twenty-four hours. He turned to Bobby and said, "Can it be one of those fake ones?"

Bobby stopped and considered. "You'll want the real one. You don't know what happens next. I do. Trust me, you want the beer."

"Is that a yes or a no?" Jamie said looking at the bartender and not at the man he was talking to.

"Your funeral," said Bobby, and so the bartender brought the near beer. When he'd opened it and set it in front of Jamie, Bobby said, "Drink it."

Jamie looked at him, communicating that he knew what beer was for, and took a long slow pull, his hand covering the part of the label that says non-alcoholic. "All of it," said Bobby, and without stopping for a breath Jamie did just that, finished the drink in a single pull. It didn't taste bad, sort of like a beer-flavored soda.

Bobby pointed at the bartender, "Can you open four more of those please?" The bartender shrugged and did as he was told.

"Drink another one," Bobby said to Jamie.

"Didn't I just do that? Can't you just loop it or something?" Jamie said, looking straight ahead into the filthy mirror in the bar, looking at himself.

"Don't be hostile now. You chose this," said Bobby. Jamie looked at him. He wasn't angry or even forceful. He was only patient. Jamie picked up another of the non-alcoholic beers and swilled it down, and then with no prompting picked up the one next to it and did the same thing. Though the label swore they were all but free of alcohol, Jamie's head was swimming just a little. He hadn't drunk that much of anything that fast since a party in a field some years back.

Bobby looked at the cameramen and confirmed that they'd gotten the footage, that it was as good as they hoped, and then said something into his walkie talkie, confirming that someone or something was in place. "All right we're good in here," he said to the whole room. "Jamie, let's go, next shot's in the parking lot." Jamie nodded and climbed to his feet.

By the time he made his way back outside, the camera crew was in front of him and set up to film him making his exit. Though he was inside not half an hour, Jamie's eyes had grown used to the lack of light, and he threw his hand up to shield himself. And when he pulled his hand away, Jamie saw that he was standing face to face with perhaps the largest man he'd ever seen.

He had to be six foot four and weighed three hundred pounds if he weighed an ounce. He had wide-set large eyes and a shaved head. He wore a white t-shirt a size too small that the crew had selected specifically because it made his skin look darker.

"Hi, I'm Robert," the giant said.

Jamie introduced himself, stuck out his hand to shake. Instead Robert threw a right cross and dropped him to his knees, and then apologized for it.

Jamie screamed and asked in not so many words for an explanation.

"Sorry, Jamie," Bobby said. "We have to get a natural reaction. Part of what makes it work. Stand him up and hit him again, Robby."

Before Jamie had a chance to even look confused about it, Robert complied, pulling him up and setting him on his feet, then hitting him again, this time in the stomach and then over the back.

Jamie coughed and spit blood and managed to ask why this was happening.

"You know, we're not sure just yet. Truth be told, it's just the kind of thing people want to see, a redneck getting his ass kicked by a large black man. It scores well with a lot of key groups. I'll explain later." He asked the crew if they had enough footage, got a noncommittal answer, motioned to Robert for one more go 'round.

"Like I said, I sure am sorry," Robert said. "I, I want to get into television too."

Jamie tried to smile, but his cheeks were too swollen to let it happen. "It's all right," he said. "You hit like an actor."

Next he remembered, Jamie was in the van, and Bobby was taking another one-sided phone call. He saw Jamie sit up and started talking without turning around. "You did good back there. I've been planning this for a long time. See, the truth of it is that no one wants to hear the truth of it. I've been at this since the very beginning, seriously, I was a cameraman. We thought we were doing groundbreaking shit then, entirely new. Back then we just used to put them together in the house and wait. Film and film and wait. We pretended that we were waiting for them to start acting like themselves, but it was always the opposite. I've seen months of my life spent behind a lens cut to nothing in an editing room, like it never even happened. And what was left wasn't the most honest part, just the most compelling.

"And then we thought to start showing it to them, the footage we cut and that was what really did it. Because as soon as you showed them who they were supposed to be, it got so much easier, so much quicker. And the show didn't get worse, didn't get less real, whatever that's supposed to mean—it improved. They meant it harder once they knew what they were supposed to mean.

"And then I figured it out. That it was some deep animal thing. A need for story and meaning and whatever, but also something else. Like how when you pass the wreck on the interstate you always look for a body, always. I think we like reality because it's both at once, an excuse to believe what we know can't be. But really that's not the point.

"So that's where the plan came from—why the pretense? Why the lie? Why not make reality TV in reality? You, me, these other gentleman, we're professionals. And so from now on. No more bullshit.

"This is a new show, and the new show is the old show without the moping and the crying and Lyle's stupid chin. We're going to give the people what they want. Like that back there. I don't know how we'll cut it yet, but it's like this. People want to know why this town's got zero people of color, and if they don't want to know it's because they like it that way. We show a black man and you fighting, we get both sides. The ones that wanted there to be black people get to see a black person, the ones that liked there being no black people get something to be afraid of." And then almost before he stopped he added, "It's not racist, it's just pragmatic."

Jamie thought about it for a minute, his first thought being that pragmatic wasn't the opposite of much at all. Mainly what came to him was how out of the ordinary it was for any one person to talk so long without stopping. But it all more or less made sense. So he said, "So who kicks my ass next?"

Bobby laughed out loud. "I knew you were the smart one."

"We're heading back to your place so you can get a shower. Then it's either the Indian casino across the border in Tahlequah or the honky-tonk in Ozark by the freeway. Your call. But between the two of us, it'd be a real solid if you'd take the casino—it's way less work all the way around."

Jamie didn't give himself time to think about it. "Oh, hell, let's do both."

Bobby turned around and looked at Jamie. He tried to share what was supposed to be a meaningful look, but Jamie didn't know what it was supposed to mean, had trouble thinking about much besides his aching jaw.

Bobby turned back. "I knew you were the one," he said, and then, "oh, and we'll shoot the intro at your place before we leave."

When Jamie got out of the shower he found clothes laid out on the bed, overalls he was sure weren't his, the old steel toes he used to mow the lawn, no shirt.

Outside, his front porch had been neatly appointed with amateur taxidermy and a sea of empty beer cans. In front of him, they set up the big lights to counter the ensuing August night. It took a while for his eyes to adjust enough to see the cue cards.

Briseño

"Y'all, I useda work at the gear factory down in Paris, but that closed up and since then, well, I been getting by. Don't matter what, don't matter how, if there's money to be made or a good time doing it—well, I'm the one to call. I'm Jamie Mallett and this here is *Logan County Raw*."

He couldn't help but think of last season, so long ago, when they would ask him to repeat himself so as to sound natural and the very concept had cinched his eyebrows together. But acting was a skill like everything else. And now, Jamie was surprised to find he did it exceptionally well.

"One take," said Bobby. "One take! I knew it! I knew it! All right, we've got to get to the casino. If we're lucky, we'll be done with this tonight."

Miles away, responding to something as different as could be, Jason Johnson let fly a pained yet joyful whisper, "Aww, Bubba."

And we the town say, *Amen*, which means about the same thing. Down the road a piece, Lyle and Cathy are yet to speak to each other, and again all of us say, *Amen*. Martin and his daughters and his wife are feeding Riscky's Barbecue to a mule named Horsey. *Amen*. Fr. William is saying mass by himself in a chapel not large enough to accommodate another, and it is all our prayers that he lifts up. In the name of the Lord. *Amen*.

Season 2, Episode 12:
It Means the End of a Thing

Marla had been on the show since the beginning. Martin stared at her confused, in shock, and nearly shaking from the drive. It didn't begin to feel real, not even that next morning when he woke up wrapped in her arms, more complete than he'd perhaps ever felt. It wasn't real even with the camera in the corner, catching the glint in her morning eye before she said, "Get out—this is no pay per view," and proceeded to make love to him in a way that hurt in its emotional weight. His body remembered things about her that he'd forgotten and though what he wanted was a cup of fresh coffee and a long talk, he found himself made to feel as though everything was in some important and elusive sense better.

Yet even still, with his family reunited, it felt like a bath in needles. Dread was inevitable like rainclouds, but along with it was something nagging and it took him a great while to realize that it was honest and unadulterated sensation. It felt damn stupid to say he hadn't felt things in quite some time—just yesterday he'd felt angry and confused and panicked as well as dismayed in a general sense. But it was more than true that he'd been more or less reacting to simple stimuli since the day Marla had left him. Had he punched Jamie and then had him arrested for the pleasure? Was he gainfully employed at the Outpost out on Route 22? Did he own a mule? And why had so very little of this mattered before? He looked at his daughters, skinnier than he thought was right but recently scrubbed clean by their mother, their cherry-wood curls tamed and softened, the literal manifestation of a mother's love.

And then there was Marla, glowing, smelling exactly like herself. And so for a night and a day he let it wash over him, let it happen, while the tape in his mind whirred in a simple rewind. Throughout all of it he was naturally on camera. But they never asked him to step into the van to talk about it and he spent time with his daughters and he soaked up the stultifying August sunshine and noticed everything was still blooming here, not dried out and dead in the bake of the sun. He watched his children disappear and his wife turn a corner with a bottle of champagne and a smile.

And together they sat in the window of the little house, knees touching on the bench seat. Through all this his mind kept spooling, spooling back, until with a soft click it stopped, and he looked around anew and saw his wife—his wife—how she gave off pretty like heat and he felt it just bouncing off him, her greenish eyes flickering in a light meant to resemble candles. He took her hand, felt the weight and the warmth of the thing and said what had finally at long last occurred to him. "You could've come back to us."

It wasn't a question, but it wasn't an accusation, not yet. "You could have, six months ago—before the gas station and Jamie and, and you could have been there. You could have—"

She nodded and dropped her head, and then met his gaze. "You're right, I could have."

And then there was a pause here, but not one big enough to fit even a single *We needed you* or a *How could you*—space only for a solitary "Why?" which Martin whispered before she went on.

"They told me not to." For a spell, Martin was so far removed from it all that he wasn't sure who they were. "They said that you would come to me. Come any day now, any moment. You would pack and leave and we could be together. They said that the show needed it, that it made it better, that it was good for Paris if I waited. They kept saying they needed you to earn it."

"But, but you left me because you didn't want this..." he said, unsure already if what he was saying was true.

She looked at him softly, put her hand on his cheek. "Baby, I've been under contract longer than you have."

As it turned out, they'd offered Marla the exact same thing they'd offered Martin—everything she'd ever wanted. In her case, that had been enough money and a good reason to leave Paris behind forever.

She explained all this in an offhand manner, as if it were obvious, and really it should have been.

What Martin felt just then went well beyond all the words he'd ever known, and yet here those sons of bitches go, right in front of God and everybody. It seemed as though he ought to be choosing something, deciding whether Marla's betrayal, if that was the right word for it, was significant enough to merit drastic action, or if she had earned as much, as in his own way had he. Still if this was indeed the woman he had wrapped his life around for so many years, if their love had in fact survived, then what did that mean? It occurred to him then that when she had left him, that in that moment in the living room formerly known as theirs, when she had turned away from him, it was then that he loved her the most. Loved her for the strength it took and the conviction it came from, the fierceness of her belief that had made her all that she was to begin with.

And yet how could he blame her for doing exactly what he'd done. There was that other hand, counterargument upon counterargument and the vast array of static hum that builds up with such a line of inquiry. He needed time to sort this all out, to weigh one thing against the other. But as it turned out, it wasn't up to him.

Marla came up to him with a sweet smile and said, "The girls are in their car seats, and Horsey's in the trailer. We have to get back to Paris in case the Outpost gets robbed." She gave him soft beautiful eyes that hid nothing and she held his hand, but she did not pull. And so he rose on his own and went with her and even though it was the bright middle of the day, he was asleep before she'd found the freeway.

For the third morning in a row, Jamie woke up sober and early and drove over to the church to clean up what mess might have accumulated since yesterday. Fr. William met him at the church's front door, an extra dose of limp in his gait. "Radio says storm's coming." With no further explanation he led the way to the garden shed to point at a ladder, which Jamie needed to latch the shutters over the stained-glass windows. Even from a few feet off the ground, the air had a different flavor to it and clouds were stirring in the west and south. Jamie didn't need a weather report, just common sense. Still, for now the late summer weather was cooler than it ought to be and Jamie felt almost chilly in his shorts and shirt, looking in backwards at Jesus falling for the first time. The sun shone around the clouds if not through them, and it was pleasant to be outside and meaningfully if not gainfully employed. He worked quickly, was finished before noon and started to walk back towards the office where he expected to find Fr. William.

But Father was in front of the church on the benches next to the walkway, facing the square, looking at nothing in particular. When he heard Jamie coming he slid over so Jamie sat down. They sat together sharing the opposite of conversation. Jamie thought very briefly of his own father and the priest spoke, "So which is it? Are you the good guy or the bad guy?"

"I don't rightly know. It's the bad guy on the show. They got me acting a fool just to make us all look bad. But I ain't been drinking, and I talked them out of having me set somebody's hay on fire. I mean they'd have paid for it and all, but it didn't seem right.

"They let me come here every morning so far, and the boy that runs it, Bobby LaDue, he's a son of a bitch, but he wants to do his job the right way and I can live with that."

Father nodded and went back to not speaking. After a while he said, "Jesus loved whores and tax collectors so I suppose you're in good company. Doing right and doing wrong, they're probably both better than not doing."

The white van pulled up and Bobby rolled down the window.

"I guess that's me," said Jamie as he got up and dusted his hands against his jeans. "I'll see you tomorrow, then." He turned and walked slowly towards the van.

"Wait a second, son."

Jamie turned and watched the priest climb to his feet. Who even knew how old he was. He'd been at this post as long as Jamie or any of us could remember. His back was still straight, but he took longer getting over to Jamie than seemed exactly right, the timing slowed to match music none could hear. The priest walked right up to Jamie, close enough for a handshake and then closer. Jamie could see the milky yellows of his eyes through his glasses. "Bow your head, you damn jack," the priest said, and once Jamie had, he felt the priest's hand on his forehead, the callused pads of the fingers.

"Lord, bless this child and protect him. He's asked for a way forward and I'll ask with him. Show him the way ahead, whatever that might be. Father, Son, Holy Spirit."

Jamie lifted his head, ashamed he didn't feel any better. But the priest nodded, seemed satisfied, and so Jamie turned around and headed for the van. Fr. William made his way back to the bench where he sat, watching the clouds leak out over the sky.

Jamie opened the door and nodded hello at the four men in the van. They were all nice enough and it was good to have coworkers again. In the last two days they had filmed enough material for three full episodes, complete with reaction shots and voice-overs. Jamie had been thrown out of a Waffle House, a Walmart, and all three bars. He'd lost his shirt literally at the Indian Casino, traded a trailer hitch for a tattoo, and had, as Bobby kept putting it, "trimmed all the fat from reality" and "made an exciting product."

"So, boss, what are we doing today?" Jamie asked.

"Crossover. You and Jason Johnson are going to buy a bunch of liquor on a Saturday and then bootleg it on a Sunday," said Bobby.

Jamie nodded, almost used to the strangeness of his own actions, but he still couldn't help but ask, "And we're doing that on a Wednesday?"

Down and Out

"Confirm. Bootlegging turns out to be a felony, and we can only film you committing misdemeanors," he said, distracted by something he was writing on the clipboard. Jamie nodded, pleased he wouldn't have to get punched or change pants. He couldn't help but think about what used to make for a good day at work—a lack of accidents, a smile from a coworker, not noticing the passage of the day. Really there weren't too many good days or too many bad days back then. Now, you always had one or the other. He didn't feel sorry for himself then or now.

That was what was on his mind until they pulled into the Johnsons' driveway, when what was on his mind instantly became the three boys. Junior, Ricky, and Dale were all three wearing nothing but cutoffs and a thick shaggy coat of River Valley mud. They had each other in a three-way chokehold, each boy with his hands on another one's neck, looks of dangerous determination in their eyes. "I'm gonna kill you!" shouted Dale as he lunged towards both his brothers and the three of them fell over into the mud. From the better-lit side of the scene, the Johnsons' camera crew was set up with two different cameras capturing different angles of the mayhem. The boys stopped as soon as the van pulled into the driveway, pulled each other up, and waved.

When the van had stopped, Jamie walked over to them. "What you boys doing?" he asked.

"Oh, we didn't have much better to do so we figured we'd just come out here and play in the mud," said Ricky. He was the oldest of the three, and when he spoke the other two looked at him and nodded when he finished.

Jamie looked at the camera crews, now filming him talk to the boys. "Nobody told you to play in the mud?"

"Nah," said Ricky. "'Course once they came out and filmed it, we figured it'd be a good idea to act mad some, just in case, you know." He stopped, spat a wad of dirt into the mud puddle. "What y'all filming today?"

Jamie told him that he and the boys' father would be pretending to bootleg. The boys hemmed and hawed knowledgably. "A Wednesday for Sunday shoot," said the little one. That made Jamie smile, and he would have stayed there talking to them for a while longer, but Bobby came up behind him and told him to make his way to the porch to talk to Tammy.

Four production assistants walked ahead of him and entered the house. To do so, they walked either around or right over Tammy, who was sitting on the porch smoking a long thin cigarette. They acted so confidently as if she weren't there that Jamie wanted not to believe his eyes. One of the PAs came back almost immediately and reported to Bobby, "He's still at it."

From the porch Tammy sneered, "I could have told you that."

Bobby also stepped over Tammy, and as he did he told Jamie, "Comfort her," without looking her direction. Except for the children and the cameras, then Jamie and Tammy were alone.

He wanted to go and sit with her, felt that would be most appropriate, but didn't because the two hadn't spoken more than three dozen words to each other in as many years of living down the road from each other and it felt right to play by the old rules of politeness rather the new rules of television.

Jamie thought to run his hand through his hair and stuffed both mitts deep in his pockets. The silence, all too natural when they weren't being directed, took hold. But then she said, "So they gave you the spinoff." She waited for a reaction that didn't come. "Suppose they would. Most things you work hard at don't come out right." This wasn't bitter, just factual. A nod to a life spent well and half spent up.

Jamie looked for a way to contribute to this conversation, but all he could come up with was to gaze above the roofline. "Storm's coming. Looks bad."

Tammy nodded and reached for another cigarette. "That's what they say."

Bobby leaned out onto the porch and threw his chin in Jamie's general direction.

Jamie answered the silent command and said *Excuse me* as he went by. Then, without really knowing why, he turned to her and said the thing that came to mind, his father's words, "Everything will be all right because all right's what we'll call how it'll be."

She searched out his eyes to give a silent kind of thank you. This was the second twinge in Jamie that he didn't understand, this one strong enough to make him wonder if he wasn't medically ill even if he was fairly certain that this was all a mental thing.

Once inside Jamie was hustled upstairs, where he and Bobby and a two-angle crew were crammed into the Johnson's bedroom. Jason Johnson was under a blanket in the corner.

Rich explained matter-of-factly. "You and him are good old buddies from way back in the day. He's having a hard time, you're going to cheer him up and then the thing with the liquor."

Jamie looked at Jason as best he could. From under the

blanket Jason asked, "They put you up to this?"

"I was gonna ask you the same thing," Jamie said.

Jason retreated further into his own shadow. "Yeah, but you didn't, did you? They must think I've gone soft in the head." This puzzled Jamie.

"Is that the same they as put us up to whatever it is we're put up to?"

Jason nodded, which is to say the blanket he was under shook up and down.

Jamie thought it easier to finish the thought than risk an open-ended situation. "Is they the show?"

The blanket nodded profusely.

Jamie thought for a minute and shrugged. "Well, hell yeah, they put me up to it. That's what you and me call a job these days. They put me up to a fair amount. But, by God, a man has to work if he can and so I say the two of us go and see what we can do to put some food on the goddamn table." He held out his hand and because things had taken on an easy kilter in the last day, he expected nothing less than complete cooperation. He did not expect Jason to throw the blanket off, thrust his head to the side, and spurt, "Tammy fucked Lyle Younse." And then as if settling any lingering doubt, "It's true."

Jamie turned right to the camera. "Well, what in the hell's the move here?" But the camera and the man running it and Bobby behind him said nothing. He turned back to Jason. It was the first time in several days that he realized he wasn't just on a television show, that what was going on around him was in most ways actually going on around him. "Well, hell, I mean, that's, uh, Lyle did that? I would never have thought, you know. I just."

From beneath the blanket again, "They made her." A

whisper, and then again. "They made her." That time a scream.

And from downstairs and maybe outside at the top of her considerable voice, "You made me. You fucking told me to. You, Jason Johnson, and you shot yourself while we were at it." As she spoke, her voice got closer and her footfalls landed in the cracks between her words and then she pushed past the camera and was pulling at the blanket, screaming, "Get out here, motherfucker, and tell them it's true. Say it. Tell them how it really happened."

Jason clung to the blanket, hollering all the time, and when it was words it was, "Not on camera. We can't give them any more."

The camera crew watched this the same way they'd watched everything else. Bobby was already in deep consideration as to how to best use such excellent footage.

Jamie looked and saw only the pain—white hot and naked—looked and saw Tammy rip the blanket away and Jason curl up into a far tighter ball than you would think possible for a man his size. Tammy was ready for murder, just look in her eyes, but as soon as she saw her husband curled up like that, she sprung onto him and started heaving in sobs. "I'm so sorry," she said and, "I didn't mean it, I swear." Jason wouldn't move his hand from his face to look at her.

Jamie saw that and he saw Bobby seeing it and he wondered if Tammy and Jason were both right. What if it was equal parts conspiracy and your own goddamned fault? And the main question, looking at the two of them not even yet able to hold each other, their children outside and alone with strangers watching them, was what would it take to make it all right again? Or was this the situation we all had to adapt to now?

We will never know the truth about what Jamie was thinking then, because he never told anybody. But it had to have been right there that whatever it was broke. It had to have been.

Finally Jamie said, "I'm not supposed to be here." And he walked back outside. The three boys were no longer in the mudpile, but were trying to clean up under the hose; the eldest had found his shirt.

Jamie looked at the three of them, nodded. A thing had clicked into place deep inside of him, a shift of perspective that brought a sudden misleading sense of understanding. And even in that first moment before he knew just what he'd decided and long before he'd known why, it felt not dangerous or destructive or painful or wrong—rather it felt like sweet undeserved clarity, just this side of holy, almost like redemption.

He saw through the open door that his camera crew was saying goodbyes to their camera crew.

He looked at the boys. "It'll be all right. I promise. It'll be all right." He heard the echo of his father but he swallowed it. It had taken him all these many years to understand it wasn't meant as fatalism, was at least halfway about hope, halfway about Fr. William's mess about making tough decisions. But kids didn't need bitter drink philosophy. He didn't know it all, but he knew that. The camera crew poured out of the narrow doorway, looking neither happy nor sad, only busy and out of place. Jamie looked at them, and it all got easier, a little more straightforward in his mind.

"Don't worry, boys—I got me an idea," he said, and they looked up, neither confused nor surprised nor expectant.

Down and Out

"Jamie Mallett—Storm Chaser," he said. And with no further conversation and a pause only long enough for a slow panning shot of the sky, which had turned a stomach-twisting color like the worst possible decision at the frozen daiquiri stand, a color that tells a deep part of you to run and to hide. To see it was to feel guilty for what maybe you didn't know but probably you did. It felt wrong. And so they filmed the sky, that color of green, and then Jamie climbed behind the wheel and off they went.

Lyle and Cathy still hadn't talked. Cathy was using the silence and the space it opened to reinvest herself in cleanliness. If she'd been thinking about it, she might have said that she was sorting things, taking charge in her way. So many things in her life that had gotten out of reach that the black stain tattooed to a cookie sheet could be a metaphor. The silence wasn't just on the outside anymore.

Lyle for his part was holding together not so well. From the corner of his eyes, which was the only way he felt safe looking at her for very long, he kept seeing something that wasn't supposed to be there. Not just a glare or her new absence of a hairstyle or the darkening circles under her eyes, but more, a face. An entirely different face, a different person, a stranger. And it felt like he deserved it. And it felt like he knew why but couldn't remember. And it felt like it had been this way forever and could never no matter what change and that's when he decided it wouldn't matter, couldn't, and so he turned to her ready to ask for a forgiveness he didn't deserve, or at least to say something, and there she was, this other person. Another. An other.

He watched whoever it was using a spatula in a manner other than directed and fuming at everything. Behind her framed in the kitchen curtains was the sky.

And then the hail started almost without a beginning. The tin roof whined and hollered under the abuse and the other saw Lyle. And seeing Lyle with his goddamn mouth open with every stupid excuse stuffed into his stupid cheeks, thinking whether to beg or maybe to run away, she almost, almost, didn't hear anything at all.

And then the pressure dropped and the windows were beckoned outwards and shattered and it made for a moment a glittering halo behind her head like the Virgin Mary appearing where she was least welcome.

She saw him shout something, which she realized had to be her name as he dove across the table and knocked her to the floor, covering her with his body. She felt the roof lean against itself and felt Lyle's lips whispering something into her ear, not an inch away, felt the air move from his lips to the soft hairs in her ear canal, but she heard only one sound, a sound just like a rushing train.

Martin and Marla and the girls and the mule were making good time. If you take the interstate through Oklahoma, Fort Worth isn't six hours from Paris. But Marla had decided while her husband slept that they would take the long way, through the mountains and down Petit Jean. Once Martin started driving in Texarkana, Marla was all but constantly turned backwards talking to the girls, coming up with games to play, pointing out landmarks, cramming months of mothering into the back of the family SUV. On anyone else it would have seemed stilted, fake, too little too late, but for Marla, thrown all the way into it, it brought out a light in the girls that Martin hadn't seen in far too long. The lavish amount of attention made them beam and somehow this made Martin feel guilty and a bit jealous but also fairly certain that the decisions he hadn't really gotten a chance to make were the right ones, would lead to no regret.

Every forty miles or so she reached over and touched him, and it was the familiarity of it that struck him, the way his skin remembered hers. She made sure the radio stayed on music, asked him if he still felt all right. She did things.

They called the road over the mountain the Pig Trail because it slid over and through the hills like the tail of a hog, or maybe because only a wild animal could have dreamed such a circuitous route. At the start of the trail a sign warned that the road will be crooked and steep for some sixty-two miles. Climbing up the ridge, loblolly pines craned over each other searching for light, and underneath it was cool and looked the same at six in the morning as it did at noon. Martin drove slowly, feeling the weight of the trailer resist the incline, lagging around corners.

As they approached the crest, Marla turned around and talked to the girls.

"Did you know we're about to pass the highest road in the whole state? From the top of this hill, if it was clear enough, you could almost see our house from here."

Martin wondered how she came to know such a thing, whether it was gleaned from one or another polite conversation or a fun fact adorning some diner place mat, but he suspected in the way that feels just like knowing that she'd made it up right there. He was wondering if this was another parenting strategy he wasn't well enough versed in. Questioned whether he was telling enough lies to create enough wonder in his daughter's eyes. He stole a look at the two of them in the rear view, all loose-tooth smiles and pigtails looking out at the coming vista. Then they were there and it turned out his wife was right, that they could see all the way to what had to be Paris, all the way past what must have been Fort Smith. But he looked at none of it. He saw clear blue sky like ice in stop motion, trapping the sunshine like a diamond. Then he looked in the rearview again, and behind his daughters he saw green sky.

And then he did his damnedest to push the accelerator into the asphalt.

"Martin, that thunderstorm doesn't look good," said Marla, fully turned around in her seat. She had her bottom lip in her teeth, but her tone was even—she was not alarming the girls.

"It's not a thunderstorm," said Martin. "It's a tornado." He kept his tone just as even, but more from a lack of attention.

"Well, do you think it's such a great idea to keep driving?"

"Don't have a choice."

"And why not?"

"It's coming this way."

He watched as the sky grew darker and then menacingly lighter, watched as the trailer spilled around the wrong side of every curve as its weight pushed forward and towards the guardrail. Along the outside of the road every mile or so, he saw an exit lane that lead only to orange barrels labeled runaway—a last chance for truckers out of gear to keep from plummeting. He did not see his daughters holding each other in a tight ball, whispering Hail Marys at each other, or Marla watching on, wondering who had taught them to pray.

But the pace proved valuable. They made it most of the

way down before the rain caught them, and were on the straightaway a half mile from the home stretch when the hail began, softly at first and then in chunks big enough to dent the hood and send tiny spider cracks down the windshield. The rain came so hard that visibility was notional. "We have to stop, Martin," screamed Marla. "How can you see to drive?"

In his mind, so full of adrenaline, he reasoned that the storm was all but upon them, that if they couldn't get to some kind of shelter that a lack of vision would be among the least of their problems and that further he had lived here for his entire life, that he felt where the road was, or at least thought that he could. What came out of his mouth was, "Too late now."

And so it was that in a blind rain, Martin and Marla, Layne and Stacy, sped across the approximate middle of the Arkansas River Bridge, hail pounding. Behind them in the old metal trailer, Horsey the mule was not afraid. The rain came in through the worthless roof and wept out the back gate, washing over his hoofs and ankles. The mule had seen worse, and was too old to worry. He chewed slowly on nothing in particular and shook the water off his hide.

Martin had thought to make it home, or if not home then at least to the Outpost, or a barn or anything at all that would stand between his family and the storm. But he could tell there was no time left, and so when he felt the tires leave concrete for asphalt he cut the wheels to the left and slammed down what he hoped was the path to the boat ramp under the bridge.

He was almost right, in that all of his left wheel and half of his right found the dirt trail down the embankment. The other half-wheel found only falling rain. The truck bounced, and all four wheels spun, none finding purchase. Only gravity kept them aimed down the hill and towards what Martin was only guessing.

The car came finally to a stop about halfway down the hill. Martin cut the wheel again and aimed the car to what he thought was under the bridge, and then it was hard to figure just what happened just when. You couldn't tell whether the cab of the SUV slid under the edge of the bridge out of the hail and the rain, or if the wheels found purchase and started pushing the truck up the slope as close to the roof of route 197 as it could get. Couldn't tell whether the trailer started to slide or to tilt to one side first, whether the water and the mule slamming into the side wall was a symptom or the cause of the whole rig losing the last of the momentum that kept it going forward, the last that held them still, and took to slipping. Couldn't tell whether Martin started blaring the horn trying to push the truck up the hill with his own hands or the girls screaming started first.

Under the bridge now it was a waterfall on either side of them, nothing to see but rushing water. Below them and behind, the river lashed at the bridge's supports. A mile wide and all of it whipped white and frothing like a canyon stream, bouncing and tossing all manner of trash and river life out and back down. Martin had never been more sure there was a God. Marla had never been more sure that there wasn't.

Martin poured his will and his energy into willing the vehicle forward, or at least no further back. But the embankment was too steep. Nothing could keep them from the river.

"Get out!" he screamed at the top of his lungs and kept

screaming as Marla ripped open the girls' safety seats, and pulled them into her lap. No one knows how she did it, only that it was done and that all three of them tumbled out of the car. As soon as they were gone, Martin tried to do the same. But the car lurched back when he let off the accelerator and his arm got caught in the seat belt. He was twisted around and somehow landed sitting under the truck, dragged down with it by the door. He heard Marla call his name and had time to wonder whether he would be knocked unconscious before he drowned in mud.

The mule was still at peace. Even when the trailer had started to tilt against itself and Horsey fell sidelong against the wall, he only watched it happen to him. He had known all along. He cried out only once, as the waters reached his chest, the only bray that Martin and the girls ever heard him make, a sound that should have been sadder.

Martin shook himself free of the seatbelt and pressed his body flat into the bank. He felt the tire roll over each of his legs, felt his own fragility at the true weight of things and then there was a splash and the truck and the trailer and the mule were swept away down the river and back out towards the storm.

Season 2, Episode 13:
Aftermath

They say they dance, tornadoes, jump up back into the sky only to touch down some other place. Some were certain it had to be more than one, that only God could be in so many places at once. It was the first thing in some months that seemed worth discussion, when a camera couldn't prove you wrong. Not that there wasn't footage.

It would be easier, far easier, to tell you what survived, what remained when the sky cleared and the sun came back and we looked out into the startling brightness.

The old factory was gone, hardly so much as rubble left in the field. The Coin Laundry and the Mini Storage had changed places damn near board for board. All of Church Street was a pile of broken. And when I say that what do you see? Is it neat piles of sorted debris? Do you also see the wedding photos and the socks that used to be behind the washer and the plastic kids' toys? Can you smell gasoline and burning everything and the rain coming down like vegetable oil? Is it personal enough before I get to the dog kennels and Mrs. VandZandt's cats, most of whom survived, most of whom were seen wandering the streets for some years later still looking for what all of us knew?

For what felt like days but was likely less than hours our concerns were immediate. You started by opening your own cellar or bathroom door, pulling yourself loose from the rubble. From there it was your family, your kin, your dogs, some thought to whether your house was still standing and then to your neighbors and then in pairs and crews, taking to searching through the neighborhood looking road by road to see which of us would need help. The first person to declare himself and the rest of us lucky was Jason Johnson.

He and Tammy and all three boys had climbed into the storm shelter behind the Mallett place moments after Jamie had left at the wheel of the white van whooping and hollering. Jason had seen the storm coming and just like another shot going off he rose up and shepherded his boys and his wife into the five-by-five storm shelter he figured Jamie wouldn't have much use for. As he looked around before closing the doors he told his camera crew, "There ain't room enough, so y'all do the best you can."

And when he opened the door and saw that the land and the trees and the grass and the ridge behind them were still there, all vivid sharp, realer than they had a right to be—it was then that he said it. Jason saw his porch collapsed, his truck overturned, his house standing. He offered praise. The camera crew came sheepishly from his back door, timidly filming the wreckage around them.

When the windows broke and the storm came inside, Lyle and Cathy finally looked at each other and in this moment there was a whole lifetime. His eyes held such deep pain, such terrible awareness that he had ruined the only thing that could ever matter. She read that and said back without ever having to say that he'd done nothing alone, and that he never would. There was more love and understanding in that moment than in who knows how many hearts and then all there was to hear was wind, thunderous rivers of it, and they held each other waist and shoulder and pulled themselves down the hall towards the bathroom.

They walked past the sitting window as the curtain rod worked loose from its screws and launched off the wall and into Lyle's neck just behind his ear. He fell towards the floor but into Cathy.

She felt the sudden weight of him and began to crumple before her pupils dilated and she rose and bore all 190 pounds of him the last six feet into the bathroom, swung the door closed behind her, and laid him on the linoleum. She scrambled on top of him as he opened his eyes. She pushed her face right to his and whispered his name.

And though they couldn't hear each other screaming much further apart, he could feel her words on his skin. Feel every "I love you" and "I forgive you" as sure as he felt her hot tears slip from her cheeks to his.

And he wanted to answer her, but all he could feel was his neck and the pain radiating from it and he wondered if he were able to move or just struck silent. Then the roof made a sound that almost no one has ever heard but that is instantly recognizable as imminent catastrophic failure. And it turned out he wasn't paralyzed as he heaved himself up and over Cathy, shielding her on hands and knees as the sheet board and the rafters and the leaking shingles came down on and all around him.

And that's how we found them, at the bottom of it all, under a thousand pounds of manufactured home. He was sprawled over her, spread eagle, her fingers interlaced around his head.

How either of them was still alive, none of us could say. But alive they were and Cathy was conscious enough to keep screaming for help until we dug them both out. Jason Johnson had almost driven by the shattered bent remnants as being a lost cause had he not heard her cries.

It took six of us an hour to find them and by then there was a helicopter to fly them to Fort Smith. We didn't hear them say it themselves, but they were lucky as any of us.

Lucky as Martin and Marla who walked into town each carrying a daughter, all of them filthy, silent, but unharmed. The SUV had rolled over both his thighs, but only pushed Martin into the dirt and gave him a bruise you would never believe. Blessed was the Lord for that one, we whispered. Only a truck, a trailer, a mule. Only their house, as it would turn out. A gas leak had lit just after the rains stopped so everything had burned, so there wasn't a thing to salvage. But they weren't there, you see. Think what could have been. Praise be.

And then there was Jamie.

He wasn't exactly sure what he was up to when he stepped on the gas and turned the white van up Old Military Road towards the place the sky seemed to be spinning around. Or he didn't know why he was up to it.

"Well, America," he said into the camera. "This here is Jamie Mallett and I figure it's about time I saw me one of these twisters up close!"

"That's brilliant," said Bobby from the back seat. "Let's get a little closer, you can holler out the window, we'll move the storm closer in post, maybe add a cow or two. This will be outstanding. Jamie, baby, you're making us rich. Do you know that? Filthy fucking rich."

Jamie nodded and decided it didn't have anything to do with Fr. William and his advice. It wasn't anything any one person had said or did. As soon as the thought entered his mind it was like a seed grain in a science show, shattering in slow motion as a crystal solid pushed out everywhere all at once.

It felt freeing like the greatest weight lifted from his shoulders. A plan, a simple, clean plan.

"This is pretty close. Why don't you slow down, and we'll just speed it up, so it looks like you're going way too fast."

Jamie nodded, he knew this was part of it. He looked at Bobby, wondered if he should think about this more. But he didn't. He just said, "Aww, hell, I thought this was supposed to be reality TV." And with that he opened the door and stood up in his seat, leaning out of the car and into the wind. "Hello, you fucking tornado. I'm James Robert Mallett and I thought I'd come and introduce myself. How do you do?!"

As yet there had been no tornado to speak of, only the solemn promise of one. But like it was reaching out to shake hands, a finger of wind touched down and shot black soot and soil upwards for what seemed a thousand miles.

It was one of the cameramen who said, "Dear Jesus."

"Get back in the van, goddamnit," said Bobby from the second row and after a long moment Jamie did. "All right let's turn around and hopefully that thing doesn't catch us and destroy all this goddamn footage."

Unable to press the gas while conversing with the storm, the van had coasted to a near stop. Jamie reached for and fastened his seat belt, took a deep breath, and floored it in the now certain direction of the storm.

"Come on, now," screamed Jamie over the wind and the protest of the other four men in the van. "I thought y'all wanted excitement. Let's see how close we can get to this son of a bitch."

Down and Out

For a full three seconds no one moved as the van accelerated towards the dark horizon and rain fell a pondful a time on them. Then Bobby screamed, "He's going to fucking kill us!"

Jamie hadn't thought about that part, oddly enough, hadn't fully considered that there would be the others still in the car, just as he hadn't thought about any number of other things other than just how well his plan seemed to fall together. He thought about changing course based on this new information, but then decided it was much too late for all of that.

Bobby lunged for the wheel but Jamie was ready for him, caught him by the throat and held him off. Looking away from the road, the left front wheel found a rock and took to a skid long enough for Jamie to see the sterile, nearly clear polished whiteness of Bobby's teeth in his open, screaming mouth. Then the van slipped around its axis, drifted sideways and then toppled over itself. With all the wind it was hard to say for sure, but the highway patrol figured he had to be going ninety at least and they were certain that the van had rolled at least three times.

Jamie felt his nose break before he heard the airbag deploy, watched his arm get caught between the camera dolly and the roof and snap and fall like a green limb on a short tree. And then he didn't see much else.

The passenger airbag likewise deployed and in so doing saved most of the footage, which turned out to be hugely valuable.

The final episode of *Down 'N' Out* closed with this recovered footage, which went dark before the audio gave out, just long enough for someone to say, "Oh no." The episode won four Emmys, swept the Realsies, and was viewed more times both live and on instant replay than any other reality television event to date, excepting wrestling. Though he had only six directing credits to his name, a Lifetime Achievement award was given to Bobby LaDue posthumously, and a moment of silence was held for him and the city of Paris and its fallen at a black-tie ball.

None of the four crew members were wearing seat belts. Two were sitting on crates holding sound equipment in the very back when it flipped. None of them survived so much as the first tumble. It was said to be relatively painless.

Jamie was found unconscious and in shock, hanging limp from the seat of the van, which had finally skidded to a stop roof down. The patrolman who found him assumed he was dead without checking, thought his help was most needed elsewhere, radioed it in and headed on, ended up helping to dig out Lyle and Cathy.

Yet still when they got back to him, they found Jamie with a pulse and when they loaded him onto the back board and into an ambulance he opened his eyes and said, "It's a miracle," before losing consciousness for some three weeks.

He didn't remember saying it when he came to, or much of the preceding month. But the highway patrolman put it together for him. The storm had passed right over without so much as touching them. It had only been a car accident. Only four surgeries and an arm that couldn't hold or open a beer, not that Jamie ever drank again. Only a year in a rehab hospital, and the house his father built gone. Miracle for certain. Say a rosary.

All in all the town was only maimed. It would survive.

Down and Out

The funnel had jumped and skipped over some of us. Many were just fine, many more miraculously only scathed. It was a time to count our blessings, or so said the sign that someone put on the edge of town, just before you got to all the wreckage. God Bless Paris.

So it was true that when we first headed to the church it was to pray thanksgiving. Most of the town had been found by then. We knew the score. Several of us had driven by the church and crossed ourselves when we saw that the stained-glass windows looked to be still intact, the roof only missing a few dozen shingles, and we'd kept going, all of us experts by then at triage.

And the church was preserved, still standing at a time when such seemed its own little impossibility. We found Fr. William slumped over the altar in the act of saying mass. We'd heard tell of high winds driving tiny bits of straw through beams of fence and we searched for such an explanation. But the coroner reported, once he'd had sufficient time to catch up, that William Colquitt had died of a coronary failure attributed to old age. The Lord works in mysterious ways.

The bishop from Little Rock came up to say the funeral, declined to wear Father's black vestments, insisted that Fr. Colquitt's life was deeply meaningful and full of joy. It felt all wrong but then we couldn't hold it against the bishop. He was young and he hadn't known Fr. William and besides it was the eighth funeral he'd done that week and since both hotels were gone he was having to drive in and out a fair ways.

The dead in the end were buried. Those that could went back to going back to their lives. Many things changed. Some didn't. In the end the land was the last to remember.

Briseño

Some messes are never quite cleared away.

Yet by then, for better and worse, we were on television. And people on television always get happy endings.

So let's say that with the show money and the insurance money, Lyle and Cathy partnered with Jamie and bought a fair amount of land on the side of Mt. Petit Jean and hired a boy from the university who swore up and down that the climate on the mountain would grow grapes that would make wine.

The young man focused on a single variety of grape, something called Cynthiana. It was a local native, naturally growing in hollers all around the county. If known at all in the circles of winemakers the grape was rootstock, hardy vines to grow others' fruit.

Through luck and the internet the young man proved capable of selling the wine he made and it provided a mostly steady income to Jamie and the Younses. Slowly others of us followed suit, and one winery turned into four and then eight, and then a bed and breakfast and the Grapevine reopened and we got written up in *Wine Enthusiast* as the Redneck Napa Valley. We do good business during the summer, and it's usually enough to last the winter. Some of us moved off, as some of us would. Plenty new have moved in, as we had to expect. They paved Old Military Road, and Jamie got them to rename it Fr. William's Way.

The town kept moving as it would, as it had to.

As for the show, it certainly tried to do the same but you might be surprised as to how much damage a tornado can do to continuity. They tried shooting everyone rebuilding, but it was far from riveting. The truth is everyone wants to look at what a tornado does to a town. But no one wants to keep looking. Besides, none of the stars were interested in renewing their contracts for a third season and it proved difficult to replace all the cameramen.

There was never another episode of *Down 'N' Out*, though there are negotiations underway for a *Where Are They Now?* Special. The storyboards look like this.

Most of the former employees of Doyles' Gear have found some way to keep the lights on. Some drive to Dardanelle to work at the Tyson plant, and others work the fields.

Martin and Marla and the girls buried Horsey's water bowl and then moved off to Texas. We don't see them anymore but we imagine they have fairly nice lives. The girls are twelve and fourteen and only Layne remembers the tornado at all. They both remember the mule and bake a birthday cake for him every May 29.

Jason and Tammy and their boys, Junior, Ricky, and Dale, slogged through another season of low-rated *Logan County Raw*. Their performances only increased in quality and audacity, but the audiences never came back, something about the brand being tainted. They were successful in making a small talk show tour and three paid appearances at trade shows. They managed their money well from what we can tell and Junior is set to attend the University in the fall, his brothers two and four years behind.

Jamie had his father's house rebuilt and lives there alone. He is not known for making conversation but is polite when spoken to, doesn't grumble any at the load he bears, and goes to church every Sunday. He wishes there were more to say, wishes there were someone to say it to.

Cathy and Lyle rebuilt their home as well, adding on a third bedroom. With the extra money from the show and then the winery, they could finally afford fertility treatments. They named their first-born daughter Abigail Jean Younse after nobody and a mountain. Lyle has trouble keeping up with his daughter, what with the cane and all, but he and Cathy smile a good deal now.

It could stop here. It could have stopped a lot of places. But here in particular, it would feel good. Just that right blend of sweet and sorrow and hope above all. We could say *Aww, Bubba* and *Amen*, and that child Abigail Jean could be a symbol, could stand for what this town might become, for the bright future we might someday all of us have. It could stop here. But it didn't stop there. It never stops, never. This is the miracle we prayed for and must now accept. After all, everything will be alright because alright's what we'll call how it'll be.

THE END

Acknowledgements

I owe thanks to so many for so much.

An earlier draft of this book was the bulk of my dissertation at the University of North Texas. Gracious thanks go to Miroslav Penkov, John Tait, and Javier Rodriguez for helping to mold this book. Drafts of this book were critiqued by multiple workshops at UNT, and this book would not be here without that process or the insight of my fellow students. To Zach VandeZande, Courtney Craggett, April Murphy, Justin Bigos, and the rest of the Bummer Club—I don't get to write these words without you all.

Thank you to Kyle McCord and Nick Courtright and the rest of the Gold Wake Press family. Thank you for making my book a book, and for running such an amazing small press.

Thank you to my family, all of you, I have taken small bits of you without asking and built this book upon them. Special love to my mother, Cathy, who can never say again that she is not in one of my books, to my father, who taught me to tell stories, and to my grandmother Ruth Hernandez, who sacrificed her whole life to give hope and opportunity to her children and their children.

Several of the characters in this book share names with (but are not based on) folks I know or have met in real life. Miles Francis, Dustin Younse, Whitney Tevebaugh, Abigail Allen, Jamie Mallett, Fr. William Wewers—if you find yourself reading this, thank you.

Extra special thanks go to Erin Stalcup, my editor. You have put so much love into this project, and it shows on every page.

Finally, to my wife, Emily Allen. You believed in me so long before I could. I will love you long after the stars burn out.

About Gold Wake Press

Gold Wake Press, an independent publisher, is curated by Nick Courtright and Kyle McCord. All Gold Wake titles are available at amazon.com, barnesandnoble.com, and via order from your local bookstore. Learn more at goldwake.com.

Available Titles:

Sarah Strickley's *Fall Together*
Talia Bloch's *Inheritance*
Eileen G'Sell's *Life After Rugby*
Erin Stalcup's *Every Living Species*
Glenn Shaheen's *Carnivalia*
Frances Cannon's *The High and Lows of Shapeshift Ma and Big-Little Frank*
Justin Bigos' *Mad River*
Kelly Magee's *The Neighborhood*
Kyle Flak's *I Am Sorry for Everything in the Whole Entire Universe*
David Wojciechowski's *Dreams I Never Told You & Letters I Never Sent*
Keith Montesano's *Housefire Elegies*
Mary Quade's *Local Extinctions*
Adam Crittenden's *Blood Eagle*
Lesley Jenike's *Holy Island*
Mary Buchinger Bodwell's *Aerialist*
Becca J. R. Lachman's *Other Acreage*
Joshua Butts' *New to the Lost Coast*
Tasha Cotter's *Some Churches*

Hannah Stephenson's *In the Kettle, the Shriek*
Nick Courtright's *Let There Be Light*
Kyle McCord's *You Are Indeed an Elk, but This Is Not the Forest You Were Born to Graze*
Kathleen Rooney's *Robinson Alone*
Erin Elizabeth Smith's *The Naming of Strays*

About J. Andrew Briseño

J. Andrew Briseño grew up in Southside Fort Worth, Texas. A graduate of Subiaco Academy and The University of Arkansas at Fayetteville, he received a PhD from the University of North Texas. He is Assistant Professor of English and Creative Writing at Northwestern State University in Natchitoches, Louisiana. His short work can be found in *Waxwing*, *Smokelong Quarterly*, *Acentos Review*, *The Boiler*, *Nat. Brut*, and others. He likes dogs. Find him online at jandrewbriseno.com.